The Place

A Story About Dwelling

Alice Scheffey

Levellers Press

Cover art by Elizabeth Scheffey

Published by *Levellers Press*, Amherst, Massachusetts

Printed in the United States of America

ISBN 978-1-937146-71-9

The Place

A Story About Dwelling

alice schaffey
june 2015

for the meek who shall inherit the earth

Contents

Preface

BOTH THE SCIENTIST AND THE MYSTIC ARE explorers of space. With deepening exploration they come to see that the way we experience space is an indicator of our states of consciousness. Our views of reality influence the questions we ask about how we are living on the earth.

It's also the task of poets and philosophers to examine these questions, to see if it's true that we are on the path toward the higher consciousness that alone will allow survival of the earth as a human and animal dwelling place. The ideas of two of these seekers have hovered over the writing of this story. (See Heidegger & Goethe, Bibliography.)

First, in searching to its origin the word 'dwelling' –its meanings now clouded by technologies–one thinker sees dwelling as life lived in caring for earth and sky and other humans and for the gods either absent or present in their absence. This poetic way of life would be lived deeply in sparing and preserving things and other beings, a way of measuring ourselves by life deeply lived on a place.

The work of the second thinker liberates itself from mainstream methods of analytical science by involving a reversal of will from active to receptive. The receptive will allows the necessity of the phenomenon to be apparent and shared in the researcher's thinking, a sensory rather than intellectual organizing activity. This embraces processes of coming-into-being, of qualitative wholenesses relevant to our ecological crisis.

These thinkers have indicated that our world is moving into its night; that the time for building alternatives to save it is upon us, now. The great tragedy is that in our history, places, and things are disappearing at an accelerating rate, into abstract images and into production to be counted as part of the money flow. Images of things and the things themselves that inspire our deepest non-verbal thoughts and dreams, the thoughts that construct new levels of consciousness, are dumbed down to uniformity or hidden inside electronic pathways. What can inspire our care for Things and Places, inspire us to stay at peace with them, preserve them from harm? In this story, the characters find "traces of the fugitive gods" in ordinary things –the blue fence, the trumpet vine, the falcon, the ship rock and the sky god – things which become a true refuge of safety in their struggle. Each character is, in different ways, struggling to allow the original Light to shine through. The Place is a larger than life character in their story.

Alice Scheffey, 2014

Part One

A Certain Slant of Light

"Here are your waters and your watering place.
Drink and be whole again beyond confusion."
Robert Frost, *Directive*

1

Lidia

It was late summer and I had been standing beyond the overgrown field for a long time, watching the empty house. My body was still but my mind was on a journey remembering other houses and how they had changed my life. The images moved here and there in my memory, opening and closing, most of them just fragments now. This reverie was taking place through the changing light of the summer day I had returned again to the abandoned house. I'd just found it a few days before on one of the back roads outside the town of Garrison, the small town where we live at the foothills of the Green River Range. The place was coming alive to my eyes and in my heart.

There are places that have known love and wait for it to come again. These places wait for love to hold them and listen to their dreams. I know this because I've listened to the dreams of many places. They have not always belonged to me but I've been touched by their dreams and their desire. I know dreaming doesn't happen in the absence of desire. Desire runs deep. Desire is a dark energy that moves toward light and reaches out.

Unfulfilled desires left behind by the ones who move away hover around an old house and reach out to make their claim on you. It may be just a ravine grown over with honeysuckle or the husks of an ancient apple orchard. At the field's edge there may be a flat rock that looks like a ship and then, something from childhood reaches out. If you accept it, the claim of such a place will transform you with a mingling of desires.

Don't you know that every heart holds an imagined place away from the world and open to the stars? For so long I'd been searching for that place. I knew it existed. It existed in a way I would recognize when I found it. And I knew it would be just as I needed it to be at this time of my life.

It was the stars hanging low over Blue Mountain that led me to it. Spread out at the mountain's foot, along the river, lies the village of Weir sheltered from fierce storms out of the northwest. Blue Mountain is old, smoothed down to a landmark that's like a loaf of bread risen high at the center. As the mountain's northern end slopes down into the Rangely Hills, it forms a bowl-shaped hollow that protects the village within. It was here, just a few miles above the village that I found the place, and the way it caught hold of me and breathed desire into my body made me feel the discovery was no accident.

It was summer when I first saw it. How the place looked then remains clear in my mind. Around the house was a thicket of wild raspberry and grapevine. Vines reached over the stone walls, over stumps and shrubby growth and coiled together with pale green tendrils that held as fast as the frame of an old building. Vines grew in through the broken windows, making an interior green lattice when sun fell on the cracked panes. Vines had pulled at the stonewalls and some of them had fallen. But high above this turbulent confusion, the canopies of five old maple trees sheltered space that was dim and still, filled with rays of filtered light that fell on the sculptured forms below.

I discovered that the house was built in 1820, not old for houses in New England. Someone had sited it with a wise and gentle eye. Facing southwest it rested in a hollow like a backdrop for the thorny shapes growing around it. I've always preferred thickets to any smooth or cared for open space. Only in the farm pond across the road, where sedge and cat-tails had grown in, could I imagine clearing to get a smooth reflection of sky. There was an abandoned dog-house beside the brook and a barn, silvery gray and strong. There were horse stalls and a loft.

The stone doorstep at the front of the house was old and worn. There was no way to lock up the place so I wandered through the rooms. Though in total disrepair, for me it was perfect. In the kitchen was an iron pump in the stone sink, and the fading paint of a corner cupboard shone blue in the dim light. I took away with me the power of that blue.

It stayed in my body like enlightenment and moved me into the unfolding story of the place. There was no way I could let it go.

My story is about the triumph of a place that waited for someone who could begin to fulfill its dream. I don't think everyone will allow a place to gather the things it needs. Not everyone will keep these things near and close together in the world that place is making. Sheds, tools and fences, machinery of fields and garden and animals. "Look, you can keep horses in the barn, Richard. And there's the hitching ring right at the front door! It'll be like your old summertimes." I would say this when he returned from his work of photographing desert plants in the north of Mexico and we had found our way back to this place. I could not keep myself from leaving town and going back to the place. I soon noticed a short figure who walked, a bit painfully it appeared, up the road a short distance and back down again. She kept her eyes intently on the house. I followed her one morning down into the meadow and waited as she arranged her heavy body on the big rock and sat there very still. Hadn't I seen her face before? It might have been years ago. The white hair escaping from an old blue scarf lay soft against deep wrinkles of her skin. She looked steadily at me, her eyes glittering like the eyes of a tamed hawk.

"The sky comes down very far here. Do you see? From here you see the rise and fall of light. It's an open place." She moved to make space for me on the rock, and when she spoke again I heard the faint old world accent in her voice. "I've seen you before. Long ago. I'm Piri Olevsky. I'm watching over this place. Sit down. I want to know how it could be managed right."

It was clear that Piri Olevsky was the messenger bearing a sign that I had at last come home. As though she would never be moved she sat firmly next to me on the rock like an archetypal symbol of some future revelation. I felt her so deeply rooted into the earth as to reach a center of darkness there. And strangely, I felt her as an adversary and that some transformation must take place in me before we could move into a higher space together. The spell of the place had fallen on us both.

It's clear to me that places are bound up with eternity, with time, and if you have the whole viewpoint, with the entire universe. You can't say where the hidden messages of a place end. Or, how the messages change with new understanding. Richard and I were in the unfoldment of a path, yielding to that natural flow which becomes reality if it contains truth for a person. Among our present truths were the circumstances of town and house where I was brought up and, on the other side of a great river farther south, the very different sort of place where Richard was growing. All this and what we thought we had freely chosen –our travels, our children- had been providing for this moment.

As our past had allowed us to recognize each other, the same truths would allow us to recognize our place. We understood that dwelling meant to care for, protect and preserve the land. This was a thing given, shared between us that would need no further understanding. We would stay with things as we found them, we would let them be.

I saw that this place had grounded itself and through its history had preserved a presence. That presence was apparent even in the great dis-repair of its spaces and old barn and overgrown location, set down and sunken slightly into the earth under the sheltering trees. Such a place would direct its own changes from what was already present there. We would feel what all new householders feel, that truth would happen to us in the making of the place and that slowly we would be transformed by it.

I believed it would be a refuge, a safety, a small release from the danger of the world. Wasn't that really what my search was about, a safe place for Richard? A shelter to contain us, to bring the world and other people in, to bring near much of the far world we had traveled. As the nature of the place revealed itself, it would be a way of letting peace appear. Perhaps most important of all would be the way of peace.

Growing up, I did not feel safety around the boundaries of my space. I felt I was not safe, that my world was not entirely safe. It was not about physical safety. I could run faster than anyone. I would escape danger and evade any apparent threat, and I was proud of proving that. I sensed my danger coming from those around me, those who most professed love, who most believed they would do everything in their power to give protection. I felt, in that very protection some life constricting force, a swirling dynamic of both veneration and fear. Without doubt, turbulent family histories were responsible for vague clearly manifested anxieties.

That was part of the psychology and super ego of the Victorian era. But I felt a special resentment which translated this way: I was not a chosen child. I might be left out. I might be disappointed. It would be said now that what was not given was the natural birthright of unconditional love. How could I feed myself? How could I get enough? Those feelings led to concerns, underlying sadness, some surreptitious behaviors and mostly, a brilliant tenacity of sheer will and talent to survive. Also, they led to confusion. Like the person who "knows" there will never be all the love, or any love, that she needs, that will and survival talent could be turned toward taking or destroying things that appeared bright or desirable. And there was the confusion of feeling disappointment in others arise strongly without seeing clearly what was so deeply hoped for from them.

It was a milieu into which one was "brought up." A child was, or became, what she understood, searching for and acting out the many possibilities of meanings that fill the world of a first-born. In later years, some who cared deeply noted the lack of hope and asked, "Who taught you to hide the truth?" and "Why are you always so good?" The enigma I would at last uncover was why my need to continually help others was so overwhelming. No one had ever required me to say 'I believe' or 'I feel.' Little I knew of how wounded were those around me, or how wounding they were to myself.

In early photographs there is slightness of form, the face thinning to a point giving the figure the furtiveness of a small animal which might suddenly dash toward one, snatch something and run quickly away. This wildness of aspect was intensified by darkness around the eyes which otherwise blazed with a direct gaze unforgiving in intensity. An aura of mistrust was not hidden by the bright crown of hair, all giving the feeling that one should not risk disappointing this small person whose spirit and strength of will might be hiding a smouldering region of terror.

Every aspect of the house I lived in till marriage was held captive to the requirements of the practicing physician, my father who kept office hours there twice a day. I don't remember that much sun shone in. But some rooms were light, hung with filmy curtains that let filtered light enter. Perhaps the only place of light was from the south, in through the dining room, in under the big sugar maple tree onto the blue patterned rug where I played the Great China Wall with old mahjongs. As the sun rose and fell, its light moved in patches over the blue rug. Sun also came in from the west and at the end of day, shone in through two tall casement windows. It was heavier, mellower, golden light, thicker than the clear butter color of the earlier sun, more like honey. I watched dust motes drifting there and, as I remember now, there was a sadness that I didn't feel in the lighter sunlight. In that light I was always doing something or on my way but the western light flowing in like that made me stop and wait there, watching the dust sink slowly. It held me still, not thoughtful but on the very edge of someplace large.

The Great Depression began the year I was born and contributed a spirit of rebellion to poor, unemployed and homeless people who quickly became "dangerous," above all to those who believed that "of course anyone can get ahead if he's willing to work." My father, especially angry, pounded the dining table and exclaimed that certain people should be "treated like dogs and shot." I came to believe the President was a terrible man who was bringing ruin on the country, that life was no longer safe. My father took me to the Portside of town to visit his friend who made the red wine he loved. I saw their hilarity and affection, what they called a "meeting of the Social Club." But then I heard about Dagoes and Jews, and always in later years the pronouncement "no daughter of mine is going to associate with that kind of person!"

A strange light shone out from these "others" who entered so briefly into my life. Their light drew me in fascination and filled my heart in defiance of boundaries drawn so clearly for my protection. I hadn't seen any people with skin blue-black and eyes shining, like the black men who came to shovel coal down the cellar shute from the outside. They smiled and then laughed widely as I laughed back not always understanding their words. The ice-man, arriving at our back porch with a dripping burlap-covered block of ice in his sharp tongs, would drop the ice in through the tiny door to the box inside our pantry. He was kind and offered me chips of ice to chew. Others I watched from the safety of the kitchen window where my head barely reached above the sill, the men who came to ask for food and work. With bleary, yellowing eyes and blotchy skin, their faces cut, bloodied and dirty, one at a time they came to sit on the top step and devour fried egg sandwiches that Anna, the maid, was instructed to make for them. There was never any work.

There was confusion in the jocularity I saw between men and women, in the differences between my family and other people and what I could believe about them. In later years I saw they had done good works, my father treating his patients equally and not requiring payment from those without money, the legendary works in the church and old peoples' homes of my mother. But to find what they believed, who they were and what was true, became my long effort to dig out from under the emotions and pronouncements ringing through the dark halls and stairways of the big house. Clearly the world described and offered was not the real world. I was aware of distance from so much. But I believed there were places of brightness and came to know from books that this was true. At last my purpose became clear, to voyage through the world to discover how things really are. Even then, I knew a big part of the discovery would be to return and write the story of what I would find.

Much later, when I came so abruptly into the place of love, I didn't know if it would also be a place of safety. I had learned from others how little is known about love. And how little can be known. As we approach it, love retreats. It becomes invisible to us though others may continue to see it clearly all along. Love possesses, entwines and folds itself within the body and becomes its very flesh, how it grows and moves in space. When love arrives it brings awakenings to the body to which every experience will forever be compared. Though Richard and I were, as was observed, total opposites, it seemed to me we were a joining that disclosed points of coherence and amplitude with a logic of its own, secret, difficult and only slowly knowable.

I didn't understand all this then as I do now, only that nothing I would learn about or share with Richard could alter my heart. The times were changing with new styles and values following the end of a terrible war. Old habits were breaking, there was a race to space and the first man to walk on the moon. For awhile anything was possible. Anyone could have foreseen that in less than ten years a young teacher, as full of purpose and vision as Richard Warrington, might rise to chair a conference of national concern at the White House, or would successfully guide an academic committee of forty men chosen as scholars in their fields to bring direction to the fragmentation of existing government services.

Richard was teaching a class at the university where I was a graduate student. I thought his name was lovely, suiting his substantial body in tweedy jacket with elbow patches, a person who paid attention to the condition of his used leather shoes. Passing me in the hall after the first class, he stopped, saying "we always have a party on Fridays, would you like to come?" Of course, though aspects of the old terror loomed, I would. Much of what I saw that afternoon and evening might have given further rise to terror but it was too late. There he was, tall and listening carefully, with deep gray eyes expressing what he was feeling but not always clearly able to say. His hands were square in the palms and long-fingered, his brow and bones of the face were strong. I felt, on a deep level that his appearance was an equivalent to principles he embodied, principles that might sometimes be too large for his body to contain. What I saw was determination that others live up to highest ideals; there was deep emotion and something that seemed on the edge of nobility.

Events passed and soon afterward it became time for the meeting of our families. My father, his eyes unusually twinkling, said "Yes, I can well see you care for this man. I'll tell you this, he reminds me strongly of the British Prime Minister." It was a cold and snowing January day when we married and went directly to a warm country and then to another, returning with two children, after years of service in government posts, all of us now homeless and in the lair of parents who would say predictably, "isn't it time that this family has a home of its own?"

So at last Richard and I stood together under the maples trees in front of the house he had not seen before. By then the leaves were beginning to turn golden. As we stood there, a slant of mellow light was rolling off the tin roof. "Look Lidi, how the light rises up into the trees! Beautiful." I knew then that all I needed to go forward was a dream. And it soon came, as real to my eyes and smell and touch now as it was then.

*I put my foot in the stirrup and throw myself high up
on the horse's back. The tangle of leather is complex,
reins and saddle thongs smelling of oil and sweat, darkly
interwoven, the saddle creaking. It is night. I turn to see
that all is ready behind me. I am riding high up in front, on
the dark horse of a pair drawing a small coach. There is no
coachman. I am prepared again to carry the mail, to carry
through the night what has been entrusted to me. I am
small, wiry, sure, clear, ready. I know what I have to do.
The word "postillion" comes flashing into my head. I
start on the journey.*

So from being the dreamer this place again became the dream. The place
I'd found, dreaming and at rest, played upon like an Aeolian harp by
wind and rain, quickly became a process of lives unfolding. We called it
Stone Hill and began to make it a world around us. The neglected fields
grew into sweeping spaces some as soft as the lawns of ancient country
houses. The new clapboards mellowed to a deep gray. A new wing for
the children, soon three, was set back and into the ground. At night its
row of low windows lighted up like the milking parlor of an old hillside
barn. We laid small raised beds for herbs and vegetables between a web
of stone paths, and the stone terraces on two levels bound the house
securely to the earth. Not a thing was spoiled but we were setting it all
in motion.

2
Piri and Merle

You could say to me, "Piri Olevsky, you're foolish." And it's true.
A year went by before I could accept that someone else might own that
place. I'd been watching over it for Lorion and me. We're old now. Ready
to go back in the barn they used to say in my old village. I'd been looking
for land along the back roads out of Garrison. This place kept pulling me
back.

I dreamed of dancing under the big trees there and milking goats in
the barn. It's like Batowice, the Polish village where I grew up. I'm more
than sixty now. I've learned not to get caught in the net of all my desires.
What really held me back was my feeling the place needed children.
Seven were born there I learned at the town hall. Two more had died.
Their name was Sutherland. The place was abandoned and no one knew
where the Sutherlands had gone. One man told me Charlie Sutherland,
a tin cutter, had repaired his roof and told him how 'dishearted' he was
when two of the big maples went down in a storm. He wanted to 'up and
leave the place'. When I found it was for sale and some other folks were
looking at it, a spirit took hold of me. It wouldn't let go. I couldn't sleep
for wanting and watching the place.

A few families with young children drove up while I was there but
none came back. Most of the new people around here are afraid to live
far from the main road. They're not used to seeing buckling floors and
walls open to the sky, or a cellar where salamanders and snakes rest on
the stone floor.

One evening when I was walking there a woman drove up and
stopped her car below the house. She got out slowly and sat down on
one of the low stonewalls by the barn. It was almost twilight. I saw the
sun's last rays add light to her hair. It was dark, that color of the red oak

leaves in autumn. The red of it mixed with the sun like a fiery cloud around her face. She sat so still I saw she was listening more than seeing. A few days later she came back with a tall man. Again they left the car away from the house. When I walked past them I was surprised. I saw it was Lidia Skiles, the oldest daughter of the doctor Lorion and I have known for a long time in Garrison. She didn't recognize me. "I'm Piri Olevsky," I said. "I know your family." In a few minutes I asked, "Does he love this place as much as you do?"

The tall man moved forward. "Richard, Richard Warrington." He didn't smile but he held out his hand. I saw that he had kind eyes. "I see you know some things about my wife."

Well, I thought, yes, I did know some things about her. I'd watched her as a child playing around her father's house in Garrison. How strange now to feel that her destiny on that place was so closely tied to me. So right away I talked about it to Lorion. He's an astronomer. But seldom does he play the hand with me his high education has given him. He accepts my simple understanding of things, even astronomy. It's what my life has allowed me to see, that chaos and order are part of the same pattern. For me it explains everything. It simplifys everything. I knew he wouldn't see what my way of thinking had to do with the Sutherland house. He didn't have the passion I had for the place. He said in all our years together nothing could match the fierce hold on me this place was taking. But he listened carefully. I remember our conversation very well.

"The place is holding more secrets than the eye can see. I wonder. I wonder if she will allow it to unfold itself? I'm sure it's going to be theirs now."

I remember how Lorion stirred so impatiently in his chair. "Allow it! what d'you mean Piri? If it's going to be theirs now, well, all house-holders impose themselves, try to make order. A place has to be efficient. Who are these people?"

"She's Lidia Skiles. I don't remember her married name. You know her father, Francis Skiles, the doctor in the old blue Victorian house on the main street in Garrison."

"Yes, he's a good man. Well, she'll care for the place, I guess. Is she alone?"

"No, the man with her is named Richard. I would say a closed person. It'll be her place. I can tell by her way of listening there. She loves it as it is the way I do."

Then Lorion said something I'd always remember. "Piri, I love your spirit. But let that place go now. You're pre-occupied and I miss your attention. We're looking for a simple way to live and I need you to help me keep it that way."

Of course he was right. Lorion's so clear. The thing he does is pull me back from flights in space. You'd say it's a contradiction for an astronomer. I always put up a struggle but this time I listened. I kept on looking till I found a small piece of land for sale. It was off the main road and downhill not too far from Sutherlands. To buy it, for Lorion and me, was a small and practical decision. It was the right choice for two childless old people. And still, Lorion said, I could "have" the Sutherland place nearby in the best way of having, that is, holding it without needing it to be mine. So we bought that little piece of land.

By now I've known Lidia awhile but still, my connection with her isn't strong. It's the connection between people who share the coming and going of seasons and their demands on the body and spirit. I go to her place as I did from the beginning, to buy eggs and the soft cheese she makes from goat's milk. I see the place growing with a strange and wild beauty. Except for stones, the backbone of the earth, wild beauty flies the fastest. I saw that when my old village was destroyed. Even there, a certain slant of sun or moonlight made some of the old wildness come alive.

I watched many things at that place and I began to feel that sadness is part of its beauty. If you've stood long in the silence of a place, you know what I mean. Something close to sadness comes out and creeps over you — the true life of the place, what's stored there. It will never disappear even after total destruction. My body still listens through that sadness.

Both Lidia and Richard are beautiful in a way that's similar. I think that's not usual for a man and wife. The beauty comes from their bones, strong under the eyes and especially the neck. I think the neck tells most about a person. Lidia's is long and curving, Richard's is tighter and tense around the jaw. He's tall and dark with thick hair like a lion's mane. He's always moving. It's hardly noticeable but it's a gentle rocking, rocking, from side to side.

She's quick around him, graceful like a child. Her body looks frail but it's held by a powerful will. She listens and makes me feel worthy in her presence. There's something about her that's searching for a thing always out of reach. This was true when I saw her as a child, brightly afire like a young star roaming the heaven. From the glow around her small body, I sensed her center burning furiously, like a star. A star which swells to many times its size when energy moves out from its burning core. Lorion told me that such a burning star will collapse. It loses gas into space, and what survives is called a white dwarf, small, and able to shine only faintly.

She hasn't changed much since those early years. Her skin still shows the faint clustering of freckles that turn bronze in summer. There's a network of thin blue veins that show under her eyes. Her hair's still the shade of red I remember. But now, when she moves quickly, I still see the faint outline of energy quivering and trailing behind her body. It's a reddish glow almost like the light from Mars. It's a cost to her, the growing cost of always bringing her light and giving order to the place. Maybe she feels everything is possible there. Maybe she wants to be the mother of it all. I understand that. But I want to help her find the place in herself more dark and moist and shadowed. That's the place that can restore what's emptying out.

And the man Richard. He makes me feel sometimes what I have to say isn't important. We've never had a serious talk. He doesn't rest in the beauty of that place. He's got a devil dog at his heels. To see them together I'd say that she would become an artist with unusual powers of observation. And that his work would continue out of a deep sensitivity to the principles he holds.

You can see for yourself how involved I am. I don't meddle but I do ask myself questions. Is there a conflict of hearts? Are they young enough to believe that everything's possible? How did they know each other before they found this place? Sometimes I go to listen, to sit on the rock in the meadow where I can hear childrens' voices and laughter, and the noise of animals from the barn. It feeds me, that beauty that passes quickly away, that can be wounded by disappointment. I want them to be safe. And their children too. They ask Lorion and me to all their ceremonies, ceremonies on a grand scale... always with a crowd of people. There was a winter procession with torches up the road to a great bonfire, at Easter a hunt over the wide meadow for colored eggs, picnics with a lamb or a pig roasting all day over the fire. Once there was a childrens' party with lanterns and a great piñata in the shape of a fish hanging from the trees. People come for the saunas and to jump afterward into the cold, cold pond.

I talk about it to Lorion. "They're backing themselves into a corner," he says. "Who could afford such spectacles! It's medieval."

That makes me indignant. "Lorion, you're not kind. You don't even know their place! Think of the Polish festivals we had. St. George's Day, the green holidays with the Maypole, the Harvest, St. Martin's in November!" But I don't want to find fault with him. He always makes clear to me what he sees. He knows about star celebrations and myths of primitive worlds. We sit on our porch and Lorion lights his pipe and blows a thin stream of smoke into the sunlight.

"It's older than medieval Piri. Celebrations on that scale were part of the world before any written history. In those times," his voice trails along the words, "people had no history, they were afraid to lose themselves in what had passed. The only thing real was inside their circle, their rituals returning them again and again to the present. Do you see, Piroshka?"

As always, he waits to see if it's clear to me. And it is clear – they're trying to make this place a sacred center of their world. When I put forward my understanding to Lorion he opens up a lot more for me.

"Then I'm right Lorion, that place requires ritual. Lidia feels that and I feel it too! What do you see that isn't real there?" I ask him.

"Piri, I hardly know. These times are full of fantasy. Revolutions started by poets and dreamers are always followed by violence. It's beginning now, boycotts and marching in the south and in California. Riots and burning, the poetry of the flower children turned to anger. Dreamers..." he breaks off then as if he is suddenly unclear to himself.

"Dreamers have a romantic point of view that turns in on itself, it falls to pieces. We know from our own past...we had to flee...all we built burned, ruined, killed… our people…" Then his voice is lost in the wave of darkness that sweeps over us.

(In the early morning of spring, my village Batowice, is filled with blue mist blowing up from the great open plains of the Carpathian Mountains. Poplars and willows grow, lily of the valley and jasmine and cherry. The fragrance of lilacs where the nightingales nest, is over the whole countryside. My village is most beautiful in early spring.

We gather mushrooms in summer at the edge of the heavy forests and by the lakes and rivers. In the autumn heather grows and the days are russet gold and gray.

I was a schoolgirl there when I met Lorion Olevsky's family. It was so unlikely that we would fall in love. It was then I left my village for Kraków where he was studying at the old Jagiellonian University. Soon it became clear, in 1938 after the Treaty of Munich was signed, that Poland had been betrayed. It was to be split in half. It was at the mercy of two campaigns of savage warfare such as we didn't know in modern times. When German troops began massing on the Czech border, Lorion made plans for our immediate escape to America.

In September the next year more than a million German troops and two thousand aircraft moved toward Kraków. It was the main line of attack, northeast through Batowice toward Warsaw. Three weeks later the Red Army invaded and moved west to Kraków. Behind all the troops came mobile killing units to shoot all civilians and prisoners. Most of the faculty at Jagiellonian University in Kraków was shot by the Russians along with ten thousand Polish reservist officers and prisoners, and their bodies were thrown into a mass grave in the Katyn forest. At the same time, Hitler ordered "to kill without pity or mercy all men, women and children of Polish descent or language…only in this way can we achieve the space we need." Then the occupation began. Lorian had lost his closest friends, Jarek who grew up with him, Cibor, and Kasper who was like a brother.

By 1941 a concentration camp was located near Kraków in the town of Oswiecim, known by its German name, Auschwitz. Auschwitz was the first of six camps the Nazi occupation opened in my country:

Chelmo, Sobibor, Majdanek, Belzec, and Treblinka. Poland was at the gates of hell.

Lorion and I reached Czykago where the big university took him in. We settled in that great open city in the middle of America where a million Polish and people of Polish ancestry have lived for over one hundred years. I tell you this now without emotion. This history is a floodgate that is better to remain closed.)

Finally, Lorion went on. "We lost heart, Piroshka. We couldn't build again after all we had was burned to the ground. You've been searching for years...our own *Lebensraum*[1]. Can I use that word, Piroshka? Only now, we're beginning to come out of that terrible dream."

I gathered myself together, to come back and answer him. "Lorion, maybe that place is just what the times require. A place that's centered, removed from the fear and the burning. Maybe what's needed now is just to celebrate that land."

"Maybe you're right. Piri? maybe you're right. But can these people do it all alone?"

I feel fearful about what Lorion sees. I'm aware of Lidia's isolation. Very few others bring lightness into the weight of living there. Merle who helps me, is one. Maybe another is her friend Lucretia –Crete- she calls her, that fiercely meddling woman! I try not to worry because it gives me joy watching all they do. They're ahead of the times, ahead of all these hippies who talk about going back to the land. I'm going to help them more and I'm not waiting to be asked.

It's Merle Fowler who's pushing me forward. A week ago he was drinking coffee, standing crookedly against my kitchen table and suddenly he stood up straight and looked me fiercely in the eye. "Piri? Lidia is sufferin'. I don't know why but mebbe it's somethin' you could help with. She needs you to. Ask her to come up here. Ask her t'come next week, when we open the tower. She'll like that won't she?"

---

1   *Lebensraum*: space for living, room to exist and function freely. (Hist.) territory which many German Nationalists in the mid-20th century claimed was needed for the survival and healthy development of the nation. Also, room for living, room to exist and function freely.

That's alot for Merle to say. Merle has few words and he never has a fierce eye. He's putting me in the place I need to be. When I give him a hug the look in his blue eyes is triumphant. But I wonder, just how clear is Merle's eye? It never fails with the weather. Is he right that's something's stirring up there?

Merle Fowler has been helping me for years, doing all the heavy work of the seasons' changes, mowing and keeping the woods back so the sun comes into our small clearing. He can fix whatever simple machinery we have. But mostly he helps me gather and dry the herbs and flowers I sell to the weavers for dyes. He stops every day to see if I need help. He walks three miles to get here. Merle has weakness around his heart but he has tireless legs. I say, "Merle, you're a young chicken. Just wait ten years and you'll be like me, with tireless heart but weak in the legs." He laughs and goes on telling me what the doctor says about his precarious heart. We have saltines and coffee. Merle adds four teaspoons of sugar, and we talk a little about old things or weather or something sensational in the news.

The Fowlers are one of three families in the village living by wit and living poor. Their houses line up along the main highway at the edge of town, Elmer Cordoniers, Enos and then Fowlers. The Fowlers are all sickly but tough. Merle's father, Reuben, is a drinker. He has the meanest disposition on earth. It's clear to me Merle was whipped and ridiculed, put into slavery because of his gentle ways. His brother, Harlan, was the clever one. Then a tree he was felling came down on him and Merle said Harlan had a steel plate put over part of his brain that was crushed. Harlan talks very slow now. They have no car so they walk miles. To get cat-fish in Harmon's Pond and trout in the rocky east fork of the Weir River. To pick blackberries along the railway tracks.

Right away Merle began doing haying for Lidia and helped around her place. He'd go up during the day with a basket of catfish cleaned and fresh-looking on a bed of sweet fern, some wild raspberry blooms, a flat rock for the terrace they were making beside the house. And long before me, she ignored his smell of barnyard manure and the greasy cap that covers his balding head indoors or out.

"You take care now," Merle always says and bows his tall body as he backs away. "He's a saint," Lidia says to me. "Merle's one of the saints, living his difficult life as though it was easy." Under the skin they're two of a kind I think.

Except for Lorion, no one I know can match Merle for gentleness. His blue eyes are filled with the lights of a person who's overcome in order to survive. I would say Merle's almost fifty now. It's hard to tell in a person with skin as smooth as a baby's but who's blessed with a balding head. His tall, thin body gives the impression of crookedness when he stoops over you. Really he's straight and firm as a fencepost. Merle is what I would call a person of light.

He never went to school so none of his...what is it I want to say, his sensitivity, was wasted. Merle's survival depends on his sense of objects moving on the landscape. It's beyond the sense of the average person. The movement of things comes up into his body. He moves in a vibrating field of objects like a prism for their energy. Others see him as a misfit but I see qualities in Merle the earth cries out for. Like his dark closeness to all beings and allowing them all space in the continuing creation. What I learn from him is worth the leap I take to enter his reality. I've put a lot of time to understanding him.

As it turns out, he's right about Lidia's suffering. I called there and she said she'd come. She said she wanted to come. It'll be the day I love most in the year, when the brilliance of light floods into Lorion's tower. Even if it's cold, Merle and I open the tower every year on the first day of spring. We pull back the heavy panels around its sides and open skylights in the roof. The light pours down on us, and the birds who've wintered there sing out their hearts. It's like being born again. At that moment I'm a knower about light. And I remember why I keep feeding and cleaning up after those birds all winter long.

Lorion and I are so much enjoying the spring. A great part of it is how much I love having him at home. If any man knows how to relax mind and body, it's Lorion Olevsky. It's why I married him. It was clear after our violent history that we'd have a long and peaceful life together. Lorion has a sense of balance that held us together from the beginning. He has a gentle spirit fixed firmly in one place just like the stars he studies. But later in summer, when the ponds warm to swimming temperature, his whole being changes and he takes chances. I've seen it happen before. I'm sure it's related to the grief and loss in his past.

Most of the time he's happy with a well set table and familiar friends around it. How else could it be for a man who's fixed on objects so far out of reach? It's why our cocktail hours and the sauces and condiments at dinner are so satisfying. I make these things for him, a cumberland sauce with claret jelly for the pork roast, for dessert the puffed clafouti of cherries my mother made in her Polish farm kitchen. Lorion's used to the respect and order and stability of that old countryside. It's old world hospitality, you could say, tables set out with the small potato pancakes called bliny, and kasha and barszcz, the beet soup served with sour rye peasant bread. With sour cream on everything, on pierogi and the rich babka made with apples for dessert. When I tell him it's forbidden to eat green apples before St.John's day in June or else a frog will grow in your stomach, he laughs and calls me a "komorniki", a tenant farmer. He knows that will rile me up. He knows I come from generations of land-owning families who kept bees and made their own kvass, the beer we brewed from black rye bread.

The Olevsky's are from Gdansk on the Baltic Sea. Just south is the town where Nicolas Copernicus was born, Torun. He studied where Lorion went to school. He said something new in the fifteenth century, that the sun was the center of the Universe. Maybe that's one reason Lorion became an astronomer but I don't know. He has the Olevsky's pale skin that darkens in the sun. Like the old days, he always wears white in summer. It's only when he's surprised that he raises his voice. In this part of our life, it's rare that surprising events happen.

Astronomy's an art and I think magic plays a large hand in it. But it's just like life. Order and chaos are both natural, ordinary events, do you see? Being an expert, Lorion has to travel, and this time it's to Hawaii. A team of astronomers is searching the extinct volcano, Mauna Kea, for a site to locate part of a network of giant infra-red telescopes. They need Lorion to approve the choice. I always go with him. When I say I'm happy to stay home for this growing season he looks down and smiles.

"Piri? I know why you want to stay has to do with growing, but not in the plant kingdom. You're involved with souls and I don't think I ap-prove. Your friend Lidia's troubled I'd say for one so royal a person. I saw her in town today with her friend, that tall woman who braids her hair. Are you wise to muddle in their lives?"

"What do you think of her, of Lucretia?" I ask, not answering his question.

"Well, she isn't clear like Lidia Skiles. Striking, but a little overdone. Highly derivative, I'd say. It's something, I don't know, something that might have softened in a woman her age. So many ornaments, so many words, a staged figure perhaps."

Goodness, I'm glad Lorion see's through that woman! He's not impressed by her looks.

"What's for supper? I do love you, Piroshka!" How Lorion laughs when I put my arms around him reaching just above his hips. It's like hugging a tree in my kitchen. That man is a blessing!

The morning before he leaves for Hawaii, Lorion calls me sharply from inside the shed. "Piri! Merle Fowler's in the hospital. His aunt just called from Lithia Springs to say he isn't coming. He was going for a check-up and collapsed on the sidewalk in town. Yesterday. No one helped him, Piri, he crawled to the hospital. His heart again."

"Poor, poor man, how can people be so…"

"Well you know, he does look frightening, so bent over, thin and pale."

"I'm going right away to see him, it's the second time in three months. But he's strong, he'll be alright. Poor, poor man, his life is terrifying."

Merle had already been dismissed from the hospital so I went back to his house. I seldom go there. It's such an encounter. Past the pig pen and piles of kindling, past cages of birds in every corner, some high up in the trees. No-one answers my knock so I push open the door. It's dark inside and hot. Clearly Merle chops all the kindling and keeps the woodstove burning for his father in all weather. Cans of food are stacked everywhere but the room is neat and clean. I can dimly see Merle sitting in light from the only window high up on one side. When my eyes adjust I see Reuben slouched down on the bed.

"Hello Reuben." I fear he might reach out his hand. Only his small, pale eyes move, over my body from head to foot.

"How're you, Miz 'Levsky? How're things at your place?"

"I'm here to see Merle."

"He's fine, sickly, no-account." Reuben spits brown juice into a can.

Merle stands up slowly, waving his hand toward the door. "Sorry Piri, I couldn't breathe. I'm fine now. Let's go outside."

"Don't leave here boy," Reuben whines. "I need you."

Merle doesn't answer. "Piri, I have some new birds, pretty ones. Come see them." I can see he's fine though very pale. "Well they say I need a new heart. I have to wait awhile. They told me it'll come."

At last the morning comes when I see Lidia walking up to my place. I feel a little triumphant watching her cross the narrow bridge up to our meadow. Yes, I tell you, at last I feel chosen. Chosen because I can feel it and call it out – the suffering that a person hides away before getting on in this world. And doesn't Lidia see that? doesn't she believe I can help? that she wants me to help? I *won't* frighten her. I want her to know my way of seeing and that it holds truth for her. Merle? Oh, there he goes, that wise man, leaving us alone.

"It's been so long, Piri, such a cold spring."

"Yes, but this morning feels timeless, doesn't it?"

"It's the tower I think. It's from another century." Lidia pulls a faded blue jacket closer around her. "There's an early chill. Tell me again when Lorion built the tower. Then I'll tell you about my dream."

She rests her hand on my shoulder and I look up a little to see into her eyes. The sun's rays gleam out as I begin the story I love to tell.

"Well, it was the summer you came to Weir. He started piling stone before the Perseid shower of August stars began. He had a dream of the tower. He started building it, stone by stone against the house. When the roof was almost finished he pushed the doorway through at the second level. Then the panels on tracks and pulleys that make openings to the woods on either side. See, there's a narrow balcony. You could sleep there. Lorion never talked about it. He never struggled with it. The tower was something growing out of him."

"Yes," Lidia breathes the words, "opening to the stars, another world. The skylights and the glass roof screened for the birds! It's a living thing," she said, pressing her forehead against the warm stone.

"It's a living thing for him, part of himself. The clear and steady part." I'm enjoying my satisfaction of telling her about Lorion. But then I see something hidden and unfinished in her face.

"Piri! I had a dream about a tower. Listen, I have to tell you."

She begins as if the dream is part of our morning.

> Two men are leading me through a dark wood to a stone tower. We climb up circular stairs to a room burned by fire. Black timbers and charred holes are everywhere and there's a hole in the wall where the fire escaped. At the top of the stairs stands a woman with rags bound around her head. The lower part of her face is burned. She doesn't speak and I don't know if she can speak. Her eyes are light blue and blaze at me. Then suddenly I'm laughing, dancing in the light near the ceiling high above the stone floor. Then the men lead me out past two huge dogs guarding the tower. We keep on walking through the dark wood.

I thank Lidia and say nothing more. I can see the dream is her life, a consuming fire, a dance of bravery. It's clear she's driven by a hot, dry wind. Oh how I want her to trust me! I see my own need for her. I want to let her know.

"Let's sit here. Lean your head back, Lidia, over the stone. It's warm."

She stretches back on the long grass wintered soft and smooth. I watch a few moments and then take my courage and reach out to stroke her throat.

"Lidia, you're a white swan, a beautiful white swan."

"Yes." Her eyes are closed. I feel her opening to a wider space. Moments pass before, suddenly, she startles me.

"Piri, do you remember the light, how it was when you were very small, just moving and unfolding? Piri, do you think the light has an eye of darkness?"

She rests quietly, waiting, but I don't know what to answer. Then her body moves quickly, throwing off its peace like a cloak thrown to the ground. "I can't stay now. I'll come back soon." We walk a way down the road together till the sky begins to cloud over. Then I let her go on alone.

It's breathless for me going back up to the house. It gives me time to sit and think about the memories I have of Lidia. Mostly, it's the feeling I always had that her life would be a struggle. Everyone in Garrison knew the doctor's three daughters. They had such beautiful hair. My feeling when I saw them so young –and I remember it now- was that the particular color of Lidia's hair would be a cause of sorrow. It was what they call auburn, the color of oiled teakwood. The middle sister was blond, a dark shade like wildflower honey. The youngest sister's hair was a mixture of lights, mellow like autumn leaves on a dark pond. How could they carry the praise their father heaped on them? so much reverence and nothing that was real. I never heard a man so pride-full of his children. That would bring harm to them for certain I said. Of course you have to judge for yourself. What's harm to one person, that specialness, might not be harm to another. It's how you carry it, some different from others. If my feeling is right, I'll find that out.

On the first day of spring the tower is full of new light and singing birds. Lidia's back. We sit on the cobbled stone floor watching the weaver finches. They're building a nest with sticks and some dried grass Merle left there. Lidia begins talking in a low voice. Her story makes me feel like a child myself. It seems so unconnected to the world.

"I was born under the fire sign Leo. The doctor told me years afterward there was a certain air of royalty around my birth, a child with strong bones perfect in formation. He said I was listening when I was born, I was listening. Piri, do you know that listening is a trait of queens? It's true that my dreams are full of royal offerings, like a glass slipper inlaid with shining stones and royal jelly molded in tiny diamond shapes. I don't invent them, Piri, these signs were set on me long before I was born."

I'm thinking then, hadn't I guessed right? From childhood she'd felt her power, like a center that rayed out into the world. She went on.

"On the day of my birth my father was five hundred miles away on the Ohio farm where he was born. His father, Isaac Skiles, was dying there. I don't know if my father felt grief or joy for me. There was no way I could know. He never told us stories or talked about his past, only the barest scraps. How the family wept when a sudden hailstorm flattened their crop of wheat, how my grandfather's rough ways and the high black leather boots he wore in all weather angered his elegant wife, Lovina. The saddest thing was the loss of my father's little brother who rolled off the back of a moving wagon and was drowned. That's all he told us about the farm. Mostly my father talked about obligation and duty."

(Survival was the bedrock. There was a large sense of family, of origin, of earth and the rhythm of the seasons. But for the five generations who followed David Morgan Skiles from Virginia and then to Chillicothe, a town south of Columbus, survival was what mattered. The Skiles were Welsh and like others from the eastern seaboard, they went west to find good land. Under the English system it was Benjamin, the eldest, who inherited the land and then the younger sons came west to settle: Vincent, infantryman in the Revolutionary War, Henry who was gay, Davis, Evans, Isaac. Even their cattle were tough and of many breeds. The Skiles and two other families formed the Ohio Company in 1803 and sent a partner to Darlington, England, to purchase Shorthorn bulls to improve their native beef stock. Before the opening of the Erie Canal and the arrival of the railroads, the herds were driven on foot from the farm to Pittsburgh markets. The journey was made dangerous by cattle thieves and highwaymen. The Skiles were a scrappy group, smart, eccentric, and they were tough; their rule was 'Don't tell how many bushels, tell how many dollars.' They were women chasers; their own women were the money managers and were enduring. But at last this history tied through hard labor to the land was changed, diminished in space and time, by a throughway, a gravel pit and sewage plant, the great airbase at Lockbourne, creeping outward growth of the city of Columbus. The land still in the family, was split in pieces. Some homesteads remained but little land was farmed. Survival had turned away from watching the breathing of the earth, from listening to its sounds, had turned away from touching and encouraging the earth's offerings.)

"Mostly I learned about my father from photographs. They were black and white, but when I looked carefully at them I saw faint colors glowing around his body. Some were in Portugal where his Navy ship was stationed. The ladies wore large hats and summer clothing or old-fashioned bathing suits. They were running and laughing, playing on wide lawns that swept down to the sea. In another picture, his white naval uniform gleamed from the shadows of dark cedar trees hanging around the Ohio farmhouse. Horse-drawn wagons moved in the yard carrying beautiful ladies in wide skirts with small children on their laps. I found only one picture of him holding me, in winter with deep snow, and he had on a heavy, dark overcoat. In another, we sat in the garden when it was spring. Apple blossoms fell around us and I was reaching for his gold watch chain."

I stayed silent, listening and watching Lidia move back in time. Her voice rose like a child's. Her hands fluttered around her face. I saw Merle again, but when he saw us talking he backed away into the shed behind the house. It was clear Lidia needed to tell one more story as she murmured to me, "Piri, it was wonderful going to my father's farm." I knew this was the place that, so early, she had taken into her heart.

"I was five that summer and my sister, Rillis, was almost four. It felt like she'd always been my responsibility. We were surprised at everything. The roads going west were two-lane highways then, ribbons tying the squares of green farmland together. The highway was red, red brick for hundreds and hundreds of miles, the same red as the earth. It was a long journey. It was hot. Rillis got carsick. We stopped at farms along the road to ask for water drawn out of barrels taller than our heads. There were buttercups on the hillsides. We drank glasses of buttermilk with yellow flecks of butter floating against the glass. The people were kind and gave us hard-boiled eggs to crack and honey dripping out of the comb.

Piri, it was like a dream to arrive at the farm, to lie in sweet-smelling grass listening to the calls of doves, to drink cold water from the pump behind the farmhouse. There was a creaking wind-mill turning high above the muddy pig-sty, and calves eating the clumps of thistles along the paths to the sharecroppers' place. The Shirkeys had been sharecroppers on the farm for years. Their children were Naomi with the dark skin, and Cecil with a tight cap of blond curls. They taught us to make necklaces of pink and blue wax drippings and held my hand and Rillis's when we climbed to the top of the hayloft. Up there the dim light was filled with floating dust.

Rillis and I slept with our freckled aunts and cousins on a sleeping porch on the second story of the farmhouse. We were wakened by currents of air moving through the cedars in the early morning, by the soothing of doves and by Cecil Shirkey's rising call for the hogs, Soooo-ee, Soooo-ee. I didn't think of happiness, only that each day was endless and free. I was like a rolling wheel under the wide Ohio sky. I was the center of the wheel and held everything together."

At last Lidia's breathless memories came to an end. I thought that never had I seen anyone so swept away in her own delight. But there was more.

"There's one thing more Piri…the trumpet vine! It grew outside the summer kitchen where Rillis and I played with small stones we collected from the dirt paths. Sunlight fell on the vine on a weathered shed nearby and I stood alone watching the light pour down on it. It was a mass of large trumpet-shaped flowers, dense coral-red and orange and light streamed out from the very center of every flower. The whole mass was lighted from within. The vine was old and thick and twisted around the shed. And suddenly I saw how it held on because people over many years had given it their care. I could see those people watching me there in the sunlight."

I knew she had to go on telling these stories. I know how stories of places we've loved become a refuge for the body. Their images weave into the body and strengthen it. Then they belong to us. And so, what could I bring into this space of revelation? I sit still as Merle comes around a corner of the house, raises his arm and disappears once more. There's a lot I want to say, but time will allow it. I want to say that I can't see anyone in that Skiles family acknowledging anything as a gift. They didn't see their own selves were the only things they had to give. Lidia didn't know the things she needed most *couldn't* be given. I know it takes a sorrowful life to learn those lessons.

I didn't tell her the truth then, how a place can become the history of a person. That it can begin to unfold her true self. Or how those summers had been a gift of passage greater than all her father's stories could have been. Perhaps she knew that now. For myself, what happens on a place is at the very heart of desire. That desire can bring tragedy or it can become the very passion of who you are. I can see Lidia needs space for her desire to grow, and then she can reach the well of sorrow that lies under her light. I ask her to return to my place soon. She says yes she will. I need to know more about that man, Richard. What is it she wants from him?

3

Crete and Lidia

I GOT TO LIDI'S HOUSE LATER THAN usual. The changing light as it moved across the fields at Jenkins Flats slowed me down and I watched it for quite awhile.

"Crete, the sun's going down. Look, you're standing in the last pillar of light. It's lovely. Help me get this grain out of the car and we'll go up to the house. The cheese you want is there."

The sky's dark as indigo now, a blue veil falling that draws in all the light. Already Lidi's house and the trees shrink a little in the dusk. The dusk makes this clearing precarious, like a small raft floating on the sea. I don't know a place that holds light in suspension like this as it falls to the ground. For me, there's nowhere that allows more feeling of mood and reverie than Stone Hill.

Sometimes I feel sadness coming from this light. It enters the windows of Lidi's house with a sadness like light through stained glass. It changes objects so they aren't what they seem. Do you know? It's a mystery I have to break through so I can get it on my canvas.

I only mean, for an artist like me, there's nothing simple here in New England. My work was easier in the golden California light. The beauty of Stone Hill is rooted in dark. It's confining, a confining freedom I feel when I come up this road. Woods on either side, then the brow of the hill opening to a full view of the meadow, a still, intense beauty that falls on you all at once, spectacular. But it's clear that beauty is full of contradiction. I'm trying to find my way in this landscape, still trying to feel at home.

Lidi looks beautiful, her dark auburn hair against her skin, gold in the lowering sun. She's always intense, immediate to the moment. Hearing her voice now, the two goat kids stand up on their hind legs, lock foreheads together and fall back pawing the ground like tiny buffalo. When we drag in the heavy sack of grain and spread hay for the horses and the goats, one of the hens flies up with a squawk and flaps around us with the white rooster behind. Lidi's laughter is sudden, and it softens her face. Her laugh makes me understand exactly how it is for her, now, in the barn, caring for these animals.

"Crete, I made a great mushroom and barley soup for dinner. Won't it be good, this cold March evening? My best work today. I'm thinking about work again, how hard it is to begin the day. To build good spaces into it that feel free. Yesterday, listen, I read that taking care of animals is absolutely the lowest form of work. It just struck me down! That can't be right, that person doesn't know."

"It isn't right, Lidi. Don't question yourself. I say work is whatever you feel it necessary to do. And why feel guilty about just "being?" It differs with people. Maybe you glorify working people, laborers; some of them have no choice. Would you like that?"

"Well, it makes them seem freer somehow. Inside that necessity, they're free, am I right?"

"That's too much for me just now. I can't follow it. Listen Lidi, your work is Stone Hill, real work, and no one but you can do it. We'll talk about it because I want you to stand firm."

I think about her troubledness as we walk up to the house. Lidi's a place maker. I don't know anyone so connected through her body to things around her. It's how she views the world, creating a net around herself every day of things that receive her care. It's not just esthetic, she transforms things, exchanges parts of herself to become part of the place. I watch her move a vase to a spot where sunlight can fall directly on it, or place a chair so the branch of a crooked apple tree can be seen through the doorway. It's as if, above everything else, she's here —in this place- to touch and give life to things. She told me this message from one of her dreams, 'The fruit tree is the same everywhere in the world. It doesn't take care of itself.' This care of things centers her; it's a resting place she hasn't found in the human world.

Being an artist I understand that, how objects ask for attention. They're worlds waiting to glow with light. For me, an object has value if it points to something I can transform into art. I let a thing become the center of space, let it gather a landscape around it. And I give it a resting place too. But still, it's an image. My body isn't living in it. I keep boundaries, Lidi lets things overflow. It seems like something driven. I'm just beginning to understand her, she doesn't reveal herself in words.

Up in the kitchen the light's even more dim. Richard's there, beautiful Richard, fumbling with wood for the stove, muttering as he lifts the lids off pots and puts them down again. "No, no, I'm not hungry." He waves himself into the next room and calls back, "Lidi? that desk in your study would make a good dining table. Will you help me move it?"

My observation is that nothing's ever exactly right for Richard. He doesn't locate himself easily on the earth. When his inventions of life don't fit, he begins a new project. His study won't do, light coming in the small, old panes is dim on the north side, or he's too close to the domestic traffic flow. Soon it'll be the bed that isn't right, a sag developing on his side, air coming in over his neck at night, the sound of crows gathering in the far pines every morning. I know. I've heard it already. I'm very familiar with the demands of a man like this.

"I despair of your getting anything right in this space," Lidi was saying. Richard returns to the kitchen with an empty glass in his hand.

"Physical arrangement isn't the issue, you know that!" Seeing me at the door, he speaks more calmly. "Sorry, Crete. It's school that's bugging me. All day those kids breathing on me, wanting their futures, their degrees." Pouring more clear liquid into his glass, Richard rummages for the ice.

"Where's my favorite artist? Where's Claire?," I want to know. I love Claire. She's a person, my mother Rose would say, that's made out of only true material. Her beauty is like mine was at the same age, nineteen, a mixture of opposites no artist could capture, her red-gold hair stirring gently in a breeze and her dark blue eyes flashing black. Claire's skin darkens in summer like Richard's and she has his angular face. Her brother Mouche is two years younger, a golden boy sure of his wit. I think Mary-Molly's almost twelve. She's more at home with herself than the others. She speaks her mind. Each of them was born in a different country and, like a tribe, they're a bit watchful and wary of closeness.

Richard turns toward me with a raised brow. "Predictably, Claire's disappeared." His voice is loud again. "She's only sociable with children. They don't deceive."

I resist rising to his sharpness, his need to wound. "Claire's an exquisite person. I don't think you know that."

He acts as though he hadn't heard me. When Lidi calls the children for dinner, I bend down to give her a hug. "I'll just take the cheese and go now."

As I leave Richard begins agitating. "D'you have stuff ready for the morning? A formal breakfast like we're having a formal dinner? Well, let's get on with it." In the middle of the kitchen Lidi stands straight and still, smiling.

My car's beyond the house, and driving slowly back past the kitchen windows, now bright with electric light, I see Richard gesturing with his arms in the air. The children are not in sight but from their rooms in the east wing come the mournful notes of a bugle. It's that delight of a boy, Mouche, playing Taps.

I need only low lights to see the road as it winds down from the house. It crosses over a small stream and levels out, and there I switch the lights off and stop. The stream runs south open to the sky, and its banks widen into a small, shallow pool. The water flowing there catches a gleam of reflected sky, a dark silver out of some region far above the clouds. The silver light moves on with the stream till it disappears into dark woods. I sit awhile and then drive on. Just at the main road going to Jenkins Flats, a wide band of the same violet silver light flows along the horizon, the light of early spring. I stop again to watch it resolve and pass into darkness. It reminds me how light and darkness continually turn into one another to create something new. I need to get that changing light into my work.

It brings back an old question, my struggle of how to frame my painting. In a way, I'm thinking how it's related to Richard, how he tries to impose patterns on things. I've always resisted framing a painting that grows from inside my body out. The frame conflicts with letting the forms fill their space. As for Richard, there's something about him that defies my simplicity of thought. I remember the first time I saw him. Thinking about it now still raises the hair on the back of my neck. I just wasn't prepared for a figure of such complexity.

It was a September morning, misty, too cloudy to paint but I'd come out from town to see Lidi and get some eggs and cheese. Waiting for her

I sat on the big flat rock in view of the house. Richard came out of the woods along the upper meadow on horseback. It was the white horse, a good-sized mare, and he was letting her walk slowly. Then he reined her in and stood halfway across the meadow just looking at the house. I could see his face. He sat there on the horse for a long time. I didn't want to startle him so I didn't move. Then he came toward the house and, passing unaware of me, he said in a low voice, "Lidi, oh Lidi where are you?"

At that moment there was a loud cry and another horse plunged out of the woods, galloping out of control. It was Claire. "Dad...Dad!" she shrieked. "We got into bees! Dad!" Her horse careened wildly as she thrust her arms back and forth around her head. In an instant Richard spun the mare around and raced her toward the path of Claire's horse. "Go into the pond!" he shouted. As her horse came close, he reached out, grabbed the bridle and jerked it violently to one side. "Now jump in there! Jump!" Claire slid off her horse and stumbled to the pond and went under. A swarm of bees followed her, buzzing angrily over the reeds and sedge that filled the small pond. As she came up for air Richard shouted again, "Go under! Go under!" I could see the bees scattering, some still swarming around the trembling horse. "Now run to the house," he called, and leading her horse, he cantered back to the barn.

I sat still, like part of the rock, letting those moments wash over me. The misty air, the sad nobility of his face, his words and the speed of his action to rescue Claire. My God, I thought, Lidi hadn't told me about Richard's loveliness. After a short time I went down the hill. It wasn't time for our meeting.

At the edge of town the lights grow larger now. I regret having to leave my solitude. Pulling into our driveway I see every light in the house is on and there's Ferdy bumbling about like a mother hen with our three boys. They've eaten dinner and the kitchen is a sight, but he's stacked the dishes and has a pan of soapy water ready to wash them. It all seems bright and jangling, so different from Lidi's. "How was it this time?" Ferdy plunges his hands into the soapy water.

"As always, it's like another country, I'm still learning the language. Both Lidi and Richard seem to keep their real selves out of communication, lots of facts and emotion but no connection." I really don't want

Ferdy to see how fascinated I am with them both. I try to speak simply so he can understand.

"What d'you mean, hon? No real connection?"

"I mean, they're separated by worlds of their own invention, sort of magic belief systems. They leave out so much of what moves between them and I think it's a habit now, not to give feedback. Of course, not to mention the natural tensions that exist in a marriage. I can't believe how resistant Lidi is to being known, to being loved. More resistant than anyone I can remember. Ferdy? I know you get tired of all my therapizing."

"Well, it's only the simple-minded who are really accessible, God bless 'em. Take me, for example. But do you really care about Lidia?" He doesn't wait for me to answer. "Oh Crete," his eyes look directly up into mine and his natural dignity rises up in them, "you're so grounded in the world."

I feel a wave of thankfulness to see how much Ferdy really believes that. He's so simple. Yes, accessible. "You know how I work at it. And Ferdy dear? you help me."

Getting the boys to bed I feel so distracted. What fascination, what sense of breaking, looms over me? I keep thinking about Richard and Lidia and how it was only three summers ago when I met them. We'd just moved from California. Ferdy needed east coast connections for his Brittany wines which weren't selling well out there. He travels back and forth so often to the Montfort vineyards in the south of France, and living in California made that more difficult.

It was our first spring when I met Lidi at the elementary school. We'd decided that Weir was the kind of small, rural village we wanted for our three boys. But after two years we moved into town. The location was better for Ferdy and the house large enough so I could have a studio. That first year the fair at the little school was magical. It was May and apple blossoms in the schoolyard had begun to open. Balloons were everywhere and plants for sale and things to eat. There was a tattoo artist, a wizard spinning like a dervish to the edge of the parking lot, a juggler and fortune-teller, all teachers or parents I didn't know. To tell the truth, I was looking into all their faces, searching for a friend.

The fortune-teller was Lidia. She wore an elegant dark blue velvet jacket sewn with patches of all shapes and fabrics and a blue silk scarf covered her auburn hair. Her crystal ball was a shiny toaster and my face in it looked changed. When she reached up her long fingers to hold my hand I was awestruck as any child. The ropes of beads she wore were the color of green sea-water, and her fingers played with a little bell around her neck while the crystal ball was speaking to her. She said I had come home after a long voyage, not the ordinary kind. She said I should keep myself strong and ready to do my work. "Run, run till you breathe hard. Climb the steep hill every day that reaches the sky. Eat green grapes and wash them down with pomegranate juice." Then she looked up into my eyes and spoke in a low voice, "Be patient. Come to see me soon."

The second time I saw her we were collecting our children at school and she waved to me with a fluttering white paper in her hand. We stood still while our children ran to us for shelter and away and back again. Later I learned the paper was a poem she'd written. She said later she would have read it to me if I'd asked.

I've always made it a point to choose my friends very carefully. I stand back till I see just who and what they are. It took nine years and the best therapists in California to make me into a creative person and I don't want any disappointments. It seemed to me that Lidi was clear as a mountain stream. From the beginning I knew she was the one I needed, so desperately, to be my friend.

We've had steady rain almost all this week so instead of going out to Stone Hill I phone Lidi in the late afternoons. We discuss the subtle nuances of our day and often it's about dreams. I show her how to walk into the dream landscape and encourage the dreaming body. Her dreams seem free, journeys by water or in the air on a bird's back and once she was riding the sky on a sheep. She keeps dreaming of a house, half of it lived in, the other half larger but burned or in ruin. Always a yearning, an unfulfillment, regret. I know what these dreams mean.

Right now she feels we're pivotal points for each other. Yesterday she said we're like searchlights in the night, beaming up from the horizon and crossing each other at the zenith. She says things like that, pure poetry. Lidi's so child-like and it saves her but leaves out so many adult things. She creates people and then they disappoint her. Thank God I'm not so stuck in my creations!

"Oh Mary! Mary! Come up and help me out of this...what a mess I'm in here! Will you come up now? Nothing's working...just look at this clothing. Mary!"

"When d'ye go, Mrs. Montfort?" The large woman breathes heavily from climbing to the second floor but her voice chimes like a single bell high in a mountain village.

"Oh, not till the middle of April...there's time for shopping. Just look at all these hats!"

"Will you want a hat, mum? You needn't cover that glory of silver hair. It's a pity!"

"Well, its dignified...a hat, a turban, feathers; would any Irish poet read her work without wearing a hat? She needs it to claim extra space in the surrounding air. A hat allows us to do that."

"Do what, mum?"

"It allows us the right and the ability to claim our space. Now will you fold these things for me?"

The bed is piled with silks of all colors, shimmering veils and beaded belts and turquoise and silver jewelry in one corner. "Ah, it's heaven for the eyes!" Mary whispers. "Look at these!" She lifts a soft handful of long silk scarves in her rough hand. "The reds, you do love reds, mum. You'll be sparkling!"

"No, I'm not taking those Mary. I got them out to sort through for a friend who needs bright clothing."

"And don't all of us, mum...it brings life to us! And where d'ye go with the artists this time, back to Ireland?"

"We're going to Italy, to Florence and Rome."

"Italy...oh, it'll be sunny...glorious!"

"Yes, I'm going to see light on the ruins."

It seems that the gray weather here is endless. Lidi phoned to say Richard was putting in a new stove and the house was cold and damp. She sounded desolate. A wet snow fell in the night and so I think she'll come into town. It's a hard time of year. I love looking out at the snow in town, how it connects everything. It's lovely, so abstract and geometrical. I see things differently in town. Maybe I think differently. Out at Stone Hill I have to search for the meaning, sort things out, give them direction. It's an organic mass that requires ordering of all that stuff, raw, unassorted.

"Crete! Lidia's here," Ferdy shouts from another part of the house.

The studio door flies open and our large sheep dog rushes into the clutter of paint cans and papers on the floor. Behind him Lidi is breathless with her effort to hold him back. "What a large and determined dog. I can't manage him."

"We can't either. For a prince he's totally unruly." I see quickly that in spite of her exertion, she has no sparkle, she looks neglected.

"Raj! Raj!" The dog seizes a corner of the canvas drop cloth and begins tugging it. "Rajah! come here!" I raise my voice. The dog settles down, a mound of gray shag in a patch of sunlight. The door bursts open again and Ferdy sticks his head in.

"Oh Lidia, good morning. Sorry for the rumpus of this Rajah. Dogs don't make life easier but they do enrich it," Ferdy's voice is booming. "Raj,come!" The dog goes to him. "Too long since we've seen you, my dear. A continuing rotten spring, isn't it?" Ferdy stands a moment in the patch of sunlight, then looks at his wrist watch and leaves with the dog, closing the door abruptly.

"Ferdy seems pre-occupied."

"Oh no, just a continual pall of fiddly busyness. Putting things here and putting them there, after all it's just bottles of wine. Under his polish he's a simple merchant."

"But you indulge him."

"I indulge myself." I draw her to the window. "Look at the light out there, it's full of shadows, amethyst and lavender, long, thin shadows of each tree; tiny pockets of lavender animal tracks; see,a trail of them coming from the woodpile. If we were small it would be the kingdom of heaven." I feel her watching me carefully. "But the light deceives us falling on things by chance. The external world is so seductive, but it's not such a help to me. I try to go inward where everything's really connected. I'm trying to discover how it connects to me."

"The pain of connection," Lidi sighs deeply. "Is it painful for you? Your work I mean?"

"Well you know my work is thoroughly Western, shadows, perspective, detail. But it's not how the thing looks, it's a realm of reaching for a quality felt rather than seen. I'm trying to show continuous creation, a field, a process."

"Oh, well of course, that's why you say you can't frame anything."

"It's fluid, yes, and it pushes deeper each time, distills itself through the whole range..."

"Of past and future?"

"Of mystery. Lidi you're right, my work is painful when it's unresolved."

"How does it get resolved, Crete?"

"I stand in front of it totally empty. That's all I can say now. If you're interested..."

"Well I am," she answers quickly.

Some resistance stops me. Should I hold back from her? I never have and this sudden pressure is unfamiliar. But I know well it isn't my work and it isn't Lidi I'm thinking about. From the beginning it's been clear to me she isn't strong enough to withstand Richard's seduction, his rainbow of colors. I know underneath that rainbow there's a quivering sword. I've experienced his mistrust, hatred even, of women. But I feel full of empathy for him. I want to know his beauty and, I can admit it, I want to feel its wounding.

"Well, all we really have is our own story, isn't it? And, we have to invent it. I mean, it's not just a script unfolding. You have to embellish what's happening...you have to create it."

I feel her fear and lean over to put my arm on her shoulders. "Oh Lidi, bravery isn't so useful. We have to call on outrage, a decent outrage on the spot. It's the outrage of not knowing who we are. I learned that from Rose."

"Rose, your mother? Ah, to have that kind of mother."

"No, you don't see. She was a tyrant. She called me Lucretia. She controlled everything, even the exact day I was born, on her birthday! The meaning of my work comes out of my struggle with that, undoing all the exuberance she needed me to have. She made me take drama lessons, entertain their New York friends and finally I went on the Broadway stage. It wasn't who I was, then or ever. It was Ferdy who rescued me, showed me how I'd chosen a wrong path. And once I saw how I had used my past, that my own complicity was acting against me, I could never go back. I had to discover how to be quiet, ordinary, just one of the threads in the cloth.

But the mistakes are at great cost. To get the emptiness to do my art, I still have to keep flushing out everything she poured into me. We were betrayed by our mothers, don't you see? They didn't give us light, they blocked our light! After a lot of work I learned that I was nothing, Lidi, nothing, and that's why I'm great because I'm ordinary. Strange, isn't it?"

"Yes, to work so hard to get into your sacred space." Her eyes open wider and their blueness overflows into the hollows above her cheeks.

"Sacred? Lidi how you venerate everything. It's chaos. But you're right, even chaos has a sacred aspect." I see her fear of my standing before her saying it's possible to discover yourself and then live in the discovery. "It is sacred. I come into the studio with a prayer to be empty, to let all things pass through me. And then I wait and wait for my own desire to grow."

"Desire, Crete?" I feel her strength draining as she sits down. "Well, nothing like that's passing through me now. Maybe I don't have a secret garden, maybe it's all choked up with weeds. My mother was terrible in her vigilance against fear. Her fear organized my life. What desire can grow out of that?"

"Is it the same now?" I urge her on.

"I try to see her clearly. I try to love her. But I feel her moving close to the edge, turning I call it. Even now, she's so old, I feel her turning. She takes away her warmth. She feels fear and stops it by wounding. It's an edge where no-one can go. The way to bring her back is what I can't do, simply to love her. I don't know how to love her."

"And was it that way when you were small?"

"Sometimes I stood in our dark living room and watched her lift the curtain to see who was coming up the walk. She stood looking out a long time without moving. It seemed like she missed something or was waiting for something to happen, waiting for something she'd known."

"For what Lidi?"

"Well, I've wondered if her waiting was for a kind of prey, a thing her body remembered. She was an identical twin. Maybe her body needs a psychic contact it shared in the womb life. Do you think that's strange Crete?"

I can see how hard it is for her to reveal herself. "Nothing's strange, nothing. But isn't there any kind of spirit between you? Don't you think there's a spirit connection between a mother and daughter?"

"There isn't. Not a good one anyway. My mother was drawn into my father's orbit, his medical practice. We all were. We circled without rest around him like planets around a sun. He kept daily office hours twice a day in the house and none of us could use the phone or car. He'd shake us out of our beds in the morning. But everyone loved him…and we loved him", she hesitated, "we loved him."

"Ah, street angel, house devil."

"Yes, I was very young when I dreamed he hit my mother behind the closed doors of our pantry."

"Didn't you rebel?"

"Loyal unto death, no privacy even for my body. It's not the clothes on your back, it's what you have in your head that counts."

"Well I'm clear," I say. "A man like that has had love choked off at the source so it all turns into protection or ownership…he wanted to keep three safe and perfect daughters."

"It wasn't only the doctor," Lidi smiles ruefully. "Margaret's eye and ear had been trained vigilantly against all desires of the flesh. But she had a passionate love of flesh. One Sunday at the dinner table —it was Richard's first visit—she reached out and grabbed his arm.

'You have such a lovely wrist,' she said. It was during the dessert course."

I see, from the beginning, that Lidi's relationship to her mother was overlain with a dense shroud of sadness, of pain that blocked her throat.

"I still think that seeing all things deeply is loving," Lidia goes on, "that everything or everyone truly seen is loved. I wonder if others saw her differently."

(Soon after they were married in October, Francis Skiles arranged for his wife to meet his professional community at a garden party on the long and spacious lawn behind their house. Standing quietly on the edge of a circle of the hospital trustees, Margaret suddenly dashed to the back of the rolling garden in pursuit of a large yellow butterfly, the pale green chiffon wings of her dress billowing out behind.

"So young, so lovely", the gentlemen murmured.

"So unsure of herself," the ladies sighed.

Their first child was born in July. It was late in the month and moist heat drifted over the marshlands of the coastal town. It was the third day Francis Skiles had been gone, to Ohio for the funeral of Isaac, his father. Margaret felt tired and asked Lily Tosh, the maid, to bring supper to her bedroom. She had walked far that afternoon to a small dress shop where she sometimes set aside a piece of clothing until she'd saved enough from the food money to pay for it. She'd bought a summer hat of black straw. Coming into the bedroom, Lily let out a shriek to see Margaret, with the palest skin, gripping the bed-post with one hand, her face twisting in pain. Lily packed a bag and ordered a taxi which reached the hospital only minutes before the baby was born.

What happened then Lidia could only imagine. Perhaps Margaret was nervous, alone in the hospital where her new husband had been practicing long before he married her. Or was she un-informed? so young at twenty-eight. Or was she frightened? married just nine months. Perhaps she was imperious, pointing her finger and saying to a nurse, "this is unacceptable to me!" Or insecure, not knowing dignity but trying to imagine how a doctor's wife should act. Whatever the reasons, after one night Margaret Skiles was asked to leave. The nurses could not accept the tone of her demands.

To him, P. DuBois Bunting, the circumstance was unprecedented but likely he was not dismayed. In twenty years of obstetrical practice he had become accustomed to high levels of emotional intrigue from post-partum mothers. He had enjoyed Margaret Skiles, a rather nervous patient needing reassurance, and he could imagine her awkwardness arose from being mortified by ordinary obstetrical procedures. Perhaps he sensed something missing around her, a feeling that some energy previously present had been lost, perhaps like a filly tamed at the price of its spirited soul. Yes, she was like a filly with that mane of reddish-orange hair! Dr. Bunting chose, as he did in all confrontations with birth or death, with that calm firmness of mind which moves all to equilibrium. To the head nurse he said, "Tell Mrs. Skiles she has permission to go home. She and the baby are doing well." Did he mutter to himself, "Hummm, Frank's gotten into something here, hasn't he?"

But what was around the newborn then, seized so tightly in the arms of her mother fleeing down the long flight of hospital steps to escape the indignant nurses? What aura of light would shine around a tiny being two days old? Did she look up out of her twilight world, struggling to focus on Margaret's face? Did her mother smile or reassure her, at risk of this sudden movement and surprise, her mother bound so tightly in fear?)

"Maybe all this," Lidia went on, "helps to explain my loneliness now, how I just need to endure."

"Endure?" I'm careful not to shake her confidence in me.

"There's a rawness between Richard and me now, nothing to protect us from each other. I just have to be like a rock, silent, worn smooth."

"Yes, you have to, Lidi. Because Richard wants to fly up. He's trying to fly but he can't. He's tied up."

"Do you think he's hurting himself?" Her eyes flood with tears.

"No, not yet. But I'm afraid he's hurting you. Listen to what I'm reading now. It's a Russian, Prishvin. It's by the sea Lidi. There are cormorants. They don't move from their rock to a higher rock even though the rocks are awash with tide. And there was a man who returned to this rock when he had no friends, to lie on this rock. And watched it as water ran through it, as if it was weeping. And even when he found friends and work, he would leave them and go to the rock and lay on it, and then he was able to return to his life. Isn't that what you're saying?"

"Oh Crete, maybe it's right, it's right that Richard needs a rock. Can't he share a moment of that need, the mystery of it?"

"It could be shared. It would be a gift." Through the gaps of her understanding I see Richard more clearly now. I feel how much Lidi is a place for him because he allows so little place in his own body. It isn't just the drink. That's his escape from intolerable loneliness. He's haunted by the real world."

The dog barking outside the window saves us from more discomfort. There's a deep purring sound of a heavy motor. "Another of Ferdy's toys." The old Packard roadster, its ancient green almost black, tracks down the driveway in wet snow.

"Come with me to Piri's," Lidi says suddenly. "She asked me to tell you about the dancing. They're starting soon."

I can't say anything to her now about Piri Olevsky. That she's a simple peasant cut off from her village. She's full of longing, playing the Wise Woman with powers from the Old World. How she got that lovely man I must find out. Lidi falls right into her hand. It's a strange choice of friends. And that naïf, that crooked man Fowler she so enjoys. Ludicrous! I can't account for it. Well Lucretia, one thing at a time. How wicked you are today!

"I'll go with you in a few weeks, when it's warmer." I kiss Lidi's forehead and wave her out the door, and turn back to the window overlooking my snowy garden.

The trees are beginning to drip, shining wet-black against the snow. Ferdy's tied Raj on a long lead to the apple tree. The dog is ecstatic, rolling and shaking and rolling again in the wet snow. Oh Raj, you don't need any inner control. You can just hide out in a game and be safe there. It's hardly fair. Dear Lidi, she hasn't got control of her marriage or her body. That red glow around her shines like a child's feverish eyes. It's guarding a place that's stuck. But I do see her vision. It's to help Richard realize his beauty, to help him bring it into being. It's a claim she has on him, she can't help herself. But I can help her. I know how to bring form out of empty space. That's what my work's about.

…On this blank page, moving the charcoal around a ghostly form, I make a place the form grows out of. Moving my hand back into its interior volume I build up darkness, a nest of darkness that grows outward. My hand rests in the deepness of this volume, moving in and out, back in and out over it again, slowly, slowly so the movement doesn't get ahead of my eye. A goal is lurking here but I try hard not to be aware of it. When I stand back and look, and then draw more, and stand back again…how clear it becomes now. The contours of the face, gaunt below the cheekbones, the jaw curving sharply toward the earlobe, the sense of restlessness. Why it's beautiful, totally changed. Amazing how my hand knows the shape of his body!

It's nearly the end of April. Lidi's agreed to meet me at the airport since Ferdy will be busy enough managing Mary Crowley and the boys. On our way to the car, I begin telling her what I'd discovered in Italy.

"The Italian women are magnificent…the way they dress! They don't cover up their sexuality like we do. They're beautiful…of course it's a little extreme, you wonder what's left to surprise a lover after such public display. But it's the idea, the process of celebrating the body. I really want us to think about it."

I can't keep my eyes from seeing the curves of Lidi's body under her voluminous black Indian skirt and the black rayon blouse with winged sleeves and an abstract pattern of bright colored birds. I imagine she'd chosen them carefully, for black energized her face, pale and framed with the glinting copper lights of her hair. I suspect these are vintage clothes from the early forties.

"Black is the Queen of colors," Lidia purses her mouth. "If you don't know that you ought to, Matisse said it!"

I feel gentler, seeing the trace of woundedness, so slight, in her eyes. "It's not the colors we wear, Lidi, it's the shape of our sweet bodies. They deserve freedom, celebration. You'll see what I mean."

In the dim light of the parking garage, I rummage through the luggage, discarding brushes and small blocks of watercolor paper till I find a small package wrapped with string. "Try this on, I got it at the flea-market in Florence. Just try it, there's no-one around." She opens the package and holds up a sleeveless little shirt of twilled silk, mauve flecked with pale red and buttoned down the front with carved bone buttons. The label says 'Abbigliamento, Firenze.'

"It's primordial, like a thing out of the sea! But I don't look well in this color."

"Try it." With her eyes on my face, Lidia removes her black blouse and throws it into the back seat, slipping the shirt over her head. It clings gently, revealing the perfect globes of her breasts. "It's perfect, it's right for you. Now we're going to start work on your clothes closet. It's spring, it's going to be lovely…oh, the praise life gives if we allow ourselves to follow our desire!"

"We'll see," she says. "I'm glad you're back safely. I missed you."

Richard comes to our house the next day to collect a bed. It's late afternoon. I haven't expected him and feel a little on my guard. I see right away it will be an encounter.

"I've come to collect the bed, Crete."

"Richard, dear, I don't remember you loaning us a bed."

"Don't tell me what I did or didn't do! And stop calling me 'dear!' Last year I loaned you a bed. There's no question about it, I remember it exactly. Now where do you have it?" He stands in the hall, defiant, looking stunningly clear until he sees I'm not afraid of his anger.

"Ah, I remember this now, you gave it to us for the twins more than a year ago, a gift Richard, you weren't using it, didn't have space you said."

The abused bed is located, with two broken side rails, in a dark corner of our cellar. "As always I'm robbed, robbed! And now, you add this to my teaching day." He's so straightforward in his indignation. Never giving himself to his own nature. He wants to be free. He wants a new direction.

Back upstairs I pour two glasses of gin and settle down on the couch. "One has to choose people carefully, even the ones who share your old furniture." I make the tone of my voice light. "Richard, when were you most happy?" He sits down, softening then, relaxing into the alcohol's initial deceptive gift of infinite power and ease.

"I never was. My real condition is permanent longing." His laugh is dry with a hint of bitterness. "I'm full of regret."

I keep still because I want him to feel safe with me. It takes all my strength to get beyond the presence of his physical beauty. I want him to go on, to tell me the cause of his deep sense of regret. I'm beginning to feel there's a lot of the past we have in common. It's sending a thrill up my spine but I put that down when he goes on, speaking more easily now.

"When I grew up, a lot of things didn't seem real. It was war-time. My father had a map in our living room and every night we moved the pins showing the advance of the Allied forces. My mother had close relatives in Germany and she sent for refugees to live in our house. I hated them. I did my brother's work when he went to the Marine Corps. We let the gardener go. I did all that gardening and never learned a thing about plants, worked on the clay tennis court, never mastered the game. And do you know?"

Richard's jaw clenched as though it would release something that could hurt me. "D'you know? I became afraid of war. When Korea broke out I couldn't face it. I avoided combat, I didn't go. I've always been a coward. But Christ! there was a kid sitting next to me at the recruiting station and he couldn't read! a poor black kid like that going to war, signing on for, for what? He couldn't read!"

"Why didn't you get help with that choice? Because it's fair, Richard, noble. It's like you, I mean doesn't everyone who cares about you think so? What did you do then?"

"Oh, there were ways, honorable ways." His eyes darken and he closes down, offering me no more. There's so much I need to know. I move a little closer to him on the couch.

(Richard Warrington had grown up with dogs, a pony, and horses in summertime; he kept a dovecote, a goat, some white rats and a donkey. Two brothers and two sisters also lived in the big Tudor house named The Merry House by their father. Cousins were rampant, both boys and girls. "But it was better at Auntie Peggy's," Richard always said in later years. "More fun. Not all that guilt about inheriting a little money. Not having to wear your brother's used clothes, not rolling your own tennis court and cleaning cold frames for the gardener."

All the numerous cousins, children of the five aunts, were conditioned into a culture made giddy with alcohol and social events heightened by family grief and conflict over their connection to relatives in the war zones of Europe. And Richard was, on a deep level, always alone as are those who have, from an early age, a remarkable physical beauty. What did people want from him? Why were they deceiving?

Certainly, he needed a shell of impermeability to hide the soft center where he had not made clear his own truths to himself. It was not yet foreseeable what that unformed part might become to help him overcome the contradictions he felt. A perceptive teacher saw his sensitivity to natural beauty and advised Richard to study photography. His skill allowed him an identity and acceptance in that adolescent world so cruelly strident and bound by social convention. He had a sense of entitlement and felt deeply the injustice of a similar point of view in others, particularly those who exploited rural people or the working poor. He could feel his heart growing when he made an alliance with them and could work by their side. It was inevitable that Richard's path would not be straight and, indeed, it veered wildly in different directions.

During the war he followed an uncle to live in the expatriate community of southern Mexico which had swelled with adventurers, profiteers from all parts of the world and women whose hearts were ready to be broken again. After several years he joined a young professor of botany traveling into the Brazilian rainforest in the state of Minas Gerais. They paddled dugout canoes down the tributaries of the Urucuia River to work on carbon dating of rare plant species. The work continued for a year and another year in Malaya where, by a stroke of luck, he was discovered by a well-known photographer.

The expansive years of the 60's were joined together by a net of academic colleagues determined to save the planet from further war or destruction. They read about and then became the counterculture and vowed, one after another, to go back to the land. So it was not surprising that at last Richard accepted a government assignment that took his new wife and baby to live in the muddy capitol of South Korea. Then, traveling with a second child, they set up house along the dusty streets of Oaxaca, Mexico.)

A few moments pass in silence between us. Then Richard returns from what seems to be a far distance and I see I can hold him no longer. He drains his glass, rises abruptly and walks to the door.

"Richard!" I want him to stay. I want him to admit to a certain arrogance. But I can see he's afraid.

"I take my leave M'am." He bends toward me as distinct and compelling as a prime minister.

Watching him go down to the street, I feel the strength of his bitterness but I have to laugh at his words. "Robbed! Robbed of my past." Well, he just hasn't stepped out and seized it, that's all. He thinks the world owes him joy without labor. Convinced he's unlovable! He can't see others clearly, doesn't know in his heart if they're trustworthy... things like love and freedom and independence...yes, he's really, really confused. Of course he's invented his life! Determined it almost entirely by his imagination, his fabrication of himself. I think it's exactly how he needs to see it!

He's spoiled, a spoiled visionary. But he's a superb photographer. What a good defense for someone robbed of his past! Photography makes his world available. He takes possession of it, and it softens his disorientation. But Richard isn't disoriented! He needs distance from this roiling world that can't afford his vision. He needs ritual to renew himself. Maybe the place, Stone Hill, is keeping them afloat now but it isn't keeping them safe. Oh, I'm weary of it all. I'm weary of myself today.

How fast the light's falling. It's almost dark. So much for drinking gin in the afternoon. "Is that racket you, Ferdy? Are the boys with you? I need half an hour more in the studio, it's crucial. Put that macaroni in at 350, will you, dear? What would I do without you!"

I need this time in my own space to tie up loose ends. The sun left it warm in here, mellowed the paint smells. I love the disarray of these tools. I love what I do, working with surprise at the edge of darkness. Art is a mystery, the anxiety of the unresolved. Some artists can't bear that anxiety. Matisse was one and I think it spoiled his work in Provence. He'd paint beautiful forms and then, at the very end, he'd slash streaks of pure white across the canvas. That's his Mediterranean light. He wasn't right, the resolution doesn't come from outside. We're not always in the full glare of day.

And so what is it? It's how to grasp what's less definable, the light that struggles out from the center of things. Their invisible center. To look and look and look at a thing until the tensions that hold its center together can be seen. That center is the deep heart of a thing, where the light comes from. To connect that invisible center with all light... that's my goal now. And on the way I'm going to find out about the deep shadow in Richard's heart, that's another goal. Maybe it's the same. Whatever it is, may all the players in it be damned. I'm feeling my power again. How juicy life is, and sweet! I'm going to keep on tasting all of it.

Part Two

The Field,
The River,
The Road

"...and more we know not yet
because our daies are young."
> -journal of an early American explorer

1

LIKE THE RARE AND BARELY AUDIBLE SOUND of wings beating as a bird flies low and near, the sound of spring's arrival in New England is heard only by one who lives in a perpetual state of listening. It is through the ear that the most subtle signs arrive, the sound of rain falling gently on roofs still cluttered with broken ice, swishing waterways on the back roads and the splash of brooks filling with waterfalls. The spring rain moves every living thing, and it moves the heart to listen for the sounds of this returning. Spring moves slowly into the hills, breaking its promise again and again.

People closely tied to a place watch and listen as if this slow change is part of their bodies. As cold rains snatch away the warming air the temperature rises and falls. Roofs drip outside the windows, gutters clog with icy slush, thawing, freezing, thawing again. What spring means in back hill country is repairing the ravages of winter. Gaps in old foundation stones have been pathways for hibernating animals, bats and flying squirrels in the attic, and mice who outnumber all living things inside a warm New England house. The dirt floors of cellars erupt in porous bubblings as snow melt seeks a higher level. Spring is the season of water and it is the season of fire, brush burning and bonfires. Doing these repeated tasks, hill people ask themselves, what is the purpose of this life?

It was at breakfast, after Mary-Molly's flying start to reach the main road in time for the school bus. "Just what is Stone Hill?" Richard looked up over his newspaper. "A past? a future? a point of geography? Just what are we in relation to it? Lidia?"

Lidia knew he didn't expect an answer but needed, for herself, to calm any rising agitation. "It seems to me this place reads our moods, it has an interior life, perhaps even," she glanced at him, "an etheric body. The house has its spirit, and this morning it's changed by the full moon."

"Etheric body, spirit! Lidia I'm asking you what this place really is, Stone Hill, to you, to us?"

She knew Richard's question came from a place of inconstant struggle to know himself. Time after time he smothered discomfort with questions. "I think Stone Hill is a ship," she said, "sailing east, and we're on it sailing into the high pines. The animals are on it. We go through storms and calm. We try to keep setting sail but it's hard."

"Lidia? what this place is, is confinement. We can't go anywhere having these goats, chickens, soon the mowing again. This place, my work, everything gets half done, half-baked done. Right now it's water in the cellar again, flooding us out. Again!" He stood up and thumped down into the wet cellar.

She held her mind steadily on his question. I'm the one who found this place. I decided we should come here. Perhaps it wasn't practical, no bedrooms for the children, no closets, light and air and now water rushing into the foundation. But it's ours and it connects all of us. We just need to see it whole.

She heard Richard gasp as the muffled sucking of the pump began struggling with four inches of water, more than usual for spring. She knew the water was not alarming in itself but as a conveyor for floating objects in dark corners, boots and butterfly nets and small back packs, it was challenging. How amusing this house spirit, Lidia smiled, container for all things, receiving and holding all that happens to us.

The day was good for burning and she thought of Merle, half expecting him to appear, then fully knowing he would. Claire was home from school to help burn the three huge brush piles that stood black and wet in the lower meadow. Claire liked burning and could stand for hours by a fire keeping it piled high with brush.

Merle came early. "Piri says she needs to see you Lidia." He poured a stream of sugar into his coffee. "She needs to." His face turned suddenly grave. "The river's floodin' now, after the full moon it went over the banks."

"I didn't know."

"No, you're safe up here. Down below at the bridge it's rollin' fast. It'll be all over Jenkins Flats carryin' heavy snags and logs, dangerous to put a boat in. Snow melt and rain and the ground still froze in places. A little one was swept away at Still Corners, found some way down the river, drownded. Quite a lil' fella lyin' so still."

"Oh Merle I'm sorry, I'm so sorry." Lidia's eyes filled with sudden tears.

A car drove up, stopped to let someone out and drove away. It was Reuben, Merle's father, pale, thin and unshaven, a wrathful face.

"Did you know he was coming? How'd he know about the burning?"

"From the per-mit I guess." Merle's accent fell strangely on the second syllable. "I told him there was piles to burn."

"How're ya, Miz Lidia?" Reuben's eyes glinted at her. The lurking force of his cruelty shocked her through. She reached her hand out, shuddering at his long curving fingernails yellowed with age and cigarette smoke.

"Thank you for coming."

"It's a good wind, she'll burn if we get 'er goin.'" Reuben grinned.

Thick smoke curled up from the low meadow where Claire and Richard were trying to fire the wet brush. Reuben followed Merle down into the meadow, and stood a few moments watching them poke the heavy piles with long poles to allow air to enter. Smoke swirled around them as the wind blew up but no flames were visible. Reuben ran to the heavy can of gasoline Richard had used to start the fire, held it high over his head and hurled a stream of gas directly toward the smouldering flames. The flames rose high and traveled instantly backward in a burning arc to Reuben's chest. His shirt ignited and he began to run, a wild figure with flames streaming behind. Richard and Claire stood immobilized. Running at full speed, Merle dove at Reuben's feet and brought him down on the wet grass, rolling him over and over as his father bellowed out a deep guttural sound. Claire ran to the house for bandages. They carried Reuben up to the car and Lidia drove with Merle, to the hospital.

"Poor duffer, reckless in every way. He was lucky this time." Richard began poking at the fire again.

"How can you say that Dad," Claire's face was white. "Don't you have any sympathy?"

"Reuben's a wretched sort," Richard clenched his teeth, "gets what he deserves."

She faced him directly. "Well, I think you're cruel. You don't care about people that're different. You think you're better than they are, don't you?"

"Don't put me down Claire. Better than Reuben? That's amusing. Do you know Reuben Fowler's a drunk, who terrorizes his family, who doesn't turn a hand to help anyone? They're a shiftless bunch down there. I should hope I'm better, yes. I should hope your judgment of me is clear."

"It isn't a judgment. It's what I feel." Claire's eyes blazed. "And if you care to know, I'm scared about things here. About you and Mom, how you take her energy away, what's going to happen. I think it's this place. I hate it here, I hate it!"

"Claire! What an outburst. You're upset, I guess we're both upset. Why, your mother's fine, everything's fine. Let's get these fires going and go up to the house. It upsets me to see you so distraught." Richard moved some large logs to a new space, and the fire began to rise again. "This damn smoke. I can't see anything down here. Let's go."

Early that evening Crete phoned Lidia to ask about the day. "I love this hour in town after we've had dinner and it's still light. But it sounds like you haven't eaten yet."

Lidia heard the question in Crete's voice. "No, there's so much going on." She would not share details of the morning's catastrophe or Claire's distress.

"Yes," Crete said, "maybe there's too much going on. When's Claire leaving? I want to see her."

"Claire's busy now, she has to finish something before she leaves, another time Crete." Lidia did not want to bother Claire who spoke clearly about distrust of people like Crete "who suck all your energy away."

Lidia felt Claire was so perceptive about others, that she had a gift of speaking so easily, from a reserve that drew on just the appropriate thing, a place of interior surprise, as though she always had a little joke inside. It seemed like a depth below surfaces others pass over so lightly. When Claire was away at school her presence brushed past the side of Lidia's head, not fully approving in some way, as if it knew something no one else could see, always saying it could help her. And wasn't Claire the *only* person who let her be, who saw who she was?

How often Lidia remembered her words, chanted over and over again when Claire was five, whirling in a circle around the kitchen on her tricycle. "I'm going around and around the earth. In the center there's a big hole. I have to keep everyone close to me so they won't fall in the hole. I'm going around and around the earth..."

The thought that Claire often tried to protect her and Richard was hard to accept. At what great cost, Lidia wondered.

After dinner Claire stopped on the way out to her room. "I've thought it out," she said, with a trace of emotion Lidia could not name. "Everyone has one thing they know the most about and yours is the natural world. You just don't know about people, Mom."

"Well Claire, I guess you're right." She spoke slowly. "I never did. Most of the ones I knew disappointed me."

"You could wear brighter clothes Mom. Dad said it would make you happier. He said you might like a job somewhere away from here."

Lidia turned away from her without answering. How painful and isolated this place must be for Claire. If I was happier would all be changed? I am happy. I just don't understand Richard, or Claire. I never will. How unfair of Richard to goad her that way.

When it was almost dark, she went to find Claire on the terrace, sitting alone. "It's time for us to start back to school, don't you think? Claire, you know Reuben will be fine, the burns were superficial."

"Yes, I know. He's an ignorant old man, isn't he?"

She saw the figure Claire had woven from dried winter grasses that edged the stonewalls. "Oh, a phoenix!"

Claire nodded, and then lighted it with a match and held out the burning bird till it crumbled into ashes. She looked up. "When I want things to change, I go to fire."

It was late at night when Lidia returned. The house was quiet. She gathered the pails and went to milk the goats. The barn was peaceful, smelling of moisture rich with manure and fermenting earth juices. The goats were chewing their cud, the two horses snuffling. She laid her head on the warm flank of Devi, the oldest goat who turned toward her. "Thank you for the milk, for the cheese, dear old being."

Carrying the full pail of milk back to the house she heard the radio playing softly upstairs. Richard was asleep and on his side of the bed hung Devi's old leather goat collar cracked and dusty from years of storage in the barn. She knew what he meant and laughed out loud…scapegoat, scapegoat. Then her pain arose as she saw again the length he would go to demonstrate his humility. She had seen this so many times before, it was part of who he was. But it wasn't just humbleness, acknowledging his insufficiency in the face of the world. Richard felt the choice had been made long ago for him always to please others, to please far beyond his will. It was, for him, "being put upon." He was put-upon. And for her, this understanding was like being pulled down into darkness by a deep and ugly, tangled root. How would she ever learn Richard's truth? How maddening to feel pity when patience and strength was what she needed. She closed the bedroom door and went downstairs into the darkness. In the east over the tall pines the full moon was rising. Within the hour it would reach the clearing of Stone Hill from the south and shine in the front windows. She lit a lantern and wrote…

> The moonlight is in my house.
> It falls in squares on the floors,
> in prisms on the windows, in my cat's eye.
> All we make of beauty is for our loneliness.
> Is that why the moon falls into my house?

She went up to Richard and lay down with him. He slept on, muttering, restless. She would wake him early and love him, she promised herself.

She'd try to reach the part of him that was still outside himself. Besides, she needed him.

Three or four crows began calling early the next morning from the nearest row of pines and then flew to join others calling far back in the woods. It was always a racket. A blue jay flew out of the cherry tree. Ruffled, slightly damp and disgruntled with sleep, he hopped along the edge of the roof. Lidia lay still, looking at the beauty of Richard's face, and for the first time she saw fine lines appearing around his eyes, deeper lines along the nose. She hated them, not wanting his body to be changed.

When Richard woke she reached out to him. He held her and called her a Trumpeter Swan and loved her. She demanded it. She could not go on living with him so far away from her. Not to be loved was terrible when she opened to him far outside herself and he did not receive her. It became a disease eating her, draining her blood. The anger was fury spinning her and then Richard like a whirling dervish. It became hunger and then desire and held them tightly as they held each other, rising in waves till their loving emptied them and brought them into a vast open space together.

Moist and warm, they lay breathing as one great, still animal. At last Richard stirred, breaking the smoothness that flowed around them. "We're so lucky" he said, and she, not wanting to speak, only murmured "Yes, we are."

But was it tenderness? She wanted him to be transformed and lifted, lightened to the place where he could see his loveliness. She thought this desire was part of loving him, her desire for him to open to a place far beyond one he could imagine alone. Perhaps if she could continue to see him as she had when they first met, when she had felt his charm and easiness in the world. If she could see him whole with everything she knew about his loneliness in childhood and youth, the menagerie of animals he'd loved and cared for, the painfulness of being young and taking risks in the social world where he was so sought after –- then, wouldn't their loving be different?

And if she continued to remember how it was when she, the student at the big university, he the lecturer looking up over horn-rimmed glasses to assess the newcomers in his afternoon class, how his look of vulnerability had touched her heart. How from his field work he would send long letters typed on pages thin as tissue, with plans for a weekend together over the border into Canada. How it was breath-taking to sit beside him feeling the future unfold as they drove through a forest of yellow autumn leaves. They had separate rooms at the Canadian hotel and when she asked him what the plans were for the evening, looking up over horn-rimmed glasses, he would say, "Oh, take your time, have a rest and then we'll have dinner." No-one had ever given her such space, no-one had ever...the dignity, the chivalry, the beauty!

She was born away now on waves of darkness, and tenderly, as he slept, she made Richard whole again.

On Easter Day a small flock of robins gathered on the dry grass of Jenkins Flats. As Ferdy Montfort slowed the car for the three boys to see them, he said maybe there might already be frogs singing up at Stone Hill. The Montfort twins, Quinn and James, were giddy with joy. On the hill up to the house Quinn breathed, "Ohh, I love this place."

"Why do you love it?" his mother asked. When he couldn't say, the oldest boy Fran answered slowly, "Well Quinn, don't you think it's because of the people?"

"And there they are," James rolled down the car window to call Mary-Molly sitting on the stonewall by the barn. Mouche flew out the kitchen door with a cat in his arms. "We're going on a hunt," he tossed the cat ahead of him. "Then we're having a picnic. Come on down to the barn. Claire's home from school and she's cleaning up the horses." The boys adored Claire. She made magic happen. "She's brave and beautiful like a princess," James said, "with long shining hair like gold."

Lidia had arranged chairs at a small table under the maple trees and was setting down a pot of daffodils on the green and yellow cloth. "What do you think about Easter cocktails? They're on the menu. And Mouche made maps of the gardens for the egg hunt."

"Enchanté," Ferdy beamed. "Happy Easter."

They watched as Mary-Molly and Claire and the boys started off in pairs in different directions, shouting to each other while they were in range. Then Richard appeared, deliberately bearing an old silver shaker full of martinis. They sat in the thin March sun under leafless trees.

"Cheers to all of us." Crete raised her glass.

After the first swallow Lidia jumped up, "Brrr'r…I'm going to get some warm sweaters."

"I'll come with you," Ferdy rose crookedly out of his chair.

"And I'll stay to observe the host," Crete said.

"What a bad pun, if intended" Richard began, "and what do you see?" He looked up.

"A gallant and honorable man, a man of chivalry," she answered and then added, "but that kind of man whose charm does not cover a certain vulnerability behind the eyes." Richard shrank in discomfort as the others returned carrying lap robes and shawls.

"Richard, this is quite a place," Ferdy offered after a silence, "quite a place. Anyone would give a lot to live here," he added generously. "Tell me, what're the gardens?" Ferdy had seen Richard's map in the kitchen, a series of concentric circles with colored zones containing all the landmarks: the Tree House, the Vegetable Gardens, the Old Foundations, Swampy Tracts, a series of trails linked together, some completed and others planned. The map was to scale, a reminder of projects unexamined or unfinished.

"Well, they're everywhere," Richard began, "wherever anyone felt moved to create them. Some you see from here, vegetables and flowers on that upper slope and down here the raised kitchen beds," he waved toward the house. "In the woods a way up is the Moon Garden. Mouche says it reflects rays of the moon and sun. It's a drumlin, you know? sandy soil with a species of lichen. Good campsite for the kids, too far to walk back at night."

A slow smile lighted his face. He stood tall and straight except for the slight movement of which he seemed totally unaware, an almost imperceptible rocking of his body from side to side. He continued speaking as though he was lecturing a class. "Now the Moss Garden is Claire's, moss and ferns she transplanted and stones laid out for paths and a bridge along the stream. Claire's a landscaper."

"She's an artist," Crete interrupted, "a true artist."

Richard nodded and went on. "The Hermit Thrush Garden's hers too. You find it through a tangle of blueberry on a ledge overlooking the big pond. It's marked by a rusty bell high up on a bush. What kind of bush, Lidia?"

"Witch hazel," she murmured, embarrassed by Richard's pride.

"Mine is the Stone Garden. We used the front end loader to place the big rocks."

"It's really a terrace in two levels," Lidia added. "Richard plans to cover it with glass for a greenhouse someday."

"Ummm..." Crete seemed amused at Lidia's need to confirm Richard's dreams.

"Ah!" Ferdy's eyes were widening. "And is that all?"

Richard shook the silver pitcher and filled the glasses again. "Well, there's comfrey for the goats, leeks and garlic fenced in by the rhubarb plot, and a hummingbird garden for Mary-Molly. It's extensive." He seemed pleased and went on about his ideas, big ideas for Stone Hill.

"You know, Richard," Ferdy's voice was jovial, "you have all these ideas and then Lidia carries them out. I love the reflective mind but one doesn't always have to act on it."

"Dear fellow, it's a question of time, of making order in the world. As a photographer, that's what I'm about."

Ferdy stood up, balancing unevenly for a moment, and then sat down again. "Panic, panic is the natural condition of the life of the mind. Avoid it at all cost. Sometimes its good to withdraw from the field of action." He muttered on without looking at Richard. "Seems to me you're managing this like the French countryside."

Crete moved uneasily in her chair. Though it was clearly time for food, Ferdy went on, smiling. "A good artist steps back to see when the work's completed. Am I right Crete? Why don't you let..."

"For heaven's sake, Ferdy," she burst in, "we have to invent our lives, follow our obsessions till they pull us down, otherwise we're at the mercy of..."

"But you can't live on romance, can you Richard?" Ferdy was determined to gain the upper hand. "It bites you in the back, it turns bitter and bites you! Look, all this doesn't take care of itself!" He seemed desperate to have them all understand, to understand that he was speaking from his heart which had undergone such tribulation.

Lidia was beginning to shiver. "Oh, let's go in and have dinner. The children'll be back soon." They all seemed willing.

When they straggled back, the children were cold and hungry and demolished the hot cross buns within minutes. Taking a basket of sandwiches and hot drinks they disappeared again with Mary-Molly, her face covered with chocolate. "Tree house I think, Claire's taking them down the road." Richard's voice, a bit unsteady, had an edge of pride.

The sun gleamed through the glasses of red wine. There was lamb, potatoes and peas, a chicory salad with walnuts and oranges and an almond mocha cake shaped like a fish, the same cake Lidia had made a month ago for Richard's fiftieth birthday.

"Ah, to the Pisces. Salut!" Ferdy raised his glass. In February he had been working at the vineyard in Brittany, so they told him everything about Richard's birthday party. "It was all orchestrated by Claire. It was royal," Crete said, "a procession with torches wound up the road at night, people circling the bonfire and then a dinner with five kinds of fishes cooked whole in their skins, and salads and a table of blueberry pies."

"Yes, that was all part of it." Crete saw a wave of sadness pass quickly over Lidia's face.

An hour later the children burst into the kitchen saying they'd lit the sauna and it would be ready soon. Goat kids raced by the window like a pack of horses. Lidia poured coffee and Richard carried in a tray of brandy glasses.

"You do understand the practice of the sauna?," he said loudly to Ferdy. Startled, Ferdy looked up in time to see Jamie galloping wildly by the kitchen window riding bareback on the white pony. He stood up quickly.

"Isn't it time to get the boys home? Can we do the sauna another time, Richard? Lidia, you're the *real* ascension! Thank you for that and for everything." He kissed her hand with gracefulness and moved toward

Richard, who stepped back and began thrusting his hands deeply through his hair.

As Crete and Ferdy went out to the barn to send the boys back for thank-you's, they heard Richard saying, "Invent your life! invent your life? What kind of therapizing is that?"

Driving away, Crete wondered if they would remember the sauna and go there together into the heat and then out with steaming bodies into the cold evening. Ferdy put his hand on her knee. "Happy Easter Big Rabbit." The car swerved alarmingly to the right.

"Heavens, do you want me to drive, Ferdy?" He chuckled. "Enchanté, my dear, tout de suite, tout de suite," and kept on going.

2

An evening stillness falls over the hills in late April and early May. The soft nights become vibrant with moonlight. Moths begin to fly in the open windows and light rains make the sound of lizards walking in dry leaves. The moon of the spring equinox waxes full and high over the gardens, stirring plants to rise and swell into tunnels of leaves. Vita, the most fragile of the goats in the barn, feels the kids move in her belly. She knows they are ready to be born. Moonlight falls into the goats' eyes, into the stairwell and onto the floor of the kitchen as Lidia comes down at midnight to open the door. Moonlight lies thick on the ground between the apple trees, and the trees and rocks grow heavy in the light. She sees the shape of a unicorn grazing between the shadows. A thing is most truly what it is in this stillness, she whispers. Inside the house, all things begin to stir in the thick light.

In the morning she sees the house needs to be lighter, simplified. Lidia puts away heavy rugs and winter curtains, transforms the furniture with the old white summer covers. She does not wonder why these rituals are necessary year after year. Things need to rest in different spaces after the cloistered winter. She will make the house a spacious stage for what they all might become.

On a Saturday morning Lidia heard heavy thumping and then a crash from Richard's upstairs study. She waited in the kitchen, restraining her impulse to go up. Richard came to the top of the stairs, limping, motioning violently for her to come. His face flashed with red and then turned white.

"It's fallen," he said, "the damn thing's fallen. I'm moving my study. These bloody small window-panes, I should've taken the west side long ago." The room was in chaos, loose papers on every surface, journals everywhere and filing drawers flung open. "It's the damn Ardmore bookcase, the top part isn't attached." She saw he had tried to push the glass-fronted bookcase from the bottom and the top had slid toward him and crashed to the floor.

She tried to circumvent his despair. "It's too heavy for here," she said softly. "Some things from the past just don't work any more. We can fix it, please Richard...let's sweep up the glass."

"Don't you ever agree with me, ever? I can't live with bare walls and sleep on the floor! I just need a little clutter!"

She felt his familiar desperation. But at the same time she saw the meaning in the origin of his rage. It was so large, rage at his own complexity that could not slough off accumulated desires and needs of lifetimes. Rage at the very largeness of possibilities life offered, any one of which she knew he felt perfectly able to master if they would just let him alone, if someone else would make right these practical matters. She had sympathy for his search to find the right space. She knew he longed for simplicity. She was not the target of his rage. It was humility and it was filling him so deeply that he couldn't see. She could explain none of this to him. Wasn't it enough that she understood and supported him?

"Richard, it isn't the space, it's how you're living in it. It asks for something more, a yielding."

"Don't give me that holy stuff! I'm accustomed to a little dignity, a little grace and...," he barked, "don't scold me!"

It was useless. She felt helpless, not wanting to have this understanding Richard did not have. She knew how he lived, on a rainbow of all colors, he was a dreamer. He carried opposites inside himself, needing to expand then to retreat, needing large spaces, needing small spaces secure and enveloping. He wanted the old, small rooms of the house at Stone Hill, he wanted the great hall at Ardmore where he'd grown up and where they'd danced on New Years' Eve before they were married, the kitchen with three stoves and rocking chairs, the wide bedrooms with mahogany canopied beds, the porte cochère and terraced gardens. All these spaces clamored inside him and the tragedy was, that having one he tried to make it into the other. Retreat was her best ally. She would stand by and wait.

They both became still and were sitting silently. Then Richard spoke. "Lidi, I think there's a thing you don't know," he said quietly. "Many times when a person's unable to express something it's a sign that it's their deepest truth."

Oh how she loved him! loved how he rescued them and brought them together onto safe ground.

Through all such seasonal dramas Crete Montfort came to Stone Hill to paint or talk with Lidia about the meanings of their days. To Lidia, Crete seemed wise in ways of the world. She was tall as Richard, stately, perhaps queenly Lidia thought, though more defended and full of emotional history than a queen should be. She was clearly an artist needing her own territory and hungrily searching in her work. Crete had a direct gaze that might put off a casual observer before he recognized what lay behind it, that controlled sense of self and the aggression needed to protect it. After Crete's visits Lidia felt a subtle sense of depletion she accepted as ransom for their explorations together. They both needed a friend.

"It's like Pierre Bonnard," Crete said one afternoon. "He struggled with composition. If you have that right you have everything. He said a painting needs space in the center, with people and objects capturing life on the edges. He said you must make all things beautiful." Crete explained how he did this, painting canvases of his radiators or his plain bathroom in a mystery of colors.

"Well, Crete, no one's on the edges here. We're all in the middle."

"Yes, and bigger, too much bigger than life! You're like a Chagall painting, with figures carrying hearts and roses and floating in air, like the fiddler upside down over the rooftop, the goats with a magic eye. You expect so much more of yourself than just being. You need a budget, Lidi, for projects, for emotions."

"Of course you're right. I'm sure I need your advice but it's suppertime Crete, can you come back tomorrow?"

"If you'll hear me, I will. I love this place, such a world of its own, so brave and complete." Crete bent down to give her a hug.

Lidia called outside for Mary-Molly to come in and set the table for dinner. "Mom, I was just talking to Crete," she rushed in and slammed the door. "She's so beautiful, so dusky brown with her long silver hair, and her eyes kind of green. I love the jewels she always wears, those turquoise ones. She asked me how everything is up here. I said great, it's great. She's really interested, she likes all of us. She's so different, you never told me about her."

"You never asked me, dear, I only know a few things."

"Ah ha, the California mystics, like the goat people they're all sub rosa. That means underground, M-M. Don't be bewitched by them." Richard pulled out a chair for Mary-Molly to sit down.

"Richard, the Montforts are not underground!" Lidia jumped up. Her voice rose. "Ferdy's from an old English family, very old. His ancestor was Simon de Montfort, a great knight of the thirteenth century. He founded the English Parliament and then he was killed in battle. Ferdy's name is Ferdinand Montfort, Count de Montfort if you want to know."

"I don't want to know. It's boring," Richard said quickly. "A name isn't everything, money isn't everything."

"They don't have money. They work hard like you. Ferdy manages a vineyard in Brittany." Lidia began serving the dinner, slices of warmed up lamb roast with newly browned potatoes. Mary-Molly's eyes moved back and forth between them. She was trying to interrupt.

"Dad? I love Ferdy, he's dear, how he's losing his hair, how he's so round and his eyes sparkle. Count Ferdy is sweet."

"Just how'd he get the gimpy leg?" Richard asked.

"Traveling, he stepped back off a cliff somewhere in Africa. He was leading a tour when he met Crete." Lidia waited for his reaction.

Richard smiled. "And she's from the city, right? and she has plenty to say."

"New York City?" Mary-Molly's eyes opened wide.

"Yes dear, she was an actress there for a little while and then she went to live in California."

"An intrusive type," Richard muttered." She sucks energy out of you Lidia. You don't see she's a control person, that silvery sort with a big agenda. Makes my loins scream when I see her coming."

"Dad?" Mary-Molly waved a fork in the air and looked directly at him. "You don't try to like any of Mom's friends. You make them feel like they're not important, like they have nothing to say. Dad, I'm just telling you exactly what I feel." She lowered her fork and speared a potato. "It isn't fair to Mom."

"Well, of all things," Richard pursed his mouth in mock dismay. "Am I really unfair, Mom?" He turned to Lidia. "Do I embarrass your friends?"

Lidia avoided his gaze. "I believe you're right, Mary-Molly," she said slowly. Then her voice became bright. "Maybe we can help Dad to see that goat people and mystics are valuable too."

"Yeah, and just as smart as you, Dad. Aren't I right?"

The month of May unfurled its growing things and Richard's energy became charged and tightened as a coiled spring. Once more it was the approach of the high celebratory days of the Garrison Academy commencement. What had two years ago been customary and somewhat impersonal at the large university, now required Richard to be front, center and provocative on the stage of the smaller school. When asked if he would agree to give the brief commencement address, Richard assumed the willing expression he usually wore before his colleagues, an expression of trust in his power and natural charm.

His new associates seemed to have less of the "supremacy of mind" he had known in former associates, but he was unaware of feeling wholly unrelated to them. His strength, as always, lay in making close relationships with promising students and in his ability to think creatively beyond the boundaries of academic disciplines. He was most fitted for the type of classical education, experimental at Garrison, that combined the last two years of high school with the first two years of college. Superb with ideas and inspiration for the planning phase of these projects he took them on with acknowledged success. His five years of field work in cultural development overseas upheld all the Garrison principles of "cultivating generous habits of body, heart and mind."

His class in photography was a popular offering in the Academy's compulsory afternoon program. And so after quiet reflection the thought came to use a wider understanding of photography as a metaphor underpinning his words at commencement. He was pleasantly surprised to find how smoothly these thoughts flowed onto the page.

As Richard took the stage, the day was ordinary with bright sun, a slight wind off the river below the school and a sea of faces in the open air before him. He spoke slowly and with a firm voice.

"Welcome Class of 1962 (loud cheers) (hats in air).

Today I feel impressed with the privilege of your task ahead. And may it be known that I also feel envious of your chance to work with the raw material of life in search of a pattern that will be your own.

The contents in the first part of my talk --What is Photography?, I know well. Of the contents in the second part --'What is Life?' I know very little. (subdued cheers). I bring these areas together because, as I have made clear in my work with you, each informs the other in the way that art and life are inseparable. What is indefinable in a work of art may be what has the greatest hold over our minds. And it is the ordinary circumstances of human life --basic goodness, confidence, fear, presence-- that is the raw material that will form the patterns for your lives.

In photography we work with movement, and actually it is in the same way that life unfolds. Inside the movement is one moment when forces or elements will be in balance. While the photographer seizes this moment and immortalizes it in a photograph, in life you would say 'Stand still, this is a moment of balance that will change my life.' Perhaps you feel it as an eternal moment. You feel the need to distill the essence of whatever it is that has captivated you.

The balanced moment is a story of parts brought together in relationship, which you will bring together and re-unite in your own way. You will reassemble and then let them go out into the world. It may be a recognition of 'this is the way' or 'this is who I want to follow.' Perhaps it will be only a fleeting image seen by the brain, the eye, and the heart. Perhaps it will be all intuition.

There is no pattern for your choice but to recognize how tenuous and delicate are the ways of Beauty and Goodness.

So in closing, I offer three guidelines from your work with me and from your time spent here in Garrison. Be alert to contents in the process of unfolding. Be alert to interrelationships; intuit them in every case. Be alert especially to what is swiftly passing by.

Thank you and good luck to you."

There was one minute of silence and then a standing ovation.

As his teaching at the Academy in Garrison ended for the season, one after another his expansive projects on Stone Hill began. Lidia paid bills, urged him to get his practical affairs in order and to help with the childrens' summer plans. "I don't want anything to do with all these "shoulds." But he cooked pork chops seasoned in his special way and invited one of his brightest students, a musician from Zaire to have dinner with them. When they made love in the morning Lidia breathed in tenderness and quiet as though it was always there.

"You're like Ting Ling, my giant panda," she said.

"That's what I need, a giant panda," and he lay on her body and slept again. Their loving seemed like a wholeness but she often felt it was a shattering that moved some part of her toward him and then moved her out into a wide, lonely space. It was like space she'd known as a child with her father, in the garden back of their house.

A long blue fence ran the length of the garden on two sides and kept her and her sister, Rillis, confined from neighboring yards, kept them safe they were told, in the city. The fence was of soft old pine boards stained a weathered blue. More than once, he had perched her up higher than his head on the bare branch of the apple tree growing by that fence. He would stand back, smiling and admiring his beautiful child. He would leave her there, once going to the middle of the garden to talk with a man she didn't know. She heard their voices but could not call out. He would come back, laughing, to take her down, not knowing how her whole body burned with anger and fear. Such a wide and lonely space seemed to surround her now but what was the helplessness?

One morning a dream wakened her. In the dream a film came over her eyes and she couldn't see. In her left eyelid a worm was embedded and she went to the cellar for a small jar to save it for the doctor to examine. At the bottom of the empty jar was a huge insect struggling to flap its wings. These images floated to the surface of her mind and clung there in spite of her effort to push them down.

A letter came to Lidia from Rillis Skiles, Mesa Doblé, Ocotillo, Arizona. It was, even un-opened, unsettling. Lidia laid it aside but its energy overcame her will, and like an undertow the letter drew out a torrent of recollection, undercurrents of dreams and memories…

…Rillis, her life of pain and addiction, estrangement from her husband and beautiful angry children. Rillis alone, working, struggling, rigid, unforgiving. Who is Rillis today, my sister, myself, my shadow. Rillis a child, chubby, pure blond head, little rabbit with courage so inconstant, challenged, frightened by Lidia the quick fox, surreptitious planning and thieving, tyranny over Rillis mixed with deep care and protection and love.

Rillis so young seeming old, socially correct, a 'right way' to climb up, grand-daughter of Isaac Skiles the ruthless and god-fearing Ohio cattle driver, rigid and unforgiving to his own children. Push all to the outside, nothing is inside.

Rillis close for so many years and then the issue of control at last becomes the splitting point. Rillis commanding Lidia to sit at their father's grave when his coffin goes into the earth. Rillis sits, Margaret sits, the Ohio relatives sit. Lidia will not sit when her father's body is lowered into the earth, she will not! She stands. Rillis gestures before the small crowd of people. Lidia stands and stands and then ---submits. Rillis, her life an enormous effort, her body destructing now…

The letter went unopened for two days, then Richard picked it up and read out loud, "Rillis Skiles, Mesa Doblé, Ocotillo, Arizona…bloody interesting you'd think, epic figure on a desert mesa of the frontier! Yip-e-yi! And who is it? A dispirited woman in a gated housing development on ground made green with stolen irrigation water. Ha!"

Lidia laughed out loud, snatched the letter from him and read the contents aloud. 'Dear Lidia, I couldn't answer your letter. It's been months as you know. My body is giving out with the long hours at

Canyon Inn, all the planning, shopping, preparing and then having to be a good hostess. Usually for fifty people. Finally I'm getting a raise so they appreciate me, thank God. I see my life stretching ahead and know there is not going to be a good time for me and there never will.

One good friend is helping me but no-one knows how vulnerable I am. Please come. My apartment is lovely overlooking a golf course. The weather is great, steadily dry, ninety degrees. Mother may visit this summer if she can make the trip. Otherwise no news. With love, Rillis'

"Well, she's asked for everything but money," Richard said. "So when will you be leaving?" He paused. "Lidi you don't have to go, it's not a duty."

"No, and I would dread it." She saw how he watched her, she knew he saw that she was already allowing herself to go, facilitating the details of her absence. "Richard, it's a tremendous confusion. It's like a fabric of expectations over Rillis and me, not about how we feel or what we know about each other, it's more how we're bound in commitment. Rillis doesn't know she's tearing the fabric that holds her, that she's going to fall through it and be lost."

"But she won't know she's lost, Rillis won't listen to you anyway."

"She might hear something beyond talking about why I came across the whole country to see her. If I don't go it's like throwing a piece of broken crockery on the dump!" She flung out her arm, "Crash! Scattered to smithereens!"

Richard stretched out his legs and then rose up out of the old blue chair. "Lidi, you manage to get drama out of a dishrag." He leaned over her and looked into her flushed face. Straightening up, he rested his cool hand on her forehead. "We'll be fine, Mary-Molly can milk the goats."

The plane set down in a nest of palm trees and tropical plants that did not mask the parched earth or the hot breath of the desert. During the flight Lidia remembered the events of Rillis's life that had brought her to the desert, but why she remained as though it were home was still a mystery. The pretentious suburbia had crept further out over the vulnerable land, a jangling, glittering overlay of habitation and amusement. She thought about deserts everywhere in the world where people lived simply and survived by yielding to forces more powerful than themselves.

Nothing man-made here could strike a balance with the destruction it caused. There was no relief for her, every sight shocked her body with strangeness that gathered into anxiety at the pit of her stomach.

Rillis was waiting in a long, shining white station wagon and Lidia felt the rush of love joining them together again. Rillis looked well but underneath the cared-for look was a new fragility, the sense that she had capitulated with life by surrendering some of her invincibility. What had replaced it was what Lidia hoped to discover in these few days.

The long, bony face of the Skiles family was more apparent since she had seen Rillis two years ago. It was the arrogant Edith Skiles, their aunt, the matriarch of the Ohio farm. Rillis's face was sprinkled with freckles, her eyes were haloed with mascara, her smooth hair curled under in a page-boy style.

"Your hair, there's such a reddish glow in the blond of it. Rillis, you just look so great, so together and stylish!"

Rillis gave her a hug. "Well, I have to keep up. How I look is a big part of my job now. Anyway, let's go have a drink, my favorite place isn't too far. Is this all your luggage? You look just like one of the old girls of Santa Fe!" Her eyes lingered on Lidia's polished but cracked Chippewa boots and the old, faded hat.

"Yes,,I always carry it on my back. Don't trust airports I guess." Lidia shouldered her backpack. "Let's go."

"There's a Bergdorf-Goodman near my apartment," Rillis said. "We can go later if you like. There's a sale on shoes." The station wagon spun out into traffic along a wide highway lined on each side with creations like pictures in a child's book of fairy tales.

"The land of pleasure domes...Rillis, I can't imagine living here."

"It thins out to the south. Here we are." Rillis turned up a long sweeping drive with electric candelarios that flickered feebly in the bright afternoon light. She pulled the car up under the portico of a massive hotel and it was a relief to enter the cool, high-ceilinged adobe rooms inside.

"Buenas dias, Señora...para servirle. Es su hermana, verdad? Ella se le parece mucho."

"Buenas dias, Ricardo. Sí, mi hermana." Rillis answered and Lidia felt the proprietary pride in her voice.

"Y de donde viene usted señora?"

"Vivo en la costa este," Lidia said slowly, "y usted?"

"Mi familia es de Saltillo, Mexico," he said proudly.

"Ah, un país lindo, lo sé."

He turned gracefullly to Rillis, "Lo mismo que siempre, Señora?"

"A daiquiri Lidia?"

"Oh yes," Lidia smiled at him, "lo mismo que mi hermana."

With a slight bow Ricardo turned and left them, murmuring "las bellas hermanas, las bellas hermanas…"

"Well I see why you stay here, with people round you so full of grace!"

They had a second daiquiri served by the beautiful Ricardo and were considering a third. "When we get home," Rillis said. "It's close." And they ran giddily in the heat back to the air-conditioned car.

The small apartment was cool and dim, lavish with oriental rugs on the tiled floors, gold-framed mirrors and polished wood furniture. "I insisted on keeping these things after the divorce. There were rugs stored under every bed in the house. Of course Paul was mostly a rug dealer though he occasionally sold other valuable things. He wanted the children to have the rugs but the oldest two, Jake and Tricia, had already lost contact with me. They're not in my life now."

Rillis poured a glass of Scotch whiskey and added a piece of ice. "Lidia, it's a different world, so many unsavory people. I'm thankful not to be young any more. But a cleansing is going on, the earthquake in Armenia killing those starving people, the drug users hanged in Iran. The difficulty is it will never end!"

Lidia was silent. A deep hole opened in front of her. So soon it was clear how mistaken she'd been. Rillis would not open to anything she wanted to share. "Is this where your ideas come from?" Lidia flipped through a magazine from the top of a pile, knowing she should be silent, knowing Rillis would withdraw as she always had from a duel of intellect. In a flash Lidia saw how the whole visit would go, she saw her coming was useless.

The next day Rillis had to do a luncheon for residents at the Canyon Inn. The theme was gambling so they spent the morning setting up roulette wheels and chips and arranging flowers on every table. Rillis was organized and gracious, moving among the guests, enjoying their response to the entertainment. Everyone received a little gift, a knife sharpener with Canyon Inn in gold stamped on the handle.

"Successful but exhausting," Rillis moaned afterward. "My back is excruciating so let's have dinner at home."

They drank whisky, heated up frozen dinners and laughed at photographs of their childhood, Sunday School picnics in the backyard, their high school friends and episodes of their trip to Europe as innocents abroad. Rillis told Lidia she had gotten word of the death of Harley Skiles, the one person in the Skiles family Lidia had truly loved. Harley was twenty years older and had been Lidia's protector and adored cousin in the Ohio summers, reading and teaching her simple tunes on the piano. "He'd been very sick and died alone in a small town in Texas," Rillis said. "That's how it was, I'm sorry, I know you loved him so much." Before going to bed, Rillis gave back a watercolor Lidia had painted and sent to her long ago. It was entitled Poppies for My Sister.

"Red isn't my color," Rillis said, "it reminds me of blood. You don't mind?"

Lidia dreamed vividly, a disturbing dream that woke her in horror. Thinking of Crete, she wrote down every detail, feeling vulnerable and sick and longing to go home. Was it Crete that had told her that sisters were the shadow side of ourselves?

Under the vibrant morning sky Rillis drove them southwest toward the Sierra Estrella mountains, stopping at a dusty mining town long ago abandoned to the tourist trade. One building, a restaurant and bar, had bottles and pieces of blue glass turned over all the fence pickets. The sun sparkling through the glass was the background for their photographs, one taken of them together by a man, curious and friendly, who shuffled, with blinking eyes, out of the dark bar. To Lidia the landscape was exquisite, red and brown earth shades, the celadon green of sage and clumps of golden chamisa glowing against the dark range. The life of colors in the dry air was heightened into a vibrating weave that hung in the heat and, as the sun sank lower, each thing was illumined with its own soft horizon. They talked only about the landscape and simple things of the past. It was a timeless day, quiet and affirming.

On the last morning Rillis insisted on shopping. They visited an art gallery where she convinced Lidia to purchase an etching that had caught her eye, explaining how it would bring double in value from a discriminating dealer in the east. They had rushed to the airport, arriving minutes before departure time. Rillis had gone straight to the observation deck. As the plane moved slowly away, Lidia could see her sister waving a yellow scarf with both arms raised high. "Mi bella hermana, bella hermana," Lidia repeated the beautiful words till she could not see Rillis any more.

As the big plane rolled back toward the runway, Lidia struggled hard to breathe. She felt her heart, which had struggled so hard to stay open to her sister, had collapsed like a broken thing. Rillis had closed against intimacy like a wall of stone. It was a split that seemed like betrayal. How could Rillis betray our past, what it means to have a sister, one who trusts. I'd rather feel anger at her than this welling up of surprise and sadness and loss that's bringing tears to my eyes. Lidia leaned back her head trying to empty the emotion, trying to abandon herself to the movement of flying. As they flew over the high mountains, the great river and open plains, she slept.

She woke rested and with a sense of peacefulness. It was dark and nothing distracted her mind from its exploration into what her body had discovered, the passing from its sense of darkness into a kind of radiant joy. Turning over and over the loss in her heart of never having Rillis again as a true sister, Lidia began to understand what it meant. In her separation, Rillis had given Lidia a new knowledge of her own separate self, strengthened as a being free from blood ties to family history she had struggled to accept. Somewhere in the seeds of her family was this inner darkness and isolation of the body that destroyed so much around it, a rent in the fabric of wholeness that she could now close with her own spirit. She could turn the loss into a liberation. She could love Rillis in a way that freed them both from the dark connection.

The plane was coasting slowly, losing altitude for the landing. As it touched down on the runway, her body relaxed with a deep sigh of being home. Far back in the waiting room Richard's tall figure stood out above the crowd. The involuntary delight that always overcame them both upon meeting spread up into his face. Their words were always secondary, trailing behind.

"Long way out there over the mountain," he said smiling. "Thanks for coming back."

"Thank you," she took his arm. "Yes, it's a very long way."

The sun climbed higher over Piri's woods. Lidia was going to help her gather bark from the dye plants Piri used to supply the weaving trade. She had learned to gather plants in her village, Batowice. Polish rugs, especially the kilims with their special weave, were famous everywhere in the world.

"We'll have to work harder this summer. All those flower children going back to the land, they want natural dyes for their weaving, more soft and pure and beautiful. Mercy, thank goodness it's easier when the blooms come." Piri stood up slowly holding a bundle of jagged twigs. "But the bark of this black alder makes a rare blue. Let's carry them up to the porch. They need to soak before boiling."

She filled several large wooden tubs with water and threw in the alder. "Now Lidia," without resting Piri went on, "it's the day for us to try the watercolors."

"But you need to show me how, how you did the painting of your thicket and the old apple tree."

"There's no showing, just beginning. You make a small open frame of paper and move it back and forth till you find a view. Then you just try not to worry it."

"Not to worry it. Like we do with people we love," Lidia's voice was low.

After an hour she held her painting out at arms' length. Her brush strokes were tight, all the same weight and staying flat on the paper. The early morning light was deepening into shadows but Lidia's eye hadn't yielded to the subtle change of color. "Why it's gray, almost all gray. Piri, that isn't what you see!"

"Well, I had to learn how to let the colors come into me, scarlet mulberries, pink clovers, this moss-green stone sailing like a fish. If you're open they steal into you, yellow leaves, green land and blue sky moving together." Piri spoke passionately. "There's a way to reach the light in things. You must sit still… quiet your mind. Open it and wait…a desire may come to you from the center of the flower or the stone. You paint what you feel about their energy, not what you see but what you feel about them. Sit as long as you can, here out of view. Let your mind be still. You'll see Lidia, a desire will be there."

Lidia sat back in the grass and Piri left her alone.

> *…Shadows of trees move in the wind, the shadow of each branch down to the smallest twig is more real than the trees themselves…a swiftly moving cloud clears them from view… the sun shines out again and the shadows fade slowly back, darker against the dark trees, a web of shadows on the grass… like breathing, fading in, then sinking and fading in again… the rising wind is like hunger…my mind is empty except for the wind…my mind is hungry, open to the wind…I am all breathing, breathing in the earth…*

By noon the wind had shifted. The sky turned gray and was filled with thunder over the northern hills. They had moved indoors to listen to the growing storm. Charges of electricity flashed in brittle waves. Lidia sat on the couch kneading the pillows like a nesting cat.

"I did what you asked Piri, watching the shadows, listening."

"Ah, lovely…and what else?"

"What else." Lidia turned her head away and closed her eyes. "At the end I had a daydream. A door opened into a bright room and let in a surge of darkness. A voice said to me "you keep bringing in the darkness." Piri, do you think that's true?"

The room suddenly became dark as twilight. A violent clap of thunder boomed over the house and a flash of blue lightning followed. "Oh, it's right here!" A deluge lashed the window panes.

"Ominous, a storm like this at noon. But it'll pass." In those moments Lidia seemed to be riding the storm on the strong wind, escaping the hollow of empty light it left behind. And then she spoke in a low voice, "Piri what if the first eyes that see you are not full of light? If they make you feel shame for being born?"

What answer was there to such a question? Shame! in tiny vessels, in bones bird-light and supple as air? Lidia had come close to the core of deepest sorrow in herself.

At this moment an observer would have puzzled at the emotions flooding Piri's face. She saw that out of Lidia's reverie had come rejection instead of nourishment. Yet it had swept her toward a place of questioning that could open her grief. As Piri struggled for the courage to answer Lidia's question, she knew she was prepared for this challenge.

Long ago, Piri Olevsky had needed to form her own ideas of why people have negative beliefs about themselves or others or the world. There was much material from her own history. It was clear to her that it took violence to induce such a world view. How early in life and what is it that inflicts this violence? When she had learned about the small group at Chicago studying the connection between life experiences and experiences of the birth process, she'd persuaded Lorion that she needed to be there. She'd told him how re-creation of the birth experience was being performed by a doctor from Czechoslovakia and his wife. When Lorion had learned that the work was available in Polish translation, he'd reluctantly agreed. At those meetings Piri had learned first hand of the powerful residue that could be left in the psyche at birth. She was going to take this chance with Lidia.

Piri told Lidia the plan. "Will this be good for me?" she asked.

Piri breathed deeply. "Lidia, you have the strong and brilliant will that will make it good for you. This is all you need to do…sit back and sink into deep, deep, heavy breathing while you're listening to my voice. You will find your way back, far, far back to how it was for your body in the time before your birth, what happened there, how your body felt there. It will be awareness far back before there was any understanding. Letting go and sinking into the darkness there, breathing deeply, letting all sink away from thought, breathing deeply… Lidia sat back and closed her eyes. After a few minutes her body rocked slightly forward and back.

"It is right," Piri said.

Darkness, darkness and rhythmic rocking to the sound…
vrooma… vrooma…vrooma…vrooma…rocking…sleep…
sleep…vrooma…vrooma…vroom!…sudden shock, compres-
sion…smothering over networks of the brain spreading
to the heart…loud angry sounds, fine spasms
startle the tiny limbs…muscles tense…
fluids enter burning like fire, poison…

Force pushing, pushing, no escape…something does not want
me to survive… trembling and turning in the dark… push-
ing… I am smothered…something does not want me…
not want me to survive…smothering… I am falling…
scream!…choking… cannot receive…I am alone…I will not
live…there is nothing to receive…

It is dark and rain begins again, falling in sheets against the windows. Lidia and Piri sit in the darkness, not knowing what time has passed since the darkness began. A violent wind dashes against the window and subsides, leaving space for the mournful sounds of a train whistling at the far crossing.

"This darkness is my darkness. I let this darkness in. Cut off, not deserving love, terrified to be disappointed. It happened long before I was born." Wrapping both arms around her body Lidia rocked back and forward. "On the edge of being lost," she whispered, and then, "to survive I thought I must give up my Self. I would be good, I would be gentle, I would be quiet. I was born feeling deep sorrow for my mother. This sorrow has blocked my throat."

Her body was still now. "Yes, sorrow…hopeless…sorrow. But Piri, how was *your* birth? Some must be full of peace, and love, maybe a kind of joy, of freedom?"

"Yes. I think it's true there are powerful emotions. The body re-members and sets itself in patterns. It's difficult to undo them. Then you would be a different person. But everyone has a different pattern of blocking light."

Lidia lay back arranging the pile of pillows. The rain fell more gently now against the roof, rolling over the window and turning into drops that streamed slowly down the pane. The color which had heightened to an angry red in Lidia's cheeks was fading. All this had happened because of Margaret. Because of Margaret's anguish for her swelling body, what marriage had brought her so swiftly that was not love but loneliness; her dark fear, real or imagined, about her new husband's fidelity. It all felt so distasteful, "like being a voyeur", Lidia said out-loud, and her heart filled with sadness for her self, the small voyeur, the first-born, feeling so much without any understanding.

"Piri, I'm so tired now. Before I go can we watch it raining in the tower?

The small door on the second floor which connected the house to the tower balcony was swollen tight and took both their strengths to pull open a crack that allowed them to pry it fully open. The scene was a twittering commotion. Finches splashed in a puddle on the stone floor and the larger birds and doves, perching on small branches high up near the screened roof, flitted rainwater off their wings. Then they saw the long legs of the figure below who had taken shelter under the grain shed which also held the water supply and tools for sliding open and shut the heavy panels of the roof and circular wall.

"Merle, how long have you been sitting here, through all this storm? How are you?" Piri asked.

"Better than a poke in the eye with a stick," he said wryly, quite pleased to surprise them, "but a little wet. I knew you were here today," he said to Lidia. "I found this bush you like."

Merle stood and held toward her long sprays of the witch hazel, its blooms like curled shredded paper in tiny yellow flags along the bare, dripping branches.

"I'll leave them here. The rain's almost stopped. I'm going back out now."

"What a gift, Merle, thank you."

He nodded and stepped backward, pushing open the small heavy door then stooping down under its low frame.

"This bush flowering means spring's really here. Take care now," he said and then disappeared from view.

Lidia called after him, "Merle, it makes me happy!" She turned to Piri. "I *do* feel desire…hunger to be seen. Is this hunger part of who I am?"

Piri looked at her and, by a great mercy, she kept silent.

3

In early May, Merle came up to Stone Hill. He always walked the three miles from town to Lidia's or Piri Olevsky's place, shortening the distance to fish or gather raspberries or wild onions that grew by the fork of the Weir River. He arrived with a basket of marsh marigold plants dug from a swampy place near the riverbank, their purest yellow shining like signals in the morning light. "Cowslips," Merle said, looking up at Lidia. She was pruning branches overhanging the stone terrace beside the house. "It's the week of the wild birds, the free ones. You look like one of them up there." Leaning against one of the stone posts, he looked up at her solemnly. The terrace was washed clean after a rain and a flock of birds squabbled and fluttered under the feeder.

"Yes, look at them. There's a pair of towhees, the big one's a fox sparrow, three goldfinches, all those are purple finches and there's a cowbird."

She knew Merle had no need to name a thing or to know its name. A word, a name, was not the thing to him. Its meaning was what the thing was doing, how its life force was moving with the space around it. What he saw came from his particular way of seeing, from his mind dwelling sensually in a plant or animal till its meaning became a quality of wholeness. Watching a hawk climb and soar on planes of air he was feeling flight. With the horned owl gliding through the trees at twilight he was hunting and knowing all birds of prey. The ways of people did not fit easily into Merle's understanding, and Lidia knew that in his rich perceptual world he was sustained by the barest level of human comfort.

"You like knowin' their names," he said. A slug of blue suddenly dropped into the flock and scattered it in all directions. "That scrappy jay," Merle smiled, "I know him, that fellow's here all winter. It's their only free time, soon they'll be nesting and feeding little ones."

Lidia climbed down the small ladder and stood by his side. "The cowslips, Merle they're beautiful."

He nodded. "I came to see the cellar, the water's climbin' up in there still? It's runnin' from the hillside now you know, all this rain and snow melt, worse after Clark cut all his oak trees. There's nothin' we kin do... well, there's one thing mebbe."

"What's that?" she asked.

"Ditch it, the only way to stop it. A big ditch, four feet deep, dig 'er right across the hill."

"Well, that isn't possible," she said firmly, "you can't take machinery on that slope."

"No, have to dig it by hand," Merle smiled.

"By hand! Merle no-one could dig a four foot ditch across that slope. Why it's...it must be a quarter of a mile!"

"We'll see," he answered, "no need to go that far."

They were interrupted by a loud crash coming from the open upstairs window, and then a voice, "This is so boring, why bother with the damn thing!"

"It's Richard, he's ripping out some shelves for a new study."

"Well, he should stick to picture-taking, he's good at it isn't he?" Merle went on. "There's a right way to do this, d'ya know? Everyone needs somethin' he knows, a rock to hold to, somethin' he kin do no matter what. He should keep to it."

"What do you mean?"

"What I say," Merle spoke sharply and said no more and went to cut brush near the barn.

Upstairs she found Richard sitting on an old fleamarket desk chair among pieces of the destroyed shelving. A cut over his temple bled profusely. "Don't look at me that way. No, I'm not alright Lidia. The damn thing came at me, didn't want to come off the wall. It's like everything I try to do here, can't you see that? D'you want me to be blind, helpless? I'm swallowed up, you tell me I'm unfit and I feel unfit! I need a simple study, a place that's mine, that has light. I don't want this suffering. Lidia?" His voice slowly quieted. "Don't you see, I want to be more than I am now."

"Richard, you're not unfit. I don't think you're unfit. But you're bleeding. Here, wipe your forehead. Now listen. I put more wood on the sauna. It's ready now. We'll take it together. Will you come?"

Later he followed behind her along the path to the sauna, a small shed in the woods overlooking the pond. The heat inside was at its height, dry and searing to the skin, then making it glisten and drip with perspiration. As Richard threw water on the hot stones, the steam cut their breath like a knife and forced them down to a crouched position on the wooden platform. After each immersion in the heat they threw their bodies into the icy water of the pond. Richard stayed outside steaming in the cold woods and Lidia went back to sit in the heat one more time. Instead of lying down to rest afterward as they always did, Richard went directly back to the house to pour a drink.

"Sorry, Lidi," he said when she came in. "I feel smothered, I don't have space. Sauna didn't do it." She looked at him. "It's the place that keeps disrupting me. I just want to get it to where we can maintain it, where it keeps itself, don't you see?" Richard ran his hands through his hair.

She turned away because it was easier not to engage him, not to try once more to make him see they loved the place, that it was just a matter of their getting balance.

Darkness was falling when she went upstairs, lit a kerosene lamp and sat down on the small child's bed. She could hear Richard muttering downstairs. "Is that Frank? Frank Skiles the doctor? is that what he's sayin' to me? Keep 'im down, we don't like 'im, doesn't measure up. So let's split, kid, I wanna have fun, goin' to try to work it out so there's something like I grew up with, not your goats and dead people...not goin' to be a facilitator, trade this land anything you need, deal with your own stuff...this place is a dead end...give it to Ferdy, friend Ferdy, Ferdy Montfort with the gimpy leg. Ferdy'll manage it. Ferdy, ha ha!"

Lidia closed the door to the upstairs room, lay down and spoke into the darkness -- let me be still with him, let me send the rage out quietly and let him be. She slept soundly all night, dreaming of summer on the Ohio farm, the brilliant orange trumpet vine blooming over the old shed, the soothing doves and sounds of calves and pigs in the barnyard. In the dream the space around her felt wide and free. She woke wondering if it had come to warn her that her own space was closing in.

* * *

In all villages there are prophets who keep a constant weather eye on signs predicting the days ahead. No matter how changeable the days of early spring, they know the weather will settle on the first day of June. Cloudless days precede the rise of the Cornplanting Moon. When it reaches fulness it shines brightly enough to keep the planets from view. But even on moonlit nights, June is the best time to observe the Royal Stars, those first magnitude giants, Arcturus, Regulus, Altair, and Vega. On the 21st, rays of the sun reach their northern most angle and the sun seems to stand still before starting its backward walk to the south. The air is still cool enough to hold back swarms of black flies during the tilling and planting of gardens.

It's said that June is the crown of summer. But underneath this calm brightness there are always signs of confusion. In June, those born under variable signs must keep close account of their practical affairs. Misunderstandings, high emotions and bad judgment are a plague. In spite of the sense of settlement in June, the old wisdom that growth will come in its proper way, there are some who know the old wisdom is not always reliable.

Few people came uninvited to Stone Hill and those who came never offered to work. One of them was Ferdy Montfort. "Ah, June," he breathed, "soft days, nights with moths and bats flying, bullfrogs trumpeting in the pond. Forget everything," he told Lidia, "just live in these days. This season is a spectacle. I could roll like a lazing white seal in summer pasture, dive in and become one of the pond's reflections."

Ferdy walked with Lidia to the Ship Rock and sat pontificating like a rotund philosoper king. "Look," he pointed to a rusty hayrake abandoned far down the meadow, "nothing is ever lost. It all goes on weathering like this piece of farm machinery left out in the field. Now you wouldn't get on this old thing and rake hay with it anymore, but while recognizing you *could* still rake hay, you see its superior function is now in the realm of esthetic philosophy. Changed by the catalyst of time," he said wistfully, "time that moves all useful things into the realm of art." He paused to let the profundity of his words take effect.

"Now I have an idea, Lidia. At my family's vineyard in Brittany, every year after the hay's all in there's a hay-home supper. Don't you think that would be a good Stone Hill tradition?"

Expecting her approval, Ferdy was surprised at the deep annoyance in Lidia's voice.

"Ferdy, Stone Hill is not a collection of traditions, it's not a museum. We work hard here. Now listen to me...oh look," she interrupted herself, "I think a storm is coming, look!" Black clouds were building beyond the barn to the north. "It looks big."

Just then a car plunged up the road. Someone was leaning on the horn, then giving great blasts on a trumpet. "Oh, it's Mouche and Claire, they're home for the summer!" She flew toward them.

"Ma, it's going to storm, we got here just in time."

"Goodbye," Ferdy said, "have joy!"

The dark came quickly and a high wind blew up as the storm burst over them. Mouche, running to close the barn doors, stopped at the sight of the animals sitting in the dark light of the storm, chewing their cuds. Windrow was on the milking platform and Vita, still heavy with kid, lay in the half-light of the doorway.

"They're beautiful, Mom, the barn is beautiful. How it smells."

"Oh Mouche, I'm so glad," Lidia said, knowing it was part of herself he saw. As always, he strengthened her, seeing out of his clear eyes. Her body became centered, suddenly solid, she felt alright. And Claire's softness flowed over them. Claire in a dress of palest lavender, ran to throw her arms around the neck of the tall chestnut horse. "Mom, I'm so glad to be home now. I just want to stay here forever." The rain poured down as they dashed wildly with bags and suitcases into the kitchen. Mouche, landing on the floor, sat up and crowed like a rooster at the top of his voice. "Here Comes the Sun," he sang out, "it's alright!"

"Hela!" Richard appeared in the doorway. Mary-Molly, holding a huge burdock leaf over her head to keep off the rain, ran inside shouting, "Look, I'm blooming too!"

Slowly the place felt complete again. Full of rowdiness they elaborated the impossible and accomplished the possible in those few weeks before the summer deluge of relatives and guests. They spaded the upper garden and the raised kitchen beds near the house. To vary the rows in the larger garden, Lidia planted the seeds in squares and left a space for sunflowers at the far end. Claire spent hours on horseback following the trails of old logging roads, and she returned at twilight loosened and laughing at stories of her life at school.

"The last months don't seem real now," Claire said. "Everyone started coming to my room for advice. I had a dream that I was blind and couldn't see their faces. Sometimes I kept my eyes closed in the daylight to see what that would be like."

"Oh Claire," Mary-Molly looked up into her face. "You can't be blind, you have to paint things for us!"

"I'm not going to be, M-M, I couldn't. It was just a game. But I couldn't keep it up. I couldn't see any of the magic beings. I'm painting them now for a play next fall."

"What magic beings, Claire? Who are they?"

The kitchen was silent as everyone turned to Claire.

"Magic beings are everywhere." Her voice was strong. "Sylphs are the sky beings, rising into the sky, taking care of your breathing and helping the wind. Most beautiful of all are the undines. They're water nymphs who float across the ponds, and they are ruled by the moon. And gnomes, they live in cracks of rocks and guard gold in the earth. They keep the earth strong. You'll see them one day, when you're quiet and squint your eyes. They've been here thousands of years."

"What do they eat, what do the magic beings eat?" Mary Molly's eyes opened wide.

"Oh, they live on light, reflections of light. Except for gnomes, of course. They're heavy, stuffed with pieces of dark earth."

"Those creatures have been around quite awhile," Mouche said solemnly. "In your experience, Claire, do they help you out at all? When you need them?"

"No, they don't. That isn't why these beings are here."

"Well, I could've used their help. A terrible thing happened at the end of school. A young kid overturned in one of the canoes and we couldn't rescue him. I was in the last canoe and it was getting dark. I couldn't reach him in the fast water. It was so cold. The others went back and I stayed there where he went down. It was light before they came to search. Nobody could do anything after that. He was a good kid. I feel like..."

"Mouche," Richard broke in, "you did everything you could. I know how you feel, like you wanted to do more, but you did everything. It's hard, it's so hard." Overcome by his own emotion, Richard went to put his hand on Mouche's shoulder. His face was soft with the feeling of Mouche's pain.

"Thanks Dad," Mouche stood up to face him. "It changed the summer, it changed everything."

Claire stood next to them and laid her hand on the side of Mouche's face. "You're brave, you're very brave Mouche. I know that."

"I don't understand it," he said, "why life seems easy for me most of the time but it isn't for other people I know. It doesn't balance out." He looked at them and then at Mary-Molly and Lidia, but they were very still, unable to give any answer to comfort him.

Mouche, at seventeen, was tireless at working to make things right, to meet his own imagining of how they should be. He had a natural skill of measured precision that rarely allowed him the experience of failure. And if failure did occur, a slip of judgment that prevented reaching his high standard, his rare humor transformed the failure into success. What tall gangly figure could be at once as old and as young, as graceful at dancing squares, as full of a dignity that turned quickly to mockery or mimicry as Mouche? He was loved and easy in the world, and only beginning to discover a depth of sorrow. He wore a succession of caps backward on his sandy head, and it might have been true that he was an unrivalled prankster, both feared and admired at the Parker's Farm School. To Claire he was a close companion, to Mary-Molly a torment.

Hearing the childrens' stories, Lidia wondered...how deeply we hold each other, how deeply this place holds us. It's the whole world and it moves us, turning, like the world.

It was early in June that Lorion Olevsky was hurt. The morning Lidia went to see her, Piri could not talk. She had no strength to see anyone or anything around her. The earth she'd been standing on was suddenly unsteady ground. Ever afterwards Piri told the story simply, and always in the same words.

In the evening, she always said, I was called to the shore of Harmon's Pond. There Lorion lay, pale and barely breathing. A deep wound slashed red across the side of his head. I touched his body, icy-cold. I was fiercely determined that his spirit could not leave him. It was early enough in June that the cold black waters of Harmon's Pond had not begun their seasonal overturn. Three days before, he'd come back from the Mauna Kea observatory. He looked bronzed and rippling like a sea god. He said to me, 'Piri, I want you to go back with me to Hawaii.' He told me how they swam late at night there watching the falling stars. 'It's beautiful there. For 'scopes it's the best place on earth.'

After all his years of study, Lorion's love for how the stars look is still sublime. If you make friends with the stars, he says, you'll have a sense of your place in the universe. And that's true. Knowing the stars has made me feel there's shelter over me. It makes me feel a connection with others who wander the earth. He gave me that reliable map, but now it feels so distant.

Piri went on, I think he went into that cold pond at night to orient himself in this part of the world again. He wanted wider space to see the stars resting in the northern hemisphere. I know it was on his mind. He told me how they missed Vega in the southern latitude. It barely rises over the horizon there this time of year. He wanted to see Vega rising here. The evening felt warm but the pond was still ice cold. No one was there when he went down, just some kids on the shore who heard the thrashing. Trucks with blue lights were flashing over a crowd of people when I got there. A spotlight shining on Lorion showed the trembling of his arms and legs. How his whole body shook as they struggled to revive him. I couldn't watch. I went home and waited till they brought him back, cold as ice, with a collapsed lung and concussion of his skull. It was then I began to fall…slowly, slowly… the long, long fall of a star through distances where minutes are more than years.

When he regained consciousness, Lorion whispered to me, 'Piri, what happened?'

You went under, I said. That's all I know. You must have hit one of the rocky ledges. They said you called for Kaspar. Rest now. That's what you need. I could hardly hold together. Fear splintered my mind. I couldn't think then about why this happened.

Lorion stayed very quiet, at home with me, as the summer was passing. He helped me orient myself by locating more stars, watching their constancy and light. He showed me Antares, one of the four Royal Stars of ancient times that guard the heavens in each season. Antares rises in mid-July, a red super giant low on the horizon, trembling red through the disturbance of our atmosphere. He showed me where Fomalhaut would appear, the Solitary One that hangs alone in the southern sky, another of the four Royal Stars. I love that star, shining blue-white, the closest bright star to the earth. It's called the Autumn Star, and until it rises high over the golden trees in October the doctor said Lorion would not be completely out of danger.

Merle Fowler walked out from town every day through these months. He helped pull us slowly back. I began sleeping in Lorion's tower and on the third night I had a dream that lightened me and warmed my body that had felt cold and heavy the whole summer. The dream was of Lorion and me in the woods high up at tree level.

> *A stream moved underground below us into a building with turrets and high walls and a large empty pool. There was a system of locks and channels and small pools at different levels. But it was all empty. People came to bathe and I turned them away because I didn't know how to operate the system. The owner arrived, Jonsinger McJoy, who'd done underwater work all his life. He showed me how to use the place. I wanted Lorion to meet him. I felt he was bringing life that would be full of flowing water.*

When I told Merle the dream his face lightened and broke like a sky of scattering clouds. Even before he spoke, I told myself again that trusting in him was the best thing I've done. "It's a good meaning for you, Piri, it's sayin' you'd be a good one at helpin' people who need it on their place to find water. Lacey Simpson, over the mountain road to Lithia Springs, she knows it, she sees the water. You'd be a good one."

Merle could see that I wanted more creative energy. I could see I had to work at being more created. My identity with celestial space had been taking me farther off the earth. Now I needed it to join me with the ground. When I found I could be used it was like sap flowing through me again.

I read about dowsers seeing underground, attracted to certain spots where they look down and see the water gleam as if it's in sunlight. How the rod answers most to people who don't use reasoning. What makes them successful is yielding and allowing desire to guide the search. Desire connects the muscles and psychic body so it becomes a searching tool. That gives a response to objects just like what I see in Merle. It's handed down in families. As it turns out, Lacey Simpson is Merle's aunt.

The people around here who trust in locating have a good respect for water. They see it's alive and needs to flow free and keep its own rhythms and balance, the balance between earth and sky. Water draws them together. I think it's a feminine being, sensitive to moving with the moon and stars. Trying to locate it underground, I got in touch—after a long time—with all these rhythms. We say the Polish are grumblers. Of course. Our country has been in upheaval since the 13th century. But we're sensitive to feelings. We look inward too. I had a certain sense about finding water. It came to me as natural.

This countryside is rich, wealthy with water. Almost every farm has an underground vein. Usually I was successful and it made me feel joy, but exhaustion too. My heart beat fast, the tingling in my arms and wrist was like what happens when you hear about a deep cutting wound. I began locating deep veins, one down eight feet just past Jenny Parker's kitchen. She was pleased when the water came, twenty-three gallons a minute, really pleased. I was glad Merle could see it.

You'll find it on the high ground, I told him, not the slopes. What beginners find is seepage like that low spot, there where the royal fern grows it's seepage from a distant vein. "Merle? Let's sit down here, I'm tired."

We were in a back pasture of the Tillotson farm where Fred Tillotson put his heifers to summer pasture. He wanted water there, it was so far back to the barn. It was my second day at Tillotson's and I still wasn't having luck. To see the water you can't be tired or low in your mind. It's a hard day's work. You have to consider everything bearing on it. Because Lorion's still sick and the summer's moving toward August I need to know Merle will be ready to do the work. So once more I showed him how to hold the rod and how it would feel when it was turning, like holding the tip of it under a waterfall.

"You feel it below the stomach and here by the side of your head. Don't tell me your discouragement, Merle, every farm here has underground veins. The water's there and you have the eye to see it. It's just practice." And by late afternoon Merle had located the source. "Dig for it here, this low spot that's halfway between the pasture and that old dried up pond. The veins come together here," I told him.

"A low spot?" He questioned me in his soft voice.

"Goodness, Merle, nothing's always true! You have to believe in the rod. Now, see to it that they take care uncovering it so it doesn't get filled in. Sometimes the dozer flattens it. Will you see to that? Goodness, I'm really weary."

I knew Merle would succeed. As the word spread he began to have more work than he could do. He found water on the Stokes' place and at Wilkey Lloyd's on the Clayborne Road. Families came for him from Ashburn and Duanesville and other small towns north of Weir. And as it turned out, all this walking had been hard on my legs. I told Merle I could locate from a distance, even from home when my mind knew the terrain and could search an exact place. But he didn't feel right about taking the work. Then I told him a dream I had. About stars reflecting on underground streams, how the streams joined a river carrying the stars toward the open sea. He didn't say how that allowed him to accept the work, but I knew why. He saw how dowsing had rooted me to earth. It had channelled something far larger than my grief.

In June, about the time of Lorion's accident, Richard began work on his paper for the annual meeting of the Archeological Society. For three years, he'd been attached as photographer to their expeditions but this was his first opportunity to explain the ideas underlying his work. He'd delayed the writing, a pattern that drew everyone into the circle of his anxiety. His thoughts were conceptual and large in scope. "The

Photographer as Visionary," how does that sound Lidi? How ancient objects are emblems of hidden meaning, how their visual presentation bursts on the viewer with a new consciousness. What do you think? I've had my ideas for a long time but I don't know how I arrived at them. There's a lot of thoughts running through my mind…what do you think?"

"Do an outline Richard, please do an outline."

He worked late in his outside study, disappearing there every evening with a pitcher of martinis in one hand. He complained of headaches from the poor light and seemed dis-oriented from the summer activities. Close to his heavy breathing at night, Lidia felt the weight of something happening. The space choked up as they faced weeks ahead with the gardens and unfinished work begun so cheerfully in early summer. But how quiet it was to have breakfast alone when Richard poured a third cup of coffee and began talking to fill the silence.

"Russell Cordonnier's coming. I told him to get up here and fix that wagon he left out all spring in the rain. Saturday's his only day. What do I do with a mutilated wagon? Give these kids an inch and you get screwed up!"

"Well, look at his table, I guess he has a gift for something." Sun lighted up the bare table top, letting its red undercoat of paint shine through the worn blue-green surface. Together she and Russell had designed the table and what mattered to her was its beauty, not that it lacked authenticity.

On one of these mornings Richard's sharp voice startled her. "Potter, be quiet! Morgan!" Richard stood up as the younger dog growled deeply and began to bark. "Morg, lie down!" When he opened the kitchen door, both dogs rushed out barking at the noise of a vehicle coming up the road. It was a white truck.

"Now what?" Lidia saw the annoyance on his face transform into an emotion she did not have time to recognize. The truck pulled up slowly and stopped directly in front of the house. Richard sat down again but did not look at her. Lidia felt a sinking in her stomach. The white truck pulled a boat rack on which rested a canoe. It was the longest canoe she had ever seen and it was bright siren red.

The driver turned off the motor and there was silence for what seemed long moments. No one moved. The dogs sat looking at the truck. At last the driver opened his window and looked out questioningly at the house, and the dogs began to bark again. Richard gave a half-hearted wave through the kitchen window. He stood up slowly and without a word went out the door.

In a flash Lidia saw it all. "Oh my."

They placed the canoe across two sawhorses under the maple trees where the sun gleamed off its smooth surface. The man was tall, his body bent a little, from lifting boats in and out of water, Lidia thought. He sat hunched over on the wall and waited. Lidia went out on the porch and stood still until she could look at him.

"It's beautiful," she said. "How big is it?"

"She's a seventeen-footer m'am, the best they come."

He looked at her with kind eyes, some lines of sorrow moving in his face. When Richard went back into the house, the man leaned over to Lidia and said quietly, "I saw your face. I knew it wasn't right." She just looked at him.

"Well," he said, raising his arm as Richard returned, "just wait awhile. You'll see...she's a beauty anyhow." He walked back to the truck. Slowly he moved it forward, backed up to turn and then drove past them down the road. He looked straight ahead and did not wave. It seemed as though he couldn't see them standing there so still, neither of them knowing what to say.

Richard spoke at last, his voice pleading. "It was marked down. I've been looking at it for weeks. I just thought you and I could get away."

The canoe stayed in front of the house for three days, its glow beaming ominously into the kitchen, its shape like a sad, sad mouth so red against the green trees and meadow grass. Although it could not be ignored, its presence was not mentioned. On the fourth day Richard looked up after dinner from behind his book.

"I know Lidi, it isn't right. He's coming in the morning. I didn't think. We'd need another car, someone else to drive to take us out. But it was for your birthday."

She looked at him with a sad smile. "It's lovely, your idea. It was lovely." Her image at that moment was of a cornered deer, helpless, imploring. He needs a way out of the corner, she thought, he doesn't know how. She stood before him, her arms at her sides aching to reach out and hold him. But he moved back, raising a hand to his forehead. Was it trembling? She felt afraid.

She was drawn to a trembling thing, a tree moving at the end of the meadow when all else was still, the quavering first note of a bird before dawn, voices on the edge of emotion, all these affirmed the presence of spirit in things. To her, trembling was a struggle, something trying to be born. Richard looked up at her over his glasses. "Lidi," he said quietly, "I hope I can get past myself. Look at that glorious light on the meadow! Maybe we don't need to get away from here."

She felt fear creep in as her mind flashed back to the February morning when Richard had asked what Stone Hill was to them. It had been hard to answer. "I think it's a ship," she'd said, "sailing east and we're on it sailing into the high pines, through calms and storm but it's hard." Was something happening to weaken their hold? Did he feel the place was beginning to pull them down?

* * *

A certain trust is needed by those living on a country place as the torrent of July flows over it. As growth begins there is no time to ponder progress. Every year it's July that offers the most spectacular freedoms, the highest high to the senses. And once more, as in all Julys, country places spin out of control. Goats escape from the barn to eat the new seedlings, porcupines lumber down from the apple trees, woodchucks eat the lettuces. Children have hair-raising escapes on horses which gallop out of control down the straight country roads.

This July is no exception. As Richard directs work on the addition of a skylight and dormer to the upstairs, the scaffolding gives way, plunging a carpenter six feet to the stone terrace. One of the Maine cousins comes for three weeks and sobs through the first seven nights with bitter homesickness. It's Richard who pulls Mary-Molly out of the pond when she falls off the dock fully clothed in her long skirt. It's Richard who drives Mouche to the hospital emergency room, his finger crushed between the mowing machine and the tractor. As Richard grows tanned and younger, Lidia wonders if the way they live will ever allow any ordinary days. Soups are made for the second wave of carpenters finishing the outside study; rich stews and cornbread for guests and whoever arrives with them; pitchers of tea carried down into the field when haying begins. By the rising of the Ripe Berries Moon in mid-July, the visions of what is possible on Stone Hill are already limited.

But not the freedoms. As in all summers, they prowl barefoot in darkness on the dirt roads, brushing from their faces cobwebs that grow in the night. They paste sugar and molasses on the tree-trunks to trap night-flying moths. They swim in the dark velvet pond.

Merle came regularly to work but would not sit down for meals. He had coffee and saltines in the afternoon and the sweet baked things Lidia made for him. He observed but spoke little. He was a source of astonishment for Mary-Molly. When he took her fishing in the early morning or to see his birds, they were gone out of reach till early dark. Mary-Molly loved the freedom she felt with Merle.

"Merle doesn't tell me what to do. He says I already know. He says there's nothing we have to do. And it's always fun! Not like Stone Hill where we rake the leaves in fall, shovel snow in winter, plant the garden in spring, over and over. Mom, you know what Merle says? He says this place is eating you up."

"Oh Merle, he knows better, he knows what a place requires. But he doesn't know I grew up on a farm, a real farm where work had to be done by the seasons."

"You grew up there Mom? Where?" It was mid-afternoon and they sat on the terrace between the house and the garage being turned into a study. The sound of hammering was steady, louder than the mournful lyrics of country music on the carpenters' radio. Mary Molly lay on the stone terrace with her head under a large yellow umbrella and Lidia was peeling onions for soup.

"Well, not exactly grew up there, we went there in the summers. It was my father's farm, in Ohio where he was born. They raised cattle and corn to feed them, and wheat. It was a big farm, lots of work . My sister, your Aunt Rillis, and I were small but we learned how things on the farm couldn't wait, how they have to be done when it's time."

"Tell me about it, Mom."

"Yes, I want to. First of all, close your eyes. And look at the farmhouse...the corn fields come right up almost to the door. See? there's no other house in sight, just the fields of corn. A high wooden gate out on the main road opens to tracks in the grass leading a long distance up into the yard. The trunks of maple trees on either side are painted white to keep away insects. The main roads are all dirt, and if you and I went down to the gate in twilight there would be dark shadows falling across the road, from the moon shining over the top of the corn. Insects sing and it's hot, hot in Ohio. What d'you think about it?"

"Oh Mom, I love it there, I really do, tell me more things." In Mary -Molly's eyes a hint of mournfulness revealed her longing to be somewhere beyond the ordinary life of Stone Hill.

"I know you'd love it there, dear girl, all the smooth dirt paths leading to the barnyard and the muddy pig stys and chickens flying up to scare you. We had to hunt everywhere for their eggs. There were frightful geese, and blue-eyed kittens in dark corners of the barn. We had to open and close all the gates and every one had a different kind of hook or wooden pin to keep it shut. We'd go through them into the barnyard to see if Cecil and Naomi were working, the Shirkey's children. They were sharecroppers.They worked for Grandpa and took part of what they raised there."

"Sharecroppers. Go on, Mom." Lidia had finished cutting up the onions.

"Well, one morning we heard a terrible scream. Cecil was in the barnyard and when he saw us his face lighted up with a big grin. He dropped a long butcher knife and held up the body of a small pig by one leg. We just stared at the blood pouring from the pig's throat. Its head was flopping back and there was a gurgling sound. Rillis and I moved closer and I saw a glazed stare that took the light out of the pig's small eyes. Rillis began to cry and I told her it was all right, Cecil wasn't hurting the pig. He laid it down gently on some clean straw and said to come with him, that he had to get cleaned up. Do you know, that was just the first pig we saw killed? It was the time to slaughter and take them to market. Cecil and Mr. Shirkey slaughtered all of them, and Rillis and I heard their terrible screams and I watched them lose the light in their eyes."

"Oh Mom, go on. I see why you like remembering it, even though it's horrible." Mary-Molly shuddered and moved back under the big umbrella.

"It was horrible and I never got used to it. I'm not used to it now," Lidia shook her head.

"Now? But Mom, we don't..." Her eyes opened wide. "Ohhh...the male goats we send to market. And it's why you didn't want any more pigs, right? Isn't it hard, Mom?"

"With animals it's very hard. The answers aren't clear. In Ohio the sheep went to market too. Later that summer it was time to shear them. I went with Cecil and his father in the farm truck back to the farthest field to start the sheep moving in. The flock was very large and I couldn't see beyond their milling bodies, but I loved the movement and ran in to touch their backs. All the sheep came in around me and began to push. I heard Cecil call my name and I saw him jump down from the running-board of the truck, and then I lost my balance. They closed in over me. Their hooves pushed in and I felt wool brushing my face. I turned over and arched my back but I couldn't make a sound. Someone lifted me up and I began to scream... "how dumb, dumb, dumb they are, they don't know what they're doing!" Then Mr. Shirkey took me home in the truck."

"Oh-h my, I would've loved to be with you Mom. Can't we go there now? What happened to grandfather's farm? It's making you sad isn't it?"

"No-ooo? Maybe a little, the farmhouse was such a wonderful place. There was so much light falling in the big windows. Every room had a smell, the summer kitchen with the iron pump and the living room where the couches were covered with wrinkly gray cloth and there were striped pillows. You know? No-one told me the reason we went to Ohio in the summers was that my father had decided to sell his part of the farm, that farm where he was born."

"You mean we can't go there? That makes me very sad," Mary-Molly's long blond hair fell over her face.

"I know, I know, Grandpa was sad too but he never, never told us. His sister Edith wanted to buy it with her husband Gus. Gus wore thick glasses and a suit and he was always thinking. I ran in to the screened-in porch one morning, where they were sitting. I can see it perfectly now. That morning was so still I could hear doves murmuring in the cedars and baby calves bawling. Shadows moved across the bright tablecloth and the sun sparkled on the plate of honey oozing out of its wax comb. Suddenly your grandpa's face became dark red and Gus turned still as a stone. Grandpa leaped up and bent over and brought his fist down like an ax on the table. "Damn Crawler, you're a Damn Crawler!" he shouted. I ran out the door because I couldn't look at my father. The sound 'Damn Crawler' filled my head. I wanted to go back to save him from this terrible anger. The feeling thrashed around in me like a snake and after awhile it settled inside me and lay still."

Mary-Molly's eyes were fixed on Lidia's face. "So. Grandfather sold it to them. He was angry and he sold it. How nasty."

"No, he couldn't keep the farm. We lived far away on the east coast. We couldn't keep it."

"Where did Edith live, on the east coast too?"

Lidia put her arms around Mary-Molly and drew her close. "Yes, on the east coast too. I don't know why. I don't know why he sold the farm." She held Mary-Molly and felt slowly restored to herself, restored to her own place and what it needed from her.

Moving into full summer the air stayed moist and heavy, barely stirring the thick layers of leaves over the house. The children were leaving again, Mouche to Billings, Montana to work on a ranch, Claire going south on a work project to help design quilts for a rural cooperative. Mary-Molly would go later to visit the cousins in Maine. They were full of planning, apprehension, hilarity.

"Should we take the camp stove in the truck?" "Ma, how do you mend this tent, will you help me?" "Is summer miserably hot in North Carolina? What if I don't fit in there?"

Lying next to Richard at night Lidia was wakeful. She wanted to go with them, to be a gypsy, to work in a diner on a frontier, maybe Montana, Oregon, the desert. To feed people and send them off every day on an adventure. How simple it seemed. Of course, it would be in a lively place where life wasn't easy. Then she worried that she was too involved in their lives, the central core of herself always rising to help make them safe. No one could do for them what she wanted to do. She recognized her desires as prayer. "How is it possible to miss them so deeply, to miss them even when they're with me? They're leaving again and I feel afraid."

"Oh Lidia, it's your mother," the voice said. "How're things with you? I thought I'd come for your birthday, dear. I could arrive Thursday for dinner. Will the children be there?"

Lidia held the phone out from her ear. "Well, what a surprise and… what are your other plans?"

"I'm going on to Henrietta Miller's in Jarvistown, Pennsylvania. You remember her when we visited in Port Royal. I'm due there on Monday. I've worked out a good artery of travel. That's all I have to say, dear. News is scarce."

"Well, Mouche and Claire aren't here. You can have Mouche's room." She felt confusion, sinking, dread.

"Mouche's room? Oh dear." There was silence. "Well, that'll have to be satisfactory. I'll see you all Thursday. Goodbye dear."

"Margaret Skiles! Well, happy birthday, Lidi." Richard smiled as he came through the door.

"Don't, Richard. Look, you get along better with Margaret than I do."

"That isn't hard, you shut up like a clam, tight knots in the solar plexus," he laughed. "Actually, I enjoy Margaret, she's politically up to date."

"Oh Dad, you're a ladies' man," Mary-Molly flounced up to him in her wet bathing suit, "especially old ladies."

The fact was, Lidia thought, Margaret Skiles was a good visitor. Her disregard of bringing gifts was more than compensated for by her continual war against dirt, garbage and weeds. She worked at these crusades wherever she was. Margaret, at seventy-four, had the body and strength of a woman twenty years younger. She'd been slender and willowy as a young wife, with a shock of almost orange hair. Lidia remembered watching Margaret dress to go out to the Elmora Country Club. She wound her long orange hair up in a nest, and then held up a hand mirror to see if the back was right. The hair was puffed out around her head like a fan. Then she reached far back into the closet for the black lace gown. It made her look slender as a bullet, a shiny bullet on fire at the top. Then she put on the green velvet jacket, soft and tender as new ferns, slim except for the sleeves, gathered and puffy at the wrist. Under the gown her shoes were shiny black and open, with tiny straps to hold them on. Would Margaret be happy at the Club, would everyone there treat her like a queen?

It was Margaret's veils Lidia remembered most, stored in a secret drawer in her large cherry bureau. She wanted Margaret to wear them, to drape her body, to dance or fly winged down a hillside waving a gauzy signal to watching spirits. Her mother had a following of spirits, Lidia thought, dark and hovering. But the veils were delicate, brown spider webs and one green with eyes from a peacock's tail, some golden clouds of sparkling net and another with feathers black as crow's wings.

"Veils are like my mother, my mother is veiled. Veils give power. She keeps the veils for power over the natural world. She tries to be a witch, she tries to be a witch."

Indeed, Margaret Skiles had always tried to charm her part of the world by clearing it of noxious weeds. She worked in burning sun, the bite of stinging insects or poison ivy or the chill wind. Margaret dreamt and wrote about it: Dear Lidia, Home again after a nice visit with you. The garden is lovely. I hope you got the disagreeable weed pulled from under the hawthorne tree. It looked to be ready to drop its seed. Love, Mother.

On Thursday afternoon Margaret sped up the hill in her 1957 Dodge, spun around and parked at the garage above the house. Richard went to meet her, holding her arm and carrying her small suitcase.

"Look Ma, they both have white hair, how sweet."

"No dear, your father's hair is gray. Now go and show Grama her room."

"Whose room?"

"Mouche's room, Mary-Molly." Lidia laughed, almost overcoming the residue that always destroyed her spontaneity around Margaret. Perhaps it couldn't be overcome, something unwilled, primitive, something like a veil that happens between mothers and daughters. To arouse her compassion, Lidia always tried to remember the slight histories she knew. What came to her now, as told by a distant cousin, was Margaret's frailty, the fearful one of the twins, and how she had slept with her mother until she was sixteen years old. Lidia imagined how she might have been persecuted, with two older brothers and a crowd of cousins always underfoot in the household. Their father was a Judge, distant and occupied, of great respect in the small Pennsylvania town.

But now as usual, Margaret went right to work with a sickle in her hand, weeding the gardens near the house. She pulled out bittersweet, thistle and blackberry by the roots. At the end of the second day a light rain began to fall. Margaret came from the garden carrying her shovel and hoe, her hair white above a red jerkin. "Look Richard, she looks like Joan of Arc!"

"Well, clearly she hears the voices," he said dryly.

"She just wants the earth to be beautiful, Richard."

"Yes, by excluding certain species. They do that in small towns."

Lidia's birthday party was filled with the inevitable commotion of dogs, cats, wrapping paper and surprises. Piri Olevsky came with her arms full of daisies, all colors and sizes. Mary-Molly's friend Jessie came, and Jessie's mom. From Montana Mouche had sent a wooden harp, and Claire, had brought with her from North Carolina, an antique mirror with a fluted frame of gold. She held up the mirror and looked carefully at the tangle of her hair, dark auburn turning pale at the temples, at the fine lines around her eyes, the sprinkling of freckles.

"And now," Margaret left her chair to stand nervously in the middle of the circle. "I've been saving my present for last. Here it is Lidia." Proudly, she held out a small envelope.

"Stand back, stand back, don't jostle her," Richard said, watching Lidia's face.

She drew out the pink tissue paper in which lay a curl of pale copper hair, fine as silk, held by a tiny white ribbon. Everyone gasped at the curl of hair lying in Lidia's hand. It rose a little, fell again, and rose.

"Move back, don't breathe on it," Richard said sharply.

"Dad," Mary-Molly's voice wailed like a siren.

"Don't- breathe- on- it."

"I think it's from an angel," Mary-Molly whispered, "a heavenly angel."

"Now it's almost a half century old," Margaret's voice was firm now and steady. Her eyes shone with pride. "I can hardly believe it."

"And what do you think, Lidia?" Richard asked softly, watching, enjoying her pleasure. They all waited for her answer.

"I have no words," she said slowly, "it's as big as the world."

In the melee of blowing out candles and serving the cake, Richard put the small envelope on the mantelpiece above the stove. There was the usual free-for-all of cleaning up paper and dishes, and then a race to the garden to watch the sun go down. "Beautiful lady of the copper hair." Piri's voice burred with her Polish accent. "You're beautiful as the sunset."

"Yes Mom," Mary-Molly squeezed in between them, "and that's the truth."

"How beautiful you always are." Claire moved closer to her. "It's a magic birthday, Mom."

The curl of her hair lodged in Lidia's mind. It seemed to call her. She started looking early for the envelope the next morning. It was not on the mantelpiece. It was not on the floor. Then she remembered the burst of flame in the stove when Richard had ignited the birthday papers, and she knew it was gone. Burned! *The thing that's my very own, my own hair! After all these years, the one real gift Margaret tried to give me. To* give back part of my true self, this piece of my own tiny, tiny child that never can return. Gone, into the fire - my shining, soft, baby hair. How cruel! Why? I wasn't careful. I didn't care for myself. I didn't care, again! How can I make this bearable? How can I tell them? I can't tell them. It's too painful.

"Put light around it, Lidia," she said out loud. "Space and light so you can always gather it back. It will always belong to you then. Claire's right, when we want things to change, we go to fire."

"Well, Mary-Molly, does a thirteen year old person need this much baggage? For gathering mussels, poking in tide-pools? After all, it's a simple life in Maine." Richard spoke in his gentlest voice.

"Really Dad, can't you even remember that far back? There'll be parties, other things you know." In a sweetened tone she added, "Could you find the time to vacuum my room? It's pretty empty now."

"Maybe," Richard laughed mournfully. "I'll try."

They carried the piles of bags out to the car where Richard's sister and the cousins were waiting. "See you in two weeks, bye."

Richard was running the vacuum cleaner when Lidia came back into the room. "It's really nice work, I like it." He went on moving Mary-Molly's desk back to its place and then leaned his shoulder against the wall. "Lidi? I feel apprehensive, like something's looming. I just feel it."

"No," she looked up into his face. "It's just your Washington trip. You hate giving papers, it's too much like school. But you're ready for it. You're a superb photographer, Richard. You're talking to them about the world on a different scale, a higher plane, they're new ideas."

He wouldn't allow this praise and, as always, abruptly changed the subject. "I wish you'd seen that cat, Woody, the orange rascal, stalking a crow in the meadow. He picked the biggest one and went after him like a cougar. Lidi, there are three ducks on the pond, blacks I think, it's lovely down there now." He looked down at her. "You have a pale face," he said. "Are you tired? Are you just tired or are you tired because you're with me?"

The depth of his feeling for her was clear. She remembered Richard saying only yesterday how he loved her hands. He'd said simply, Lidi,

I love your hands, and she'd known, because her hands were freckled and cracked from the barn work and weeding, that what he meant was, I love all you do with your hands. She remembered also his saying how he loved to watch her listening, and how her auburn hair was turning in places, like embers falling he'd said. What was eroding in him? Was it the strength to prevent himself from being eaten by the world? She thought what he expected of the world was so different from how it actually was. She feared for him. He was not a warrior.

On their way to the airport the next morning, Lidia noticed he was wearing a shirt of deep Venetian red. "You never wear red." Her heart was so moved by him and she laid her hand on his shoulder. "It looks royal on you."

"It's for courage," he smiled wanly. "I feel rotten."

"You'll be fine, you don't need to worry. Besides, I'm worrying for you." Giving him a firm hug at the airport Lidia felt stiffness in his lean body. She drove back to Garrison pre-occupied by the heaviness he had left behind, and then the anger she always felt at having to sort it out. Under it all was a loneliness that seemed unconnected to any living thing.

When she reached Weir and the field where the road narrowed at Jenkins Flats, a flock of blackbirds wheeled back and forth over the corn, and lighted on both sides of her car. She turned off the engine and sat very still, only her eyes moving with the restless birds. With a rush of wings the flock rose straight up, veered diagonally and turned again and flew as one back over the spot where she sat. In those moments she felt freed. "Starlings, small black stars, black sparks of stars. I'm going to tell Merle how I almost went with them." She turned the car around and drove back toward Garrison. "He'll understand, he's raised birds all his life."

Before she left Merle's place, he made her promise to go with him the next evening. He would not tell her why. "Jes somethin' I want to show you," he said.

4

It was early evening when Merle walked up the road for her. The air was humid and resonant, the meadow twinkling with fireflies. They walked quietly down to the main road and turned left toward the place where trees were thick along the river. No cars passed them. The song of katydids was insistent, the call of one followed by a refrain in a higher key from another farther away. Merle said nothing till they came to the river bank with piles of logs and debris stacked along its edge. He helped her down the steep bank. A slipping noise and a loud splash startled them. "Otter," Merle said. "They're big, they live in the bank, prob'ly have young'uns now."

"Oh!" Lidia whispered. "Merle, look!"

A faint glow suspended like a globe hung in one spot over the river. The black water flowing around it carried the path of light away on the surface of the water. Lidia stood at the river's edge, her eyes moving along the path of flowing light and its origin in the center of the river. Everything around her seemed airy and floating, her own weight disembodied in the dark.

"Leave your shoes and hold my hand," Merle said, "the water's low but it's slippery. I'm goin' first." As their eyes adjusted to the dark they placed one foot and then another forward on the rocks. Lidia felt safe. She felt joy being led by him out onto the river. A cool breeze lifted her hair. Farther out the water was higher, moving through jagged driftwood and broken snags that had twisted and piled up on the flat rock during the flood.

"I'm not afraid," she said, "but what is it? What is the light?"

"It's for you," Merle said proudly, "a river house. Bend down now and then up, sharp." He let go of her hand, his body bent double and then he moved up and forward into the light on his hands and knees.

"Can you do it?" He spoke evenly, hiding his excitement and the pleasure he felt at what he had created for her.

"Yes, I'm coming." She crawled up after him over the tumbled logs worn smooth by the water.

Inside, the light of a lantern filled space on two levels made by the nest of logs and broken limbs the rock had gathered at flood height. The interior, scoured and smoothed by the water, had woven itself into a crude lattice with a vaulted ceiling high enough for a tall person to sit comfortably. At one end of the space, the driftwood had formed a platform extending almost five feet on which were placed pillows and a soft quilt. Through crevices in the floor and walls, the flowing river was visible and the air moved through, warm and humid.

"Merle, it's magical." In a little confusion she added, "Did you do much to it?"

"No way I could," he said, "the river made it tight, nothin' moves now."

"It's a dream, a house of trees on the water!"

"But it's real, Lidia, it's for us," Merle said sharply. She felt the sharpness covering his shyness of her in the closeness. "After the floodin' I saw it. I had to watch and see if the river'd take it away again."

They sat silently, listening to the river flowing. She was aware of the clean smell of his body, the whiteness of his thin feet. She noticed her surprise at how much she loved being there with him.

"But you did some things to make it beautiful," she said softly.

"A little. I just let it be what it is," Merle smiled. "There's this if you'd like it." He reached down into a dark space and brought up a small flask of brandy. "It's strong." He filled a tiny glass he took from his pocket and offered it to her. After a swallow her eyes opened wide. "Apricot brandy," Merle said. "It gives you courage on the river."

"Yes," she handed the glass to him, "after all we did to get here, after all you did."

"Well, I had to," Merle said. "When I found this place I knew it was for you, because..." he hesitated, "it'd make you happy."

"Oh, it does," Lidia said, "can't you see?"

"I see," he said and took her hand between his own. She sat still, watching him, watching his eyes flow with emotion, waiting for him to speak.

"What I want to say," he struggled, "is d'you think we kin love things that don't belong to us? Things that should be loved?"

They were both quiet, listening to the river. A large, pale green moth fluttered around the lantern, settled on Lidia's shirt and then flew up into her hair.

"Your eyes are shining," Merle said. "Lidia? can you...?" He put his arms around her.

Her voice came slow, faint against his shoulder. "I think I can..."

"I mean...lie down with me?"

She felt the effort this had cost him. She was silent, hearing the space around them filled with his beating heart. The meaning of what was happening was clear to her, that this moment was all of it, all there could be, what Merle had done, what he felt for her. It was large, it belonged to her, this moment flowing like the river underneath, out of its past into a future always new. She felt herself held by a deep longing. She understood Merle, she knew what he was feeling.

"Lie down here?" she asked, moving her body.

"Yes," he said. Merle lowered his eyes as she drew off her white shirt and lay down on the quilt he had smoothed out over the rough surface.

"I was right. I had to see how beautiful you are." He took off his shirt and sat looking down at her. She reached out to trace the contours of his chest, the skin burned dark by the sun around his neck. He lay close to her, still and soft and yielding as a small child. They lay together watching the moth flutter in the light, listening to the river running away over the rocks.

"Lidia," Merle said at last, "why are you so good? Why do you hide the truth?"

"I don't think I am, I don't think I do," she murmured.

He felt it was enough that he had asked the questions, he didn't need her to answer them. "Well, part of you, the best part, is my secret," he said.

He began covering her neck and breasts, the sides of her upper body with slow kisses that wakened her flesh and gave form to places that had not felt part of herself before. She lay quiet and was not afraid. At last, to still him again, she laid her hand gently on the balding spot of his head and held him close to her.

"Can I see your eyes?" she asked after a few moments. He sat up, bending over her.

"Merle, they're changing to all the colors of the night sky." She watched his eyes full of moving lights and felt her body filling with delight, glowing and dissolving, moving out beyond itself in the space between them. She lay still now, without thought, allowing herself to be held in the darkening blue of Merle's eyes.

He could not believe this was happening to him, this trembling that felt like fear, and he drew back from her a little to steady himself. This is a beginning, his body was saying, something is beginning that will come another time.

As he drew back they both felt something new enter the space between them, and Merle asked, "Are you afraid Lidia?"

"No, but isn't it getting cold, shouldn't we go back soon?"

"I don't want to," he said.

"I know."

He sat up. "Lidia, this place may break up, go on down with the river. Mebbe we can't get back."

"But we'll have it," she said, "anyway." She did not know what she meant. Did he know? She felt the pain that was trying to say she was not clear to herself now, she was not clear to him. She felt the strong pain of not being clear to him.

"We'll have it some way," he said. He offered her brandy again. "For the dark, from now on it'll be very dark." Merle blew out the lantern. The blackness was total, like blindness. They sat apart, silently, each listening to a separate piece of the darkness. The murmuring lap of the river was louder in the dark. It filled all the space between them.

They could see nothing. At the same moment they moved and began climbing out and down, and then stood outside on the flat rock. From where they were, mid-way in the river facing downstream, they could see a faint horizon line of black trees. When it became easier to see, Merle moved carefully out toward the shore, gauging each step by the sound of the river as it splayed out around the large stones. It was darker when they reached the bank, darker still when the forest closed over them. But the sound of the river did not recede. It stayed with them along the silent journey to the last tunnel of darkness which led up to Stone Hill.

When they reached the house, Merle raised his arm toward her. Trying to see his face in the darkness, Lidia put her hand on his shoulder. They stood still a few moments till Merle turned away and disappeared.

Entering her house with its closed windows, she felt there was nothing that bore a trace of her presence, nothing resonated to the desire of her body. She stood in her own flowing center and around her the house was still, without breath. When she threw up the windows to reclaim some sense of freedom, she saw the yellow jasmine had opened into clusters of bloom. She bent over it, inhaling the scent, imagining herself carrying the jasmine to Merle, "just for one evening on the river again," she would say, seeing how pleased she would be with his laughter, and then…how reckless it was, how entangling to have this desire. But she allowed it, and went back to the open window and laughed in a low voice that rose up into the night air. On the couch behind her the yellow cat woke and yawned and stretched and stood up, looking at her through half-closed eyes.

"A glass of wine, Woody? It's too early to sleep."

She didn't know what hour it was or how she had wandered so far out of her familiar space. "It's a spiritual wandering." She struggled to open a bottle of red wine. "To the River Spirit!" She drank the full glass at once. "I feel strange, dis-enchanted." With the moist night air flowing over her Lidia lay down on the couch and fell asleep with the cat by her side.

She did not hear the wind blow up. It entered the open windows, moving through the rooms to lift curtains over the couch where she slept, to unsettle papers Richard had left on the kitchen table. Later, the noise of a screen door banging on the terrace stirred the deep level of her sleep. The house was silent, the two cats slept and Potter, the ridgeback, mumbled on the worn stone doorstep by the open door. Lidia moved but did not waken.

* * *

Blowing into the bowl-shaped hollow where Blue Mountain de-
scends into the Rangely Hills, the August winds are known to
change direction. From blowing easterly against the mountain,
such a wind can shift in the early morning to blow west, down
over Stone Hill onto the village of Weir below. Blowing down to
its lowest level, the chill wind crosses the Weir River and rises
again with less force against the mountain's protecting flank.
The sudden coolness of this wind plays around the stone tow-
er where Piri and Lorion Olevsky sleep. It blows into angular
peaks of the tower's screened roof and through the open panels
around the walls. It stirs narrow leaves of the acacia tree planted
for the weaver birds. The wind circles down to flutter feathers of
the ground doves walking briskly in pairs in the dim light. Its
rushing noise rouses Piri from sleep and its chill penetrates her
bones.

Drowsing, then awakening, she hears the sound of mov-
ing footsteps and voices mumbling. No one is there in the gray
dawn. There's no sound but the wind. She falls asleep again and
the same dream begins, the footsteps and sound of voices. She
hears the words, "All parts of our body are the Sky God." Again
she looks below but there is nothing except tall stalks of sunflow-
ers and asters moving in the wind. Next to Lorion's warmth she
sleeps once more, wondering how many spirits on earth and in
the sky wait to be seen.

The wind continues blowing down over Stone Hill until dawn. In the
barn the animals move slowly in the morning light, two horses and the
goats snuffling and chewing, the rooster puffing himself up to crow for
the hens. Morgan, the scruffy, half-breed airedale, ambles slowly up to
the house and in the open door. He sniffs at Lidia and the cat on the
couch. She moves one arm onto the dog's head and then turns over and
sleeps again. It's the yellow cat who wakens her, staring with unblinking
eyes directly into her face.

"Oh Woody, what has this wind brought that's so strange? Nothing belongs to me here."

Light streamed into the kitchen through the open door. Lidia walked out to the meadow and stood still. After a time she cried out, "There's no refuge. This place is not a refuge!" In a torrent of self-pity, she started down the road. When a sharp stone pierced her instep, she saw she had set out without shoes. She went on, crossing the main road and then up into Piri's garden. The clearing was vivid and vibrating in the wind.

"I knew I'd see you on this day. The wind coming off your hill made a crack between the worlds, I could see right into it." Piri rounded the corner of her house, carrying two baskets overflowing with vegetables. "You're peaked, did you see spirits in the night?"

"Yes, on this wind."

"Good ones?"

"They took my power away."

"It's their work, to show us we do have power, to show our un-doneness that comes out on the night air. They show us it's useful to have fear sometimes."

"When did you learn that?"

"In my village when it was useful, it was necessary, to have fear."

"Did anyone show you how to have power over the fear?"

"Why yes, there was someone to show us that power and then we did have it. How else would we know?" As if clearing her mind of painful memories, Piri picked up a stick and rapped strongly on the basket's edge.

"But now, we have to yield to these spirits. They're restless, wanting us to hold on to them and make them real!"

"Are they friendly?"

"Friendly! They belong to us, they come out of our past. Don't you see?" Piri looked at her sharply.

"Yes, I do see. Because I have a spirit too. An Indian Chief, and I see him with a falcon on his arm. When a hawk flies near it's a sign that I *could* have that power."

"That's a sacred thing, Lidia, a thing to pay attention to."

They were both silent awhile and then Lidia spoke.

"This is a sacred place, isn't it? Your place?"

"Because of the dancing we do here. Mostly, the place is practical. An overgrown clearing in the woods, ordinary but useful. Come, I'll show you how it's blooming now."

She moved around the garden gently touching the bright blooms with her rough hands. "These we raise for dyeing wool the weavers use, mostly for small rugs and hangings. They all want natural dyes now that age into mellow, faded colors. Like the Polish Kilim rugs made in the 16th century and still made there today...beautiful, unequalled anywhere."

"This one we're standing on, ladies bedstraw, gives coral. Most of the plants give shades of yellow, the birch leaves, the wild apple, the mulberry. The alder bark and elderberry make blue and purple, the bark and leaves of that wild apple make orange. We plant some of the old Polish ones, madder and wild marjoram for red, and that special one is false indigo."

"How you do like knowin' their names." Merle came out from behind the house. Over his shoulders was a long pole from which hung orange-red flowers tied in bunches.

"Is this another country?" Lidia laughed but did not look at him.

"It is, Country of the Flower Angels." He turned and disappeared into the tower.

"Piri, I should go back now. I have work to do."

"Of course there's work! August requires attention. It's two steps beyond itself with all this growth. But there's something more important than the work. Your body cries out for it like its need for water. The dancing. We go just till the autumn solstice. It would bring joy to you, a place of peace you carry all day. The dancing is timeless, coming together and parting, squares for building and harvesting, spirals when we reach up to the sun."

"Why would I want to do that, Piri? Why would it be good for me?"

"Ah, the dancing is a mirror of all things in the world. It joins them in the circle and fills them with light. You feel free and without fear. It will help you see that what happened in the past connects with the future. It releases you and connects you to the spirit energy. Lidia, there's not much time now. Come tomorow."

Lidia did not answer. She had already started toward home. Down on the main road, she stopped for the mail. There was a letter from

Montana in Mouche's handwriting, with all the letters going backward on a tilt. Much folded and decorated with little stains of different colors, it had been scrawled over a period of several weeks.

August 8
Sioux Falls, S.D.

> *Dear Mom & Dad,*
>
> *Two days hard riding and we reached the ol' Mississippi at La Crosse. We cheered and drove over and went back and crossed again. Things are thinning out, great to be out of citys. The truck's doing OK, knee-deep in peanut shells. We're headin' for the Badlands. Need some work.*

August ll
Spearfish, S.D.

> *We got fired from our job at Jack Daniels. We were doing more than tasting. So now we're working as tour guides for the Cheyenne Nation in Belle Fourche. Actually, we're in Rapid City driving tourists around the monuments. Camping out it gets kinda breezy at night but one can't ask for everything at once.*

August l9
Billings, Montana

> *We just can't keep a job anywhere. We got fired from our job at the Lodge for goosing the tourists so we headed for the Land of the Big Sky. Billings is a real place. We stayed in a railroad hotel to get cleaned up but there was too much goin' on to sleep. The hippies carry knives out here! Due at Chico tomorrow*

and we'll arrive in style. Thanks for the connection you made for
us. Love, Mouche

In the same mail there was a note from Claire.

August ll
  hi ma, just thinking of you with love.
  i'm not so good at the store
  but life is really beautiful and the hard
  parts help to make it more apparent.
  i'm coming home soon, claire

Lidia laughed out loud as she started up the hill.

There was real work for her to do. The garden gate had blown open in the night and the wind had flattened the tall rows of beans. Tomatoes, sunflowers and climbing vines were dashed to the ground. The noon-day heat beat down as Lidia began pulling beans out of the tangled growth. The garden was alive with energy. The smell of earth cooled by the night wind rose to meet the heated air. She tried to free her mind into the whirl of sensations but she could not relinquish doubt, the question of why she was there in the garden at this moment. She felt insignificant, dizzy from the green shapes moving around her. Furiously she picked beans and then tomatoes and started again to finish the beans. She thinned the new growth of carrots and tried to stake up the sunflowers. Carrying the full baskets downhill to the house, she shouted into the empty meadow, "We think we are immortal! We think we'll never die!"

She felt feverish and went to the pond. Four times she swam around the banks. Floating there, she recovered a sense of herself and dove down and down again into the brown water, coming up with stems of green water plants in her hair.

In the kitchen she processed beans for freezing, tomatoes for juice. Carrying the tray of vegetables to the cellar, one thing became very clear. Both freezers were jammed full, of pork, bacon, sausage and quarts of lard from last summer's slaughter of the pigs, roasts of goat leg and ground meat, quarts of rhubarb and green beans and loaves of bread she had baked and frozen. "Lidia, you can't provide food for ghosts."

The cellar was damp, the freezers rusting in the humidity. Her body felt aroused but unconnected to anything except the need for warmth. She went up to the sun-drenched terrace, took off her clothes and lay down on the warm stones. She had a fleeting daydream, a prostitute with a painted blue face gesturing wildly for her to get into the car and go away with her. As the first lengthening shadows began to cool the stones, she woke stiffly. The goats called from the barn and she dressed and went to feed and milk them. Twilight had already filled the kitchen when she sat down to write…

> *This is our summer of sorrow,*
> *Black scarves are blowing on the wind.*
> *On the altar we built*
> *I raise my naked torso to the sun and*
> *Feel my blood running over the hot stones.*
> *Our history breathes on us and*
> *Forms a chrysalis around us*
> *That will not split.*

What would have happened, she wondered on her way up to bed, if I'd been brave enough to go with her, my blue painted lady? She was too tired to consider what the dream might be trying to say.

The phone's prolonged ringing woke her after midnight. She answered sleepily to the voice, muffled as though it spoke under water. "I can't hear you, oh…Richard? Where are you? Are you in Washington?" Her body tightened, dreading whatever she would hear.

"No, I left the meeting early. I'm at the Waterford airport. There's a limousine coming in to Garrison at 12:45. Will you pick me up there?"

A faint smile crossed her face as she recognized how like Richard it was to say limousine instead of van. "Oh…well, it's so late, isn't there always a taxi waiting?"

"Lidi, I need you to come. I'm not doing well. Something, I… there's something wrong with my eyes."

"I'll be there," she said. "Richard? don't worry. 'Bye." She felt afraid. "But whatever it is has meaning, it will be real." She shuddered as the images of her dream returned —the ugly worm embedded in the eye, the blind insect.

In the morning the sun was high up above the tree line to the east before Richard stirred. Its glow spread murky orange in the humid air, and Lidia got up to pull a shade against the August heat already coming in the bedroom window. Richard lay still and spoke to her with his eyes closed. "If I go blind, Lidi, will you manage?"

She sat down on the bed and put her hand on his forehead. She was aware of herself seeing, sparrows fluttering in the gutter along the roof, the one brave sunflower growing on the edge of the road where a circle of white cabbage butterflies hovered. She saw heat waves shimmering low over the meadow. "If you can manage," she said softly, "if it's meant to be. There are worse things. But Richard, why would this happen to you?"

"Against my will," he said glumly, "my fate, maybe what I deserve. They don't need me. I confused everything at the meeting. The paper wasn't clear."

"Richard, I'm certain you're not right. It was a brilliant paper. It isn't important now. Open your eyes, see if it's still there."

"Yes, it's the same. I see the lights now, they're flickering." Richard opened his eyes and closed them. "The spots are there, like black lace, veils of black lace in both eyes." Against the pallor of Richard's skin and the gray streaks of his hair, his eyes burned red, inflamed.

"Like they don't belong in your beautiful head." She stood up. "We'll go now. I'll call Dr. Cranford. It'll be alright, I know it will."

"I'm not so sure," he said.

Two hours later they knew nothing. The opthamologist did not recognize the symptoms and advised Richard to leave immediately for an eye clinic in the city. The drive was directly into the August sun. Richard aged perceptively and walked bent over into the doctor's office. They waited and waited through examination, questioning, consultation, the completion of minute diagrams drawn from information revealed by the magnifying instruments.

"Peele's Disease," the doctor announced, "degeneration of blood vessels nourishing the eye. It's rare in this country, we never see it, only one or two cases in my experience. Never in both eyes. We'll do what we can." He tried to be reassuring.

"The cause?" Lidia asked.

"Unknown. We'll give you medication. Don't drink any alcohol," the doctor smiled. "Wear these glasses and come back in two weeks. We'll know more then."

As days passed the high heat of August withdrew into the beginning of cool night air that lay longer under the morning sun. In the house was a new quietness and respect, an awareness that hung over every small act. If I could always meet Richard like this, Lidia thought, as though a third person was here letting us step back from each other. She tried to discover Richard's deeper feelings but he was stoic, accepting his affliction.

Crete called, back from the family's summer touring in France and Italy. Guardedly, Lidia told her about Richard's eyes, recognizing her resistance to Crete's analysis, her judgment, her necessity to be involved in every detail. "Do I only imagine that Crete needs to feed on the parts of my life that are vulnerable and raw?" Crete was insistent, and Lidia let herself be drawn out even as she saw she was giving away the very things she needed to keep. "It's a possibility he may be blind. An amazing part of it is that both Claire and I, months ago, had premonitions. I'm reading to Richard in the evenings. It's lovely really. We can manage it if he'll accept it."

"Poor dear man, Lidi, I'll come out as soon as I can. We're just back and everything needs organizing."

She's so definitive, Lidia thought, even in chaos, definitive. But she gets to the bottom of things, all the moments to be clarified. Crete doesn't cover up, I think that's my resistance to her.

She'd forgotten how regal Crete was. Seeing her the next day Lidia felt the same awe as on their first meeting. She was setting the small table under the maples when Crete arrived. Her height, crowned with the silver-gray coil of hair was impressive enough, but it was Crete's studied air of adornment Lidia had forgotten. The tones of a pale green tunic falling loosely to her ankles were matched in the turquoise and silver ear-rings and the simple chain around her neck. Crete's skin had darkened and her eyes seemed full of greenish lights. Lidia stood back and held her breath as Crete bent over to reach a sandal that had slipped from her foot. "Crete, you look beautiful." She moved closer to look directly up into Crete's face. "Talk to Richard while I get some lunch."

Crete watched Richard coming toward her across the wide lawn. Wearing dark glasses, his left arm in a sling, he tapped the ground with a cane and walked slowly. He approached her with the dignity of a tragic figure.

"Mercy," Crete said to herself, "he's bent over like an old man."

He seemed unable to verbalize his feelings. Crete moved to brush his cheek with her hand. An aura of distance surrounded him, as though he were seeing into another world. He barely acknowledged her greeting. Crete sat down and remained silent till Lidia appeared in the kitchen door struggling with a large tray. "I'll help her. Sit down yourself," and she left him standing awkwardly beside the table.

They spread out plates and glasses. "Ah, piroshki's, I'm impressed." Crete reached for a tiny triangular meat pie on top of the pile. Its crust was brown and shining in her long fingers.

"I had time," Lidia said, "and Richard loves them." They ate everything and the luncheon ended with two announcements, Richard's, that Claire had phoned and would be home in two days, and Crete's invitation to them all for a party. "To cheer us," she said, "after the gravity of our summer."

The last days of August were like a rollercoaster as the effects of Richard's medication waxed and waned. He resembled a sleepwalker moving with a hand outstretched in darkness who would suddenly transform into a giant, jangling and jubilant. He was morose to jovial, depressed to elated, constantly irritable. She knew he wanted sympathy, was frightened not to feel safe, not to have his space secure. To keep peace she became quiet around him. If he shouted, "Damn it, Lidia, can't you understand the bed in this light is torture for me?," she held back a reply. If he jumped up from the table saying, "Stop fussing over me, I feel suffocated. Just because you don't give yourself space the rest of us have to suffer," she would make an elegant picnic for them or arrange a boat trip on the North River. She watched his bursts of anger become interspersed with a wistful back-longing, like a tree falling branch by branch.

One evening she said to him, "I have a heart-ache."

"Well, I can't reach your heart," he answered.

When the children came home the place lightened and expanded again. Claire was so happy to be out of the city. Mouche brought spacious Montana sky and Mary-Molly the wind-sweep of the Maine coast. Carrying in a bushel of shells, Mary-Molly dumped them on the living room floor and disappeared to start up a telephone marathon with her friends. Mouche began his high and hilarious tales which everyone recognized as the mere surface of his actual adventures. Tall as Richard now, he was growing a straggly beard. He fumed about his name. "Mouche, no one understands that. But Morley! With that name what'm I going to do?"

They explained again what he perfectly remembered. That he had been born in France, so suddenly and unexpectedly, Richard said, he was like --une mouche-- a little fly on the wall. "Now Morley, of the Skiles clan, was an adventurer, someone your mother thought you might resemble. He left familiar territory for the tropics and bought a large ranch there, a successful bucaneer you might say." Lidia agreed with Richard, that Morley Skiles had been helpful to the world.

Crete's party took place on the evening of the full Harvest Moon, two days before there was to be news about Richard's eyes. The end of August was cooling down though the days were warm and katydids and crickets still sang. It was warmer in town and Crete had Japanese lanterns hanging far back in the garden where supper was planned. Ferdy, moist with exertion, came out to greet them. He'd finished raking the fresh mowed grass and its smell mixed with the sweet odor of nicotiana and white phlox along the garden wall.

"Where's Richard, the old boy?"

Lidia explained that he hadn't been ready and was coming shortly in the truck.

"Soooo. We have Claire and Mouche and Lidia and Margaret!"

Mary-Molly pounded his shoulder. "I told you Ferdy," she shrieked. "Don't-call-me-Margaret!"

Ferdy laughed and put his arm around her. "C'mon, help me in the kitchen. We have oysters to shuck."

"How horrible!"

Ferdy pulled her toward the kitchen as Raj, the large sheep dog bounded into the center of the group. "Raj! stay down! I'm tying him up." The oldest Montfort boy came off the back porch with a leash. "Mouche, I have some things to show you upstairs, neat stuff!"

"I did alot of drawings yesterday." Jamie Montfort came quietly up to Claire. He was eight, the more gentle one of the twins, and he adored Claire.

"Will you show me now?" And they also disappeared into the house.

Crete came down the steps carrying a large tray of glasses, soda and ice. "Raj be quiet! This dog's been hyper ever since we got back. Lidi, have a little glass of wine before Richard comes. Why isn't he with you?"

"I'm fine, quite high on all this commotion. He preferred to come on his own. He does that, needs a lead time before parties. I don't know," she raised her eyebrows, "what it means."

"Dear man, he's so noble," Crete said off-handedly. Her fingers closed around a long-stemmed crystal glass of white wine. "My heart goes out to him. I didn't know he could drive. Soon you'll know if the meds work." Lidia nodded.

They walked back up to the kitchen and passed, just inside the door, a tea cart piled with covered dishes, bread wrapped in a red napkin, relishes in tiny jars and large bowls filled with fresh, green salads.

"I love the exuberance in your house, Crete, the feeling of lavish offerings, food, art for the eye and love and abandon."

"That's the trick," Crete said, "a simple offering in lavish display. Really it's meatloaf, corn on the cob and sliced tomatoes. This town is special in summer, all the people freckled and glowing with sun. I'm so glad to be back." She dropped ears of corn into a large pot of boiling water. "We'll give Richard eight minutes and then we're going ahead."

Dusky twilight floated in the far recesses of the garden where the lanterns' glow did not penetrate. Shadows of shrubs and heavy lawn chairs began webbing across the grass. The drone and rasp of insects rose and fell with the childrens' voices. Lidia sat back in a deep chair. "Children in summer twilight, it brings back moments of the past."

"Yes, it holds them," Ferdy said, gracefully moving into Lidia's nostalgia, "as though time didn't exist. What do you remember?"

"Summer nights on my father's farm in Ohio. I was five or six. I remember grown-ups sitting in a ring, how they seemed real but we knew better, losing ourselves into sounds of crickets and the feel of moonlight on our hands. We wore white dresses and we felt the terror and joy of cousins. What about you, what do you remember?"

"The same," he said, "the garden with fireflies and there was a sweet odor of flowers blooming."

"Oh, was it white phlox?" They turned toward Claire, who sat down then with them. "Phlox, the white kind. We have it growing now, white blossoms that gleam in the dark. I think it's here too."

"You must be right Claire. I don't know its name," Ferdy acknowledged her. "Names didn't matter to us then, did they?"

"In the city," Crete stood up to begin serving the plates, "our garden opened into back-street alleys, mossy bricks and crooked walls for hiding. In the city, twilight was the same, mystery." She handed full plates to the children, buttering ears of corn, pouring drinks and making thick sandwiches out of the meatloaf. Ferdy was lighting two lawn torches beyond the tables when they heard the noise of the truck.

"Is that Richard?" They all turned toward him coming over the grass.

"Oh, he's brought Potter," Lidia gasped.

"Oh Dad," Mouche groaned.

The dog stayed close to Richard, walking steadily at his heel. Dressed in white with dark glasses and his cane, Richard appeared like an actor on stage. He was smiling, pleased at his own spectacle. Ferdy rose as he came closer. "Sorry we went ahead. The kids got hungry. Come sit down."

"S'alright," Richard's voice slurred. "I'm not hungry."

Lidia turned to Crete. "He's been…"

"Yes," Crete nodded. She took Richard's arm and led him to a chair. The dog, Potter, lay down next to him. As all their voices rose again, Richard sat back, smiling, refusing all offers of food.

Crete soon disappeared into the house and returned with a huge bowl, an antique china wash basin piled to the brim with scoops of chocolate and raspberry ice-cream. There were bowls of caramel topping and old-fashioned chocolate sprinkles. In the general melee over the ice cream, Potter the ridgeback, rose and lunged at the Montfort's sheep dog tied on a long lead to the apple tree. Raj bared his teeth and leapt up. Their large bodies connected high in the air and fell back snarling before Potter lunged again, the hair on his back standing high.

"Let him off the lead!" Ferdy shouted.

Someone moved forward and then back as the dogs twirled in a blurred circle, their teeth snapping and then biting into flesh. Blood appeared on the white hair hanging over the sheepdog's muzzle. Everyone was immobilized. The noise of the dogs was deafening.

"Get Raj by the collar!" Crete shouted.

"No, no, let them go!" Ferdy shouted back.

As Richard stood and moved toward the crashing dogs, Mouche thrust his body between them and grabbed Potter's collar. The dog twisted back and sank his teeth into Mouche's arm as he held on and dragged the trembling dog back.

There was silence. Mary-Molly began to cry, then Jamie. Crete rushed for antiseptics and a tourniquet, and Ferdy, pale and shaken, led Raj to safety in the house.

"My God," Claire moaned, "Mouche, are you alright?"

Lidia, drained of all emotion, could not speak.

"Well," Richard said , with what sounded like a sob in his voice, "I guess I ruined everything."

There was nothing to say except good-bye.

5

No one had called Merle to come up but, as always, he knew when help was needed. Water in the spring across the pond had been low all month and suddenly had drained all at once out of the storage tank in the cellar. The kitchen sink was full of dirty dishes and everyone was using the old outhouse. The spring at Stone Hill had never dried up but the water's conveyance into the house was mercurial, as described by Claire. She had learned how to blow the lines to clear the silt and get water flowing back in to the tank again. It was a seasonal event through which everyone always remained cheerful.

When Merle arrived Claire was riding horseback. Richard was alone in the cellar, cursing whoever had left a toilet running through the night. "I need help down here," he shouted. "Bring me a light, I can't see anything in this blackness!"

Merle stood in the doorway. "How're his eyes? Better now I guess." Lidia felt confused and faced him with a mixture of sadness flashed through with anger. It was a relief to talk about medical facts.

"The tests show improvement," she said briskly. "The doctors say it will be slow with some damage remaining. The cause is unknown but it looks hopeful now. He won't be blind."

"You know Lidia?," Merle said softly, "I b'lieve things like this happen for a reason. It's not a straight path, ragin' like he does against this and that that's in the way of it. You have to go sideways or you don' see anythin.' It's sideways the eyes see, that's when things stay in the mind."

"And what about the heart?," she asked boldly. She was aware of Richard's growing discomfort in the cellar.

Merle looked into the space behind her. "I guess mine's weak because I haven't found the way to use it." She held out the overhead lamp to him. Merle carried it to the cellar and stayed to help Richard till the pump was working again.

Merle was having coffee when Richard stomped through the kitchen wearing high rubber boots and carrying a shot-gun. "M-M's complaining about the snake in the pond. I'm going to get it." The screen door banged as Richard went out, and they heard him call back, "Have you noticed? It's turned into a superb day."

"Oh my," Lidia glanced at Merle. "He's a good shot really. Two days ago he killed a porcupine in the apple tree."

Merle grinned and pushed back his cap. "I guess he can see then when he wants to. But," Merle went on quietly, "he doesn't see what he needs to see. He doesn't see his own children."

"Merle?" Lidia said sharply.

"Lidia? I see a thing or two, I cain't help it."

She looked into his eyes, startling blue under the bare forehead, and she saw him withdrawing from words which he knew would give pain to her. She held the awareness carefully between them, a break in her possession of herself that changed her sense of who she was.

"I'm takin' Mary-Molly fishing. She wants to go, kids need to be free. There's a good pool down by the river. We'll bring you a trout." Merle paused and looked carefully at her. "You want to go too, don't you?"

"The garden," she kept on looking boldly into his eyes, "I have to finish the harvesting."

Merle looked back at her for a moment but said nothing. They heard the gun go off and after a few moments it fired again. When they reached the pond, Richard was leaning out over the water with a long pole, drawing toward the bank the enormous body of the snake, black with mottled spots of dull red. It was headless. "Shot in the head, killed instantly," Richard said. "You can tell Mary-Molly it's safe now."

Mary-Molly was planning a party. All her imaginings were focused on this end of summer gathering, and every detail of her support system was now being made clear. Setting up the heavy canvas tent was a morning's job requiring the cutting and lashing of several young trees along its sides. Mouche worked steadily in spite of pain from the wound in his left arm. The day before the party the cousins arrived from Maine with

Richard's sister, Belle, and her husband Clay. The cousins slept that night in the tent which had already become glorious, hung by Claire with colored cloths and works of art hastily created. Mary-Molly dragged tables, luxurious pillows and mattresses from the house, and Mouche wired electricity from the barn. They'd placed the tent on a knoll in the lower meadow, out of sight of the house, where it received the first rays of sun. "By far the best location on the place for sleeping," Mouche said.

That whole day was a carnival, the white pony and two horses galloping in the meadow, the goat kids performing ritual dances, dogs and chickens meddling into everything. Wild shrieks rose above the trees at the pond. Packed lunches made by Claire were carried to the tree house. Belle and Richard took refuge in his outside study.

Belle was the favorite aunt, the one who saved family treasures and sent them to the right person at the right time. She resembled Richard around the forehead and her eyes were the same deep gray. Belle's voice was clear, not only its meaning but its tone. Anyone would know where they stood with her. She and Clay were close, "an indivisible unit in the face of treachery," Clay joked. He laughed with Lidia at his and her status as out-laws, part of the clan when needed, but "once in," he said, "we're really always out. Wonderful, isn't it?" Lidia loved his habit of cheerful deference to his wife.

In the late afternoon of the next day, cars driven by parents began to arrive, spilling out small animated groups which clustered together in different parts of the meadow. "She's brought the world up here," Belle said, "and she's supremely at home in it. Look at her!"

From the terrace they watched Mary-Molly's effortless merging and cohesion of the little groups into one organism whose meaning and function seemed to arise out of simple proximity. Energy exploded from the boys, a spontaneous movement of heads and limbs covered in caps and clothing of which carelessness appeared the prime virtue. The ladies, as Clay remarked, "truly ladies," seemed of different vintage, standing secure and centered in their casual elegance. Mary-Molly was bringing them all together.

She wore an artful layering of shirts and shining vest over a long black skirt, and had illumined her blond hair with dangling earrings and a headband of jewels. She steered a willing group of her friends toward the grown-ups for introductions while the others moved in a small herd down to the tent, carrying pitchers of liquids, bowls of food, guitars and containers of unknown contents.

"Phew," Belle exclaimed, "did we ever so inhabit the world? Of course," she looked at Richard, "you did, Prince Charming of all the coming out parties!"

"Ahhh. I was just a lackey if they needed an extra." He mumbled, looking pleased. "Now, what kind of a voice is that?"

From the tent came sounds of a piercing nasal voice accompanied by guitar.

> *If your time to you is worth savin'*
> *Then you better start swimmin' or*
> *You'll sink like a stone*
> *For the times they are a-changin'.*

"You don't know? Well listen." The honking voice went on.

> *'Come mothers and fathers throughout the land*
> *And don't criticize what you don't understand*
> *Your sons and your daughters are beyond your command*
> *Your old road is rapidly agin'*
> *So get out of the new one if you can't lend a hand…'*

"The times they are a-changin'," Belle sang.

"Well I'll be damned! I've heard enough, let's take his advice," Richard said. "I'm feeling celebratory, shall we go out to dinner Belle?"

"Lidi, would you mind? Clay?"

"A good time for you both to escape," Clay said. "Lidi and I can keep things in hand, can't we?"

"I don't mind eavesdropping alone. I'm astonished at all this," Lidia admitted.

"Some of these actors belong to us, I'd like to stay." So it was decided and Lidia felt relieved.

They had finished a gin and tonic on the terrace and were walking down into the meadow. "It's a good party, it's a great party," Clay was saying to her. At dusk the music had subsided to strains of two guitars and a portable keyboard. Someone had lighted candles and from a distance the scene appeared like an encampment of gypsies. Lidia was moved almost to tears. She took Clay's arm.

"Lidi, you look beautiful," he said, "that crown of luminous hair above your face. Are you happy? Lonely? Are you worried about Richard's eyes?"

"No, his eyes are much better. We're over the worst. There'll be slow improvement now. I hoped he would see differently after the disease. He might've been blind you know." She paused. "I'm lonely I guess, but isn't everyone?"

"I don't think so, at least not most of the time."

Moist air rustled the heavy canopy of maple leaves over their heads. A mellow tremulo, trilling so low it seemed far away, floated under the sound of the guitars. "They're right here. It's toads," Lidia said, "they're the last to sing in summer." They listened to the sound of the toads. "Do you think things always work out, Clay?"

"No," he answered. "I don't think so necessarily." They stood still listening.

"You know? I'm smiling but you can't see it in the dark."

"Yes, I am too," he said, "but I don't know why. Do you?"

She answered without hesitation. "It's because at this moment, everything is so beautiful. It's all coming into my body."

In the morning before Clay and Belle left with the boys, Belle drew Lidia aside. "I see you have your own room."

"Yes, but Richard wants it for a dressing room."

"Oh, he's a peacock," Belle laughed. "Richard always was. I'll write you soon, Lidi. I'm worried about him. Stone Hill is marvelous, inside and out. It's so peaceful, the bare floors, the old white furniture covers and the childrens' art things. But isn't it tiresome always to make one's best effort?" Belle laughed a throaty laugh and gave Lidia a long hug.

In three days her letter came. It was to Richard. He'd left it open on his desk upstairs and Lidia picked it up and read.

Dear Richard,

> *I tried to call you on Sunday but maybe you were out in the
> woods. How much we enjoyed our visit. I'm sorry if we ate too
> much but the food was quite fine. Thanks for everything. I've
> had alot on my mind this week but most of my thoughts were
> of you. I felt sad and concerned after our visit. I've written this
> letter many times in my mind. My first fear is that you'll be
> angry with me. But something has to give and it may be you.
> Lidia and the children love you, Richard, but they need to know
> they're part of your life and all you do. The place has become
> overpowering in your life, it is your life. Nothing should be that
> all engrossing at the expense of one's family. Clay and I were
> very aware during our visit that you used 'I' and 'mine,' never
> 'we' and 'ours.' A family can't prevail over this. Lidia has the
> goats so she can have something, maybe your kids are still look-
> ing for something that's their own. There's more than enough
> love to go around, Richard, if you just...*

As her eyes filled with tears Lidia stopped reading. Out the upstairs
window she saw Richard leading the white pony into the meadow for
the night. She wanted to call him through the open window. His beautiful face looked fallen into so much sadness. The sadness floated up like
an ascending cloud and instantly the spirit of the evening was changed.
She waited for an opening, a space to call to him but then Mary-Molly
shouted up and Lidia turned away to go to her.

It was cool the last days of August, with wind, woolly bear caterpillars
and sun with scudding clouds. Lidia and Richard talked all day. "It's
more important than preserving vegetables," he said. They began in the
sun porch, moved out under the maples and back to the terrace. Richard
talked about the woodlot. They walked to the garden.

In the afternoon, Claire and Mouche came and walked with them
in the woods. They stood in a small clearing where long rays of the sun
penetrated the high pines. "I'd like to clear more of this, what do you

think Claire? Suppose we open up this stand the length of the stone wall along the meadow?"

"What a great idea, but you're so funny, Dad. It's a terrible lot of work, why would you do it?"

"Really Dad," Mouche began, "I agree with Claire. There's enough old stuff to do for awhile." He turned, watching Lidia start to run in pursuit of an orange butterfly which settled down on a tall weed near the brook. "Mom, what are you after?"

"Look, look, you know what it is Mouche, on the Joe Pye!"

"Yeah," he smiled, "let's hear it," and together they shouted, "the Great Spangled Fritillary! the Great Spangled Fritillary!" until they broke into laughter.

"How do you know Mouche, that it's a Great Spangled Fritillary?" Claire was laughing with them.

"Silver spots on the underwing," he said, "and they always sit on the Joe Pye."

With Richard leading, they started up the steep part of the trail. "Wow, I'm impressed," he turned back to wink at Claire, "what they do teach you at Parker's Farm School!"

"And there," Lidia spoke quietly so only Claire could hear, "there's my hawk, my sign." She and Claire watched the bird circling low over the pines till it disappeared.

"Yes, a good sign for you, Mom," Claire agreed.

Two summers ago, Lidia had traveled north to a healing woman who saw in her aura the same fire and emotional heat that is the life force of the falcon. The healer had seen a vision of the Native American Chief, Tretrataus, standing tall with the falcon on his arm. She told Lidia the falcon would be his messenger, giving her strength to balance her energy.

It was Claire who later told her more about the falcon as a sign of spiritual energy. Claire was learning about alchemy at school, the fire elements of the 'prima materia'. "That means," she said, "the first material of the earth, like chaos and water, like the bird and the fish and the salamander. In the Indian medicine wheel the hawk belongs to the Thunderbird Clan -- sun and fire energy. It draws you to be consumed in its energy and that means something good for you, Mom. It means change, like changing matter to its basic stuff and then re-building it again into what's more real. The hawk is a sign of strength, but to change first you have to contact your power center. It's focusing, really focusing like the falcon, to reach your desires and make them into real stuff. It's such a good sign for you, Mom."

Lidia had felt happy that Claire approved. She marveled at her clarity, and how it was so like Claire, going directly to the center --like the hole in the center of the earth she circled around and around when she was five. Alchemy was full of darkness but it moved toward the light. "It's all going toward one thing," she'd said, "and that's toward light."

The day was quiet, a relief for them all. A turning, Lidia thought. On this day it seems we do have a meeting. In the afternoon she sat drowsing by the woodstove. An image, suddenly and so clearly, came before her eyes. It was a woman, young and beautiful, coming toward her with arms out holding a bunch of yellow roses. From the old photographs she knew the face −Mary, her father's sister, mourned by him as long as Lidia could remember. It was Mary and she had come to help her.

At five o'clock she made stuffing for a fish and began rolling out dough for a blackberry tart that would be ready in an hour. She heard Richard breaking ice cubes, muddling them in the silver shaker. His voice was cheerful, wheedling Mouche to take down the tent. Mouche went out, pushing Mary-Molly ahead of him, and they raced to the meadow. Claire was in her room. In the pantry Richard began muttering, and in half an hour his voice had taken on an edge. "Nothin' goin' on here, all for kids, damn Belle anyway."

Lidia groaned. "What is it Lidi, your body again? pain? It's age, old age." He came into the kitchen looking disheveled. "Gonna get an apartment, give the family stuff to Belle. Belle knows all, Belle the Wise."

"Richard, please, dinner's ready, I'm calling the children."

"I'm not hungry. I'm taking a shower. Just need a little drink." He slammed the refrigerator shut and carried his glass upstairs.

"Is dinner ready? Ma, what's happening?" Claire spoke in a low voice.

"Nothing Claire, he's tired, angry at Belle. We had a lovely day. Get Mouche and Mary-Molly now, we'll eat by ourselves."

"Mom," Mary-Molly rushed in the door. "Mom? what's the matter, your face looks funny, are you crying?"

"Ssssh. Let's take everything out on the terrace. Get sweaters, it's cold now, the sun will be going down. What's the sense of spoiling our dinner, we'll talk about it later."

Mouche kept his eyes on Lidia's face and then spoke slowly, "Ma, are you going to ask us for any help?"

Claire burst in, "You do need help, Mom, you're so involved with Dad I hardly know who you are. Maybe you can't help, maybe no one can. He's drinking, more and more. Maybe it's the darkness of this place breaking over us."

"Well, I don't think Dad takes care of himself," Mary-Molly said slowly, "and he thinks we'll love him anyway. And I do love him too even if he doesn't let me have my own way."

"Oh how much you are a help to me." Her love for them flowed out on Lidia's voice." I love him too but right now I don't know what to do."

She went later than usual to the barn. Mouche had fed the horses and their stalls were clean. As she always did during the last weeks, Lidia ran her hand over the bulge on Vita's right side to feel the kids move. She could see the outline of their bodies. "We're late bloomers, Vita, all of us. Soon enough there'll be grain for you after these beauties come." She spread moist greens of kale and comfrey in the feeding trough, then leaned over and laid her head on the goat's warm flank. "Be peaceful, it isn't long now."

Back at the house she wrapped herself in a blanket and sat by the cold stove to write...

> *Yesterday the sun burned out. Under a sodden sky the only light now will be from the death of plant cells. Across the road a heavy bush burns out its heart, raw and red. No warmth comes from it. Inside, the house is cold and a musty smell grows in the corners. Every night I wake in the same fear from the scratching and footfalls of an animal on the attic floor above. Last night I dreamed of helping you center your thoughts on a heavy white paper. I drew a black border on it for you and showed you mine.*

*I want you to do your own. I'm young, dressed in a white tunic
to my knees. A green plant is nearby but the white of paper and
black of letters is clearer.*

The next morning, she woke at dawn and came downstairs in bare feet.
Her wool socks lay beside the empty stove, and half a glass of wine.

* * *

*Above the rising moon of mid-September, the constellation
of Orion moves higher in the sky. Lighted by bright stars, the
Hunter raises up his club and lion skin and starts the long, cold
journey west. Swirling nets of blackbirds alight and gabble in the
trees, flocking to move south. Moths flutter at the lighted windows, crickets sing with a labored chirp on the edge of frost, and
the owl's hoot is low.*

    *The first weeks of October are golden on Stone Hill. Yellow
and saffron veils fill the air and reflect in the rooms and mirrors
and windows of the house. There's a smell of wild grapes high
out of reach, the smell of late-blooming clematis hanging over
the stone walls and a smoke of purple asters on the hills. It's the
spectacle, unequalled anywhere, of autumn in New England.*

The day after Claire and Mouche went back to school, Mary-Molly
came home with a bird. "My friend Jessie got tired of him. His name's
Chipper. We need a cage, Ma. I'll keep him in my room."

    "A paraquet, so green, so blue. You'll have to keep him safe from
Woody and Claude. Especially Claude. That cat's a killer."

    "I know. Don't you just love Chipper? Maybe he'll need a friend."

    "We'll see how it goes." Lidia wondered how she could keep on af-
firming day after day when the house was filled with so much confusion.
She consoled herself by writing at night.

*The bad times have strengthened us. Isn't it enough to put a
backlog into the stove and watch it light up with a clear flame? I
love Richard, who he really is. I want him to go to that hidden*

part of himself and let it be a place for us. He coughs now, alone in bed. In the morning he'll go to school for another unsatisfying day. What will break? I stay up late and live my own rich life, not part of this world. Only the creaking floor of this house is real, the stove fire burning low.

The days were filled with harvesting, cooking and juicing the last of the tomatoes. All containers were filled and Lidia washed plastic jugs to hold the juice. Richard arrived home in the evening sunset as she came down from the garden in her old felt hat, carrying gathered kindling. "Faggots, faggots, gathering faggots," he greeted her. "Just like your mama does. Last fall you did the same." They went in to the kitchen. "Lidia, you are so un-dis-crim-inating, putting juice in plastic jugs. Don't do that!"

"How were the meetings today?"

"At least take off that mangy hat. The meetings, meetings! I come from that chaos to this. Don't-freeze-that-juice-in-plastic-jugs!"

She nodded, watching him pour gin into a glass.

"I think you've got to get out of it," she said a bit glibly.

"Oh. Well, you go and tell them. Lidia, I'm getting sick, it all makes me sick." He turned to go up the stairs. "We have a different view of things. Big fantasy the juice. I don't like juice. A big mistake, you're making a large mistake."

"Some of it's for Crete, she won't mind the jugs."

She went on preparing dinner, grating a large pile of cheese, slicing tomatoes. Richard stayed upstairs but she could hear his voice. "Just like your mama, your mama. Gather, gather, go out and gather bark. Dammit all, damn it!"

She woke about midnight and Richard was not in bed. She found him downstairs snoring in a sleeping bag in the living room. The cats were playing on the kitchen floor as she turned on the lights and began funnelling tomato juice into the plastic gallons. On her way up to bed again she spread a blanket over Richard's sleeping bag, then leaned over and whispered in his ear, "O sleep well, Richard the Lion-hearted."

Crete came regularly from town to set up her canvas and paint the light. She said the light rayed out from the center of the trees and that it differed from the quality of light reflected from their surface. She came at all hours but never succeeded in capturing the effect she wanted. She wasn't discouraged. "I have to mask my own brightness to reach the root of this light. Maybe a year from now I'll know how to do that."

"Mask your own brightness Crete? That's quite profound if I understand what you mean. But the light comes through your own body, doesn't it? Isn't it the body that connects?"

"Well, partly. It's both really. Cezanne said it, not me. He actually accomplished that, keeping himself out of the painting, allowing the forms to come forward on their own ground. It changed everything in art. Look, I brought you these golden pears from our tree," she lifted up the basket of fruit, "and this is the old recipe from Ferdy's aunt in Brittany. Cut each pear into pieces, put them in a very hot oven with alot of sugar and a little butter. After fifteen minutes they begin to burn and caramelize. Then you throw a cup of cream over them. That's it. Pears are classic. Tell me how it works."

"Mask your own brightness." Lidia drew in her breath. "What exactly does that mean?"

Piri and Lorion walked up on a warm afternoon to sit with Richard and Lidia under the golden trees. "Unequalled anywhere in the world. In my Polish countryside there is nothing like this." Lorion's voice burred softly. "We had chestnuts. Their leaves were like pale leather, and the poplars, a thin yellow. But this," he raised his arm with the palm upward, "this is like gold of the Incas."

Piri smiled at Richard. "Do you see, Lorion's a poet like you. He sees all things under the stars."

Richard reached out and took her hand. "I guess he listens to you. Lidia tells me about all you know. Sit down," he pointed to the wide bench under the trees.

Lidia came out from the house with a tray of small glasses and a bottle of brandy. Mary-Molly followed her carrying a plate of sweet biscuits and muttering, "Slivovitz, slivovitz, my dear, dear slivovitz." Lorion laughed and offered her a taste of it. He laughed again at her horror when the fiery liquid touched her tongue. "You won't believe it's made of plums, will you?" She shook her head.

"Will you teach me about the stars?" She sat down next to him.

"What do you want to know?"

"Oh, why they die and what happens to them. Maybe how they're born too. Do you know about that?"

Lorion nodded his head. "When will you come?"

"Tomorrow, after school."

"I'll be there when the bus comes."

Lidia sat back watching the two men, Lorion's large body all ease and amiability, Richard's warming from a dignified reserve into the rare and graceful laxity she so loved in him. Seldom was his body so still with her, sitting easily like this in his effort to be accessible to these dear, unthreatening people. How opposite they were. Lorion's smooth forehead held the expanse one felt on a wide hill open to the sky. His eyes were blue as the wild chicory flower, large and set far apart emphasizing the blondness of his fine, thinning hair. She imagined him standing on the prow of a Viking ship plunging in heavy seas. He had the muscled strength and energy of an explorer. Lorion was whole again after the mysterious accident at Harmon's Pond in June. Lidia wondered if the cause of his accident had come from a place in him invisible to everyone. Surely he carried so much grief about the past. But he looked strong now under the October sun.

She could not so easily place Richard in a history. Tall and thin, with a latent grace that, in rare moments, mobilized the light at his center, he was not dark but gave the impression of darkness. It issued from his brow overhanging the deep-set eyes and well defined bones of his face as if the darkness was reaching for something far off. She decided that the brow was the seat of Richard's emotions and that Lorion's was the heart.

Richard began speaking about ideas that moved him deeply, scientific theories based on the possibility of a world that didn't yet exist. He seldom had an audience able to respond to theories of cosmic evolutionary process. She and Piri listened to them talk about the complexity of forms in man and nature and how these ideas applied to their work. Lorion spoke as an astronomer with a cosmic point of view. "I know

Teilhard de Chardin's ideas. He was both a scientist and a deeply spiritual man. The acceptance of his vision requires great faith on our part.
But it has parallels in the cosmic history."

Richard narrowed the point of view to his own experience.
"Photography also changes the scale of the world. It enables me to take
possession of space and layer it till the images fold back into themselves,
dense and compressed. In the photograph it's out of time, but in the
viewer the effect creates an immediate implosion of energy. It bursts
open the consciousness. Do you see what I mean, how this applies? The
next step is to synthesize that energy into a collective consciousness.
Over time of course."

"Like our galaxy," Lorion's context was large, "pieces of the universe
that are structured out of compression into a higher unit, a contraction
of physical material. You talk about de Chardin who looks for a rise in
psychic temperature, his reflective sphere. You're applying it to images
under the same contraction. Yes, I see, very interesting," Lorion stroked
his chin. "In your work, it's images that create the compression. But," he
added, "in photography you're imposing your own standards on reality."

Without destroying its fabric, there was no way for Piri and Lidia
to break into the conversation. Lidia leaned over and whispered in Piri's
ear, "Green tomatoes? There's an empty basket up in the garden." They
excused themselves and went to finish the last of the harvesting.

Merle came on a Saturday morning to see Vita's kids. Richard was re-
building the chicken roost in the barn and asked Merle if he could help
remove part of a rotted beam in the foundation. Before going to work
they were having coffee at the kitchen table, talking about the goats. "I've
named the new does Fiona and Gilda," Lidia said. "I'm so happy there
wasn't a male this time. I can't destroy them anymore. What does that
mean for goat-keeping, Merle?" She deferred to his opinion. Merle knew
about goats but he didn't accept the practice of destroying the males,
considered useless since they gave no milk.

"It means you're done with goats," Merle said. "It won't work any
more. You don't want a herd of wild males up here." He thought a few

moments. "But they're worth alot, goats. They're calm. They'd lead the horses out if the barn fired up."

"Yes, I know that," Richard repeated. "Goats don't panic, they'd lead the horses out to safety."

"Maybe I am done," Lidia went on, "if I can get through nursing these new ones. I've raised four generations, what it takes to make them pure-bred." She leaned over and drew on paper the lineage of the Stone Hill goats. "Devi, the first, a horned goat from Texas, her origin unknown, to Jesse. Devi again to Windrow, Windrow to Mistral, Mistral to Vita to Fiona and Gilda. It is something, isn't it?" She looked up for their approval. "The new ones are pure-bred now."

"So now's the time to get out of it," Richard said.

"You learned alot," Merle said.

Just then a car drove up. It was Crete. "Ah ha, Madame Lucretia, the inventress of our meagre lives. Let's get down to the barn, Merle." Richard rose. With a faint smile, Merle picked up the empty cups, put them in the sink and followed Richard out the door.

Lidia was smiling too as she thought, hasn't he dismissed Crete now, as he would anyone who meddled in his affairs? Of course, he would resent anyone who presented such a clear articulation of life. But really, Lidia smiled again, Crete's opinionated preciseness is only the result of years of therapy. Perhaps she helps me but I don't totally trust her either though I think I still love her. She brushed away the memory of her fleeting dream image of Crete with her long, long slender finger, beckoning to Richard.

"Lidi?" Crete's tall body in the doorway blocked the morning sun. "Lidi, I'm back to paint again. I need to keep at it, I'm getting the light at last. Oh, you're busy." Lidia was starting to sew soft wool linings into some netted curtains. Their coarse weavings filtered shimmering light into the rooms but had not kept out drafts.

"Yes, it's the busiest month, October. I wish Richard were here the whole day, especially in this changing season."

"It's alot," Crete said, "and there's no time left to play. You're all so earnest up here, it breaks my heart a little. D'you know what I really think? It's that you and Richard need a bigger canvas. Stone Hill isn't big enough for all your visions. Ferdy and I just talked about it yesterday. Don't you want to be finished with this house, changing, up-grading things? It's perfect now, it's spare as a museum!"

"Crete, you're wrong. There's everything here!" Lidia jumped up and faced her. "Stone Hill is a world, it has to be endured, penetrated, celebrated, it's a radical pushing through! The meaning of it is my struggle to receive it, transform it and give it back again, changed. And then I'm changed, I discover who I am. I need the feeling of peace this space can hold. Other people need areas of peace too, it doesn't always come from inside them." Her voice was rising. "Do you think Lorion's tower is just his fantasy? Do you think Piri keeps birds in it just to hear them sing? No, Crete. These things are part of a process, part of how we grow. Stone Hill isn't a museum. Don't talk to me about a museum!"

Crete stepped back in amazement. "Lidi, you're shining, just shining! How you struggle with this. I haven't understood how you feel. I never thought of it that way. Maybe it's what old places do, they reach in and change you. But," she persisted, "that's one part of it, Lidi, and you have other parts. You need people, many people, to help you recognize them."

"Go and paint now, Crete. Try to bring all your points of light together."

The October evening light was thickening and a smoky haze of blooming asters hung over the low meadow where it sloped down into the woods. Lidia, Mary-Molly and Richard stood high up in the garden to watch the crimson sunset. Vibrant colors in the western sky moved into a mass of melded reds and lit the trees behind them with a glow of pink and gold. The reflection bathed Mary-Molly's hair and Lidia's pale skin, and turned Richard's darker skin to a shade of amber. The sun gathered into a flaming ball on the horizon and as they turned in all directions to watch the changing colors, Richard, without a word, began running down toward the house.

"What's he doing Mom? He never runs. He's going faster now!"

"I don't know. C'mon, let's hurry!" They ran down to the house and when they reached him, Richard was trembling.

"Dad, why are you going to pieces?" Mary-Molly's voice was shaking.

"The house, I thought it was on fire. How foolish," he lowered his head. "All the windows were bright red from where we stood. Of course, it's the sunset."

Lidia put her arms around him, and stepping back, she looked up into his eyes. "Poor love," she murmured, "what would you have done?"

"I don't know," he shook his head sadly back and forth.

"Dad, dinner's ready. Will you have dinner with us now?" Mary-Molly took his hand and they went into the house.

They cut wood all the next day, stacking it by the woodshed to be split later for the stoves. It was almost suppertime and Richard's second cocktail had expanded his mood. "That's good work." He was leaning on the mantelpiece, snapping the old suspenders he always wore for wood cutting. "Exhilarating and useful, why couldn't I do that for a living?"

"Yes, why couldn't you?" Lidia answered from the kitchen. "Every day would be so settled, lovely in the woods. Everyone has stoves now."

Richard sat down in the blue wing-back chair and stretched out the long length of his legs. "Come and sit with me, Lidi, you're so like yourself, already thinking like a woodcutter's wife. You never get on to my musing mind. Come, let me see you." As she came into the room he reached out for her hand and pulled her down with him on the chair. "I want you to be happy. Are you happy Lidi?" He looked into her eyes for several moments. Then his mind returned to it's accustomed track. "What's driving us here anyway? Every October there's more and more to be done. Such a little place, where's it going? I want to show you something." He stood up. "A discovery I made when I printed these last week."

He spread before her a series of photographs of the house and outbuildings, each in a different quality of light and weather, in twilight, in fog, in light so bright it obliterated all detail. Some had double images exposed on the same film, some were out of focus. They were startling, a weaving of roof lines and doorways, eerie shapes floating in space.

"Oh, they're beautiful but so strange. What do you think about them?"

"What I see is that Stone Hill is an abstraction. Without the artifacts of our life here the place isn't ours. It's just a symbol, universal and true anywhere in the world. No territory, no boundaries. In fact," his energy was rising, "the place relates more to the cosmos than it does to us! How easily we could unravel the whole thing, let it fragment. Not try to hold it together."

"Why we could, we could just let it fragment," her voice was suddenly tight. She could not see Stone Hill abstractly in Richard's analytical way. Its connection to the world was through her body's experience. She felt remote. "We could stop drawing the place together, let all its things go their own way. Then it wouldn't be whole, it wouldn't be a place. Is your musing mind saying that's a choice Richard?"

"Maybe that's what I saw, but that seems simpler than what I really saw."

It was clear how transfixed he was by his discovery and that he was trying to recover his inspiration. An idea was struggling to be born, an internalized meaning the photographs had distilled. She saw it becoming accessible to him but her mind, so divided against itself, could not yield. She struck out, painfully aware of her betrayal of the quality in him she loved most, his slow struggle to become clear.

"Is that a choice Richard? Like the choice to let other people live on this land too? To have people live here who could help us?" She knew he would rise to that, and, as he raised his arm to begin, she got up to serve the dinner.

Her idea to share the land had persisted for years. There was so much space. Richard had started planning a small community of households but it had come to no more than surveys and maps. He couldn't share the place. That would never be right for him. Once again she sublimated her desire to be with others, to be seen, this time into a need for celebration. It was still warm. It was glorious autumn. She would give a party.

After dinner she told Richard her plan. He groaned. There was the problem of invitations, how to decide on a critical mass of souls to enrich the whole. She would ask everyone, he would ask either these or those but not together. "Why is this always so damn difficult?"

"Because, we don't have any regulars." And why didn't they have regulars, why couldn't they share even one couple together in a safe intimacy? It embarassed them both but was never discussed. Lidia felt something dark lay below the problem, too large to uncover.

At last the list was shaped, edited, times considered, a plan made for inclement weather. Nothing was left to chance. The afternoon was warm and sunny and everyone came. There were two photographers, some artists and their wives, Richard's man from the garage in Garrison, the two couples who kept goats, some younger sets of parents and local people from the town.

The lawn was raked for a bocci court, badminton put up for Mary-Molly's friends, and the wide shelf of Mouche's garden bench was stocked with whisky and ice, wine and a pitcher of daiquiri's. There was a garden cart piled with cheeses and hors d'oeuvres. Leaves sifted down on the brisk air. When the sun lowered, they all returned to the kitchen to serve themselves lamb curry and tamale pie, a green salad with a cucumber and pesto sauce. They sat at small tables in all corners of the rooms. Richard was relaxed, charming, as he walked from table to table filling the wine glasses, telling a story for everyone. It was perfect because none of the couples sat together, and the sprinkling of bachelors surpassed themselves in joviality.

Toward the end of dinner, Crete passed Lidia in the kitchen. "It's so elegant, how you do all this. Did you notice the golden light? It's gathering in those nets of curtains you made. We could be anywhere in the world. The people, the food, it's timeless. Ferdy's sitting with the goat people, the Cranshaws? They're talking about farming in Brittany. Piri's telling Joe Pennington all the details about Lorion's tower. And Barnes, Richard's tractor man, do you know he's a sculptor? He's marvelous! I feel giddy, just like the old days. What a success for you!"

"Will you serve the cake, Crete? I'm exhausted. Right on the dinner plates, isn't that alright? And tell them there's coffee." She anticipated Crete's question. "Yes, some of them will ask. The cake is hazelnut with coffee whipped cream, ten eggs, no flour."

At last everyone left but the Pennington's, parents of Mary-Molly's best friend Jessie, and John Nichols, owner of the art supply store in Garrison, and the Gleasons, Libby and Fran, a young photographer who worked with Richard. Mary-Molly and Jessie had disappeared. Crete and Ferdy were on their way out. At the door Crete asked for the car keys. "You're high as a kite, dear. I'm driving."

"Lidia, I love you," Ferdy gave her a hug. "It was the greatest party."

As she returned to the others, Lidia heard Fran Gleason saying, "Anybody for home-grown? It's a sweet batch." She saw him roll a joint and start it around the circle. She began to feel disconnected. Thoughts flew in and out of her head but her tongue could not put them into words. Richard's voice was pitching higher and higher. She thought of the blackboard she'd had as a child. It had a handle to turn that brought up oranges and lemons or goats or houses moving into and out of view. You could draw them, or something they made you think of, on the empty blackboard. The images rolled and rolled through her head. She saw Mary-Molly's dear face, watching her and taking in her confusion. In the same moment, she knew clearly she would see almost none of these people again. They would not come back to Stone Hill or include her or Richard in their lives. What had Crete said? We could be any-where, it's perfect, it's timeless. And what was the use of it all, of giving herself away again. She did not want to make another perfect thing. She hadn't wanted to give a successful party. Lidia rose unsteadily and went out to the pond.

The light was dim but there were stars. A few katydids sang and a lone bird. The air was cold but the water was warm and soft. She swam to the far side and floated on her back where alders hung over the water making a black cave of stillness. Her floating body sank and surfaced as her lungs emptied and filled with air. Strength rose up to her from the depth of the pond and she began to swim around the banks, narrow-ing the circle each time till she reached the center. She dove down but could not touch the bottom and dove again into the colder depth. She was breathless and could feel her blood coursing strongly. Floating once more, she lay still in the center of the pond watching the stars.

Piri called early the next morning to thank her for the party. "Can you come down today if you're not busy? It's time to get grape and willow weavers for baskets. Merle's here, he can help. Can you?"

"Oh yes, right away." Lidia began packing a box with little sandwich-es, cheese and pieces of cake from the party.

Merle had walked down from Piri's to the crossing of the main road. He was sitting on a sprouted oak stump holding a large bunch of witch hazel. Was it a year ago Merle had found witch hazel for her? Before she asked, he answered the question. "Last fall it was and now here it is again. Witch hazel, you say? Witch hazel."

"Maybe I like it because I know its name," Lidia laughed, "and really because…it's beau-tiful." Merle said the word together with her. She felt the fragment of pure happiness burst like a Roman candle over her head. She recognized its boundaries. This is a moment.

"If I could pick you up and carry you over my shoulder I would." Merle lifted his cap and brought it down again with a snap.

"But you can't," Lidia said. "We have all this witch hazel."

"Well, your hair is shining in the sun," Merle said. They started up under the tall pines to Piri's. The leaves were falling and a bright group of greenish birds flitted up and down on the low bushes ahead.

"Sparrows," Merle smiled.

"Goldfinches maybe, they lose their gold in the fall."

"Goldfinches," he repeated softly.

Piri was waiting at the top of her road. Pairs of clippers and some large baskets with handles lay at her feet. She received Lidia's box. "Good, we can eat it all for lunch. Now, the willows, you know where they are, Merle. The grapevines are back of the house. We need different sizes, a foot and a half, long and straight for weavers and some about thirty inches the size of your little finger. If they have curling tendrils the weaving's harder but when it's finished you like it more."

She showed them how to choose the slim brown weavers, breaking them to see if there was green inside, and then to test for flexibility, around the finger for weavers, around the wrist for the basket's ribs. Piri stripped the leaves and coiled each weaver easily around itself. "And that's all you need to do," she said. "Willows are easier to collect but I like grapevines and honeysuckle best. Old honeysuckle vines are good for handles. The outside of it cracks but the inside holds strong."

They agreed not to collect willows and before long they had more than enough grapevine for beginning the baskets. "Won't they shrink up?" Merle looked at Piri.

"Not if you make them soon. If you make them later…"

"In deep winter?" Lidia asked her.

"For winter you must steam them now to soften them for keeping. I'll give you all the directions."

"I wouldn't mind them shrinking," Lidia said to them both. "The baskets would be looser that's all."

Merle had gone farther back in the woods and was pulling hard at a thick, twisted grapevine hanging in a loop. "A swing for you Piri, it's safe, I tried it."

"Merle Fowler, who would dare, it goes down and away out to those boulders."

Merle swung a little way out, holding one side of the loop. "Safe return! See?" He looked at Lidia.

"I'll go standing up too," she said and climbed up to where he stood. Piri covered her eyes. "Merle?"

"D'you think I'd..." he started to say.

"Here I go," Lidia called back.

The vine, as thick as Merle's wrist, curled tightly around and around a large white pine branch almost fifteen feet high. As Lidia pushed off, it gave a small shudder but moved her weight slowly out over the small ravine. Swinging in to the large boulder on the far side, she pushed one foot out against it and the vine moved her slowly back to where Merle stood on the bank. She smiled at them both.

"Well, I wouldn'ta done it," Merle said, "but I knew you could."

Piri shook her head. "Let's have something to eat."

They sat on Piri's porch and Lidia stretched out in the sun. "Head in the shade, feet in the sun. That's what they say," Merle advised.

Piri spoke sharply, "Well, there are many ways Merle. In my village we did it differently. And do you know this about my past?"

'Among other nations let it always be known
That the Poles are not geese
and have a tongue of their own!'

They were all laughing when Mary-Molly ran toward them up the hill, breathless, waving her arms. "Ma! I came to get you. The leaf cutter thing fell into the pond. Dad's just miser'ble, he's crying about it. It won't move. Come now!"

Leaving Piri, they walked quickly down to the main road and up the hill. The dogs were barking back at the pond where Richard sat, his head in his hands, his body covered with mud. The curved red handle of the mowing machine was all that was visible above the water. Merle quickly went to get some long, wide boards out of the shed.

"The damn thing, Lidia, it sank. I was turning too close to the edge. It went into the mud and stopped the motor. I tried pulling it," he was almost sobbing, "and it went deeper. Oh God, my clumsy stupidity...""

"It's only a piece of machinery, it's not a person. Please Richard, it'll be alright when it dries out."

They laid one end of the boards on the bank and then down into the water. Standing in the pond, Richard and Merle pushed the machine from the front and Mary-Molly and Lidia pulled the handle. With a large sucking sound the mower moved back several inches toward the bank and they all struggled its wheels up onto the boards. With another heaving push the dripping machine came to the surface. They were exhausted with the effort, soaking wet and covered with mud.

"Dad," Mary-Molly said quietly, "there's hardly any leaves out here."

"I know," he said wearily, "I was just seeing if it would fit over the stone bridge. The new snow blower's the same size. Well, it does, dammit," he put his arm on her shoulder. "We can clear snow for you to have a real skating party this winter."

"I love you Dad," she said.

6

"AND WHAT WOULD YOU LIKE TO DO on this warm night in October? That's what I'll ask them. I'll ask them at dinner." Lidia was raking leaves. The green sycamore leaves were voluptuous golden green flags, large and tough enough in summer to sew carefully by hand into clothing, but now they were dried up and wrinkled brown. They did not rake up easily with the maple leaves and kept skittering off the pile in other directions. Falling faster now, the leaves made a sound like shallow tide running out over a pebbly beach.

"Sorry I didn't call." Crete drove up and called from the car window. "Just dropped my brushes and left. Maybe it's the last warm evening." Her long blue smock was covered with paint.

"Yes, but the moon's past full. It won't freeze. Sit down with me in these leaves. I'm feeling fearful about the winter, Crete."

Crete leaned toward her. "I know how weary you feel, so used up with watchfulness and listening." They sat in silence a long while, watching the changing light. Then Crete said, "But I have to tell you, Richard came to the house late yesterday, drunk as a lord. Said he'd read thirty job applications and how unsatisfactory it all is at school."

"Why'd he come? Just to talk?"

"He was very angry. Maybe he needed an adversary." Crete straightened up abruptly. "You've got to move away from feeling helpless with him."

Lidia jumped to her feet. "I am not helpless, Crete! I'm confused about what to do. You have no idea what goes on, you have no idea! You don't know Richard. No one does. His spirit is hidden. He doesn't meet it out in the world. He drinks out of need, out of loneliness. It's a defense, to keep himself safe." Lidia covered her face with her hands.

"It's hard. And Richard's suffering too. I know this from my therapy, that the rocking, the continual movement, means an adult has been deprived of physical contact in childhood. Often the person breaks into periods of violence." Crete put her hands on Lidia's shoulders. "Will you write? Write everything now. The writing will be your space. It will Lidi, you'll see." Crete turned toward her car. "Short visit but it's getting dark. I'll go home now and bring my plants in off the back porch. I'll call you tomorrow. We have to face it, the real frost is coming." Her voice lingered on the cool air.

Lidia was arranging a bowl of tiny white autumn clematis blooms when Richard drove up. He parked by the shed and she had time to anticipate his question about the events of her day. If only she could ignore that predictable greeting, give him a hug and say she was glad he was home. Because it was true. She wanted him there always. She relied on his ideas, his way of inventing small spaces of beauty. She loved that part of him that he didn't hide. He would say, Dammit, can't you see that... and then he would say what reminded her of the Canadian hotel when he looked up over the horn-rimmed glasses, oh take your time and rest now. He would help her to choose, saying this way is safer, let's not do that. It was simply that somewhere in him was a sense that life should hold a dignity of spaciousness for everyone. If he could just see how weary she was now, put his arm around her and notice the things she'd done. But he was morose, threw down a huge portfolio and brief case and sank heavily into the rocking chair.

"I'm fagged out. Lousy meeting at school. How was your day? They voted down my requests for funding the labs, improving equipment. It's a bed of rotten stranglers. I can't run like a rat in a maze. I'm leaving in January. I'm finished."

"You're not political. It's not who you are to fight for every little necessity. I understand," she said, thinking she did not understand at all, she did not understand why men could not speak rationally to each other and be heard, and divide things up the way she certainly would if it was up to her.

"You don't understand, you don't understand! What's for dinner? Fish? Well, I had fish for lunch. Funny how that happens." He laughed bitterly. "Guess I'll have a little drink."

Lidia knew what he would do now. She asked Mary-Molly to have her supper. Then she poured a tumbler of wine and took it out into the meadow. A rosy glow lighted up the tree line to the east as the sun lowered in a ball of fire. She walked up and down and her mind raced ahead of her. Richard, your ghosts are not hidden. They're right here, choking up all your space. Please go away now. Don't talk any more. I know where you are in the house by your familiar noises, a banging door, a smash of ice. We're diminishing ourselves in useless anger. The radiance of these days is too bright for our eyes now.

When the sun fell below the horizon, Lidia went back to the kitchen. She heard Richard's voice upstairs and stood still a moment. Then she went to the stove, picked up the supper casserole and dumped it upside down in the sink. When she left the house, the cold night air entered her body like truth. She drove far north on roads she did not know. The car's headlights piercing the dark were all that mattered. She returned after an hour and the house was dark. She ate the scrambled remains of fish and vegetables and went upstairs to write...

> *I hold you like water holds all things, flowing in a rhythm that enters and absorbs every form. Without beginning or end, always new, in tides and streams that change with cycles of the moon, in full moon spreading wide and deep, in new moon pulled together. In this watery space you hang, a solid hovering form, a Piscean fish, irridescent blue and orange in the sunlight. Your shape divides the flowing water, and the fish form trails behind you. Barely moving, you hover against the current that brings you air and food without effort. The current balances your life.*
>
> *My new way of seeing you is that you are not fixed. You are in a stream of time, first fingerling, then a sparkling fish and soon, your loss of glistening flesh. I see you as not one, but all these forms existing in a moment. You are fluid as the water*

in which you live. Why are your eyes veiled from seeing me? Why are they veiled from seeing our bodies together? The veil hides you from shadow as it hides you from light. This autumn's loveliness has loneliness and indecision that heightens my vision almost to the sacred. What is it out of this that truly calls me?

When she stopped writing, moonlight was shining down through the skylight. Downstairs, Richard groaned in his sleep. Did she only imagine hearing him cry out, "Help! Help!"?

* * *

Day after day November closes in. Nothing lifts the somber weight of dark days, bitter cold under the Freeze-Up Moon. The moon's strong light penetrates the late bloomers, fall-bearing raspberries and the last pink clover blooms rigid and tightly rolled against frost. Field mice move into the kitchen, the dogs' hair grows thicker and there is the seasonal misery of fleas. The chickens' water freezes overnight and hallways are awash with thawing buckets. A chaos of winter gear fills all the rooms. To keep warmth in a drafty old house is a thankless task. The furnace rumbles on before dawn, waking the one who rises from bed on to a cold floor to poke at dead ashes, rekindle a blaze and clang shut the doors of the wood stoves.

In this year, steady snow begins at the end of November. Houses move in its fall and blow and drift like ships on a white sea. The landscape opens even as it closes the villagers in. The plow clangs up into the silence, its flashing lights illuminating the bare branches, and it rouses and shakes the houses and connects them to all other houses in the village. Icicles grow from the eaves like a collection of spears, and in the moonlight everything is crowned with stars. In the village they say there never has been such a winter. No one in the village calls this magic. But it is. The snow grows in drifts that reach the window-sills. The sight and sound of snow alters everyones' head and speech and body, and changes them, some for better, some for worse. Some are changed forever by the snow.

Lidia was fitfully asleep, dreaming of flames lifting the shape of a phoenix high above piles of burning yellow leaves, of wind moving the land and sky together, and of moonlight falling on a winter soup full of bitter love on the cold stove. The noise of a car wakened her. She heard the front door open quietly and someone come up the stairs. It was Claire. She stepped inside the bedroom doorway and leaned against the wall. She was shivering, covering her eyes. "Claire! What is it, you're angry!"

Claire was silent and then spoke in short bursts of words. "Yes, I feel angry coming here. I came for some warm clothes. I got a ride last night and they're waiting to take me back. I'm very down in my life at school. Nothing's better here is it? Aren't you sad? Aren't you lonely? I had this dream about you, Mom." She sat down on the bed. "I want you to hear it. Are you awake?" She began…

There's a gathering of people, and Dad has a beautiful dress made of black silk that all the women are trying on. Everyone's too big to wear it, and finally you notice and run to Dad and quickly slip into the dress, laughing and looking very beautiful and radiant. It fits perfectly, you're the only one small enough to wear it. The dress has a skirt and a jacket with a collar you have to tie around your neck. You do everything quickly and perfectly and when you're finished you are beautiful, the way your clear face and red hair rise up from the black silk. Then, everyone begins running, racing to some point. You run too, laughing and very happy, and as you run you take off the black jacket and there's a white blouse, and the dream ends as you're still running, and everyone is happy.

After a moment Claire stood up. "Look, I'm leaving this piece I did. It made me pleased at first because it came out well. But I don't want it at school." She held the work up before her face, an etching in black and white with shades of gray in the figure. Lidia turned on the lamp.

"Claire, it's exquisite, so delicate. The trees in the background, the woman's face. It's haunting."

"Keep it for me somewhere. It's called 'The Lost Mother.' I have to go now. I have my things. They're waiting." She turned away. "I'll see you at Thanksgiving I guess."

"Claire, Claire!" The door closed behind her. Lidia stood still, feeling that her heart would burst. When she got downstairs the car was gone. Intense pain flashed through her body in sickening waves. Its heat coiled like a flash-fire gripping her legs and back, flaming, leaving weakness and nausea. The fire coursing through her did not destroy the cold, heavy ball in her stomach that was fear.

The others were unaware of Claire's visit in the night. "I'm late Mom, I was finishing my homework," Mary-Molly said in the morning. "Don't forget my cat. Claude has so many fleas, he's crying all the time. Thanks, Mom, see you after school."

Richard gulped his coffee. "Lidi, the roads are clear. I'm late, will you keep the stove going?" She could not say anything. As he went out the door, she faced the wave of desolation spreading through the kitchen.

The furnace rumbled on and the heat rose. Lidia knelt down and crushed paper to light the stove. Claude brushed against her knee, mewing softly. "Yes I know, you need love, a warm flea bath. Well, I can give love even though I don't love you, flattened out and sneaking across the grass. You're not like Woody. You're a killer cat but you can't resist the love. You know love will make you grow, don't you Claude." The cat squalled and struggled in the kitchen sink as Lidia sprayed his body. She held him in a warm towel, his tail twitching slowly as his body relaxed against her. "I guess the fleas will all move up to your head now." She left Claude wrapped up next to the radio which was playing the mournful strains of Mahler's Eighth Symphony. It was clear to her that he was listening. "At least you're a flexible cat, you give it all back."

On this day of lowering skies, only one faint patch of sun entered the house. Lidia abandoned everything and sat there in the hallway through the morning, watching shadows of the trees move over the frozen meadow. When she heard the sound of animals scratching and running over the attic floor, she said, "Good, this house stands to serve any soul that is truly here." The remainder of the day moved slowly and its tasks hung on her like small weights.

After midnight, under a weak moon, a handful of unrelated stars and trees black against the night, she began walking the road. To keep secure footing, she searched out rough patches where the plough had scraped the ground. But a sudden dip in the road had gathered ice, and there her feet slipped out and she went down, dizzy with the stars blinking in her head.

On Stone Hill only Mary-Molly was flexible enough to be changed. She held Richard's hand on their way to the closing ceremony for his students. They were young teachers from rural areas who'd come to earn degrees for learning special skills to enrich their classrooms. It was Richard's program, the Rural Development Leadership Network. It was visionary, experimental, and tough, for them and himself. He believed deeply in its value. "What're you going to say Dad? Are you scared?"

"No, M-M, I know these kids. They've challenged every bone in my body for eight months. I'm going to tell them we need a definition of dignity in the world, and that they're prepared enough to help provide it. They have to know they're leaders."

Richard was magnificent. "He spoke from the heart," Crete said afterward. She and Ferdy came along to have a drink with them at the pub, noisy with lights and music. Mary-Molly asked one of Richard's favorite students, Chass, an Indian of the Oneida Nation, to dance with her. They sat apart from all the others. "I can't dance to this music," he said. "It would betray my people and my tradition. Do you understand what I mean?" Chass went on talking with her about what it meant to him to live on an Indian reservation.

"We live at Stone Hill. You've been there I think. There's lots of land there and I don't know yet what use it is. Sometimes my parents don't know what they should do with it either."

"Do you see," Chass said, "they don't have to know. It's enough just setting aside the land. They don't have to do any more. The land is sacred. It waits for the people who recognize that."

"Oh, they do, my parents do. We all do. But sometimes we forget. We're just one family. There's no one else to help us. I feel so relieved. I'm going to tell them what you said, especially my Dad."

On the way home, Crete invited them in for a last drink. Flushed with relief at his success, Richard's voice rose and with his drink in hand, began pacing the floor. "These kids are at the meeting of east and west, blending esthetics with our scientific analysis. I'm proud to facilitate this, the greening of the world… No, don't restrain me, Ferdy. You don't perceive it, that gleam that imagines change…"

"Richard?" Ferdy stood in his path. "It's time to go home. I'm asking you to leave now. After such an impassioned evening, it's time to leave."

As they entered their own kitchen, Lidia turned to put her hands on his shoulders. "I'm so proud. It was your true, true self."

He rallied for a moment. "Lidi, I do want to get past myself. I want to be better than I am."

"But you won't, with the drink." Her voice turned cold. "We've been alienated even from our friends now. Soon you're going to be old and lonely Richard."

"Good," he answered.

It was Thanksgiving. Claire had arrived and they were waiting for Mouche. The dinner was ready. "Let's sit down. We can't wait any longer," Lidia was saying when a car drove up at full speed. Mouche came in the door, resplendent in scarlet vest and a ragged cap set backward on his head.

"Just in time," Richard said. "I'm pouring wine for a toast."

"The table's beautiful Ma, one of your unexcelled productions. Dad, you look great. Claire too. M-M funky as ever."

"Well," Richard began, "you know how much we have to be thankful for, those we love who are here, and some who aren't with us today. And blessings…"

"Who's not here Dad?" Mary-Molly asked in a loud voice.

"…and blessings of this place as it reflects the world." Lidia stood up to get a dish from the oven. "Lidia? I have an announcement." She sat down again.

"Oh, Dad, let's eat." Mary-Molly struggled in her chair and reached out for a chocolate from the centerpiece.

"I want you all to know that today I'm adding the fifth and last parcel of land to the property, the Bowles lot abutting Camphill Road. That squares us off and we have a genuine property to manage now."

"Hear, hear!" Mouche cheered uncertainly.

"I don't feel well, can I be excused?" Claire held her head.

"Good Dad," Mary-Molly said. "You know it doesn't matter what we do with the land. It's sacred." She looked seriously at him. "It's enough just to set it aside."

After dinner they sat together in the living room, Claire, Mouche and Mary-Molly with the dogs Potter and Morgan between them. Woody and Claude were curled up under the stove. Lidia came in and sank down gratefully in the rocking chair. "I'm just reminded of something, a memory of a thing I knew as a child. I want to tell it to you and see if you have that kind of a memory too." She saw right away that Claire understood.

"Does it have to be about a thing or could it be a happening," Mouche asked.

"Either, just something you keep remembering."

"Well, I don't have anything like that," Mary-Molly said.

"Yes you do, M-M, maybe you do. How about..." Mouche leaned over and whispered in her ear.

"Ohh-hh yes, I do have something I think about alot. You start first. I do have something."

Lidia began. "When I grew up in the city we had a big back yard. On three sides of it was a long fence made of wood painted blue. The blue was beautiful, soft shades where it was repaired and painted again and faded. It was the blue of an indigo sky. The fence was so high we couldn't see over it and no one could see in. Apple trees grew next to it and a mulberry tree along the back." They were listening carefully, seeing the Long Blue Fence. "We were small then, forbidden to go beyond the fence to Murray Street or West End Avenue. I thought about the fence all the time. I loved it and I hated it. I'd walk along inside with my hand on the wide blue boards, and wonder how a thing so beautiful could keep me from being free. I still don't understand that."

"I like that," Claire said.

"Yeah, the Long…Blue…Fence," Mouche drew out the words.

"I'm glad we don't have one," Mary-Molly wrinkled her nose. "Now can I tell mine? It's OK if it's alive, isn't it? What I remember is Shulah, the rabbit we found on the road."

"Claire wasn't here then, tell the whole story," Mouche urged her.

"It was on the road to Garrison. Mom and I saw this huge animal just sitting at the edge and all the cars were going by. We stopped to see and it was a rabbit blind in one eye and almost in the other. His eyes were white and covered with bugs and dirt. He had fleas too. We brought him home and washed out his eyes and we made a cage off the ground and got some food. We called him Shulah. Mom told me it means a guardian of the house. He was really big. In spring I put him out on the grass in the sun. I think he was deaf too, because he didn't hear his name or look up unless I stroked his fur. Shulah was really happy and even began to move around a little on the soft grass. Then one morning in the summer, we found him dead in his cage. I don't think he minded being blind because he was with us, and we loved him and took care of him. That's what I remember."

"I wish I'd known Shulah, I really do," Claire smiled at her.

"I have lots of pictures I'll show you later. Mouche, it's your turn now. Shouldn't I get Dad? He's upstairs."

"I'll wait. You'll have to explain it to him pretty well," Mouche called after her.

They waited till Mary-Molly returned. "He's sitting in a chair and said he'll think about it and come down. Go on Mouche."

"What I remember is the Ship Rock in the meadow, you know the one I mean that's hidden in the trees and juts out high and big as a ship. At school I think of that rock alot, how I sat on it by myself when I was little and let my mind go out. A big rock is a comforting thing," he said quietly. "You know?"

"Well, it's still there, Mouche," Mary-Molly told him.

"But sometimes it isn't as good now," he said.

"Hurry up Dad, it's Claire's turn now." Richard was banging about in the kitchen.

"What're the rules?" he asked.

"I just told you Dad, something you remember from when you were small, that stays in your mind. Mom's is the Long Blue Fence and Mouche had the Ship Rock and mine is Shulah. It's Claire's turn now."

Claire began. "Up in the Hermit Thrush Garden, when I was clearing out brush I found a little skull. It was a fox skull, small and perfect, and when I held it out in my hand it was lovely because it was smiling. I put it up in a tree and it was always there when I went back, and it was always smiling. I brought it down and put it on the stone post by the front walk. Then," Claire looked up at Richard, "you said you didn't want a skull in front of your house so I took it back again. Maybe it's there now. I don't know why it's so powerful, a piece of bone that's smiling."

"A Smiling Skull, that's great Claire," Mouche said. "Really."

"OK, Dad, you got it now?"

"I got it," Richard laughed. "What I remember is my Green Pony Cart. It was a cart my grandfather gave me and then I got the pony, Grayling. I spent hours teaching her to pull on all the lanes around the fields where we lived. The fields are gone now but then it was open space. And I had two friends. My parents didn't approve of them but they were my best friends anyway. Their names? Their names were Nick Dougherty and Pat Scorzetti. So I started a little business with them, charging a nickel for rides, and they brought some other boys and so I made quite alot of money. After the rides I'd drive by myself to Gonzi's store and buy green mint ice-cream, the kind with chocolate in it. No one knew, and they were all so busy they never found out. It was just my own secret."

"It made you feel…"

"Good," Richard said. "Free."

"I love knowing that," Mary-Molly said. "It's so important."

He smiled at them all. "Quite a day, a good Thanksgiving, but I'm ready for bed." He rose and bent over to give Claire and Mary-Molly a kiss and to shake Mouche's hand. "Good-night, good-night."

"Lidi, won't you come up with me now?" he asked, as she was turning back toward the children. She felt the tremendous confusion of her heart. When she climbed in next to him, Richard was already half asleep. He pulled her roughly against his body and she lay with her eyes wide open. "I knew you'd choose the Green Pony Cart," she said, but he had already drifted into sleep.

* * *

On cold nights the winter sky is so near that a hill-dweller feels close to the vast Universe. The northern lights circle and stream down like scarves waving from the dome of heaven. Venus, now an evening star, climbs higher in the south-western sky. A rural villager is aware of the lengthening days, and steps outside each night to look up at the stars' circular journey. Even as winter closes in, the villager feels this slow movement and knows the circle is turning toward spring.

Perhaps a small breath of the changing season comes on the cold winds. On the night of the full moon in mid-December the wind shifts, and the moon dims in and out of fast-moving clouds. At Stone Hill the wind blows fiercely across the clearing, banging the barn door, cracking tree branches covered with ice, tolling the mournful bell in the high pine again and again. The wind flaps like a loose sail against the house, stirring the dogs who stand up stiffly to stretch and thump their bodies down closer to the cold stove. Under the full moon Richard sleeps as though dead, and Lidia dreams... she is asleep in the barn loft. A large truck clatters in below carrying a crowd of men who begin taking away all the tools. A wild woman wearing a red turban stands in the half darkness directing them. Everything is out of control.

She woke from pressure in her throat and the sound of the bed-room door creaking open. "Mom...Mom, are you awake?" Mary-Molly whispered. "I had a bad dream. I dreamed I was losing all my bottom teeth. Oh Mom, it's so cold!"

In the morning Lidia told Richard her dream. "My idea to sell the place? Maybe I do talk about it. Maybe I will. You're so literal, Lidia."

Richard thrust his hands through his hair and pushed away from the breakfast table.

"I'm going down to the bus with Mary-Molly. Then I'm going on."

"Whatever you want," he said.

Cold air burst in as she opened the door. Outside they could hardly speak against the force of the wind. "Mom, isn't Dad hurting you?" Mary-Molly shouted.

"We're hurting each other. Come on," Lidia grabbed her arm. "It's easier to run."

The main road was plowed clear, and when the bus left, Lidia began running with the wind at her back. Her body knew where to grip the ice, where to take hold with her toes, where to relax. She ran the mile up to the top of Latham's Hill and turned east to the powerline. The snowy trail had been packed by skiers. The gusts of wind lessened there but it continued blowing steadily against her back. She began running again, shouting, and her voice traveled downhill on the wind ahead of her. "Halloo! halloo! Wind, I'm giving my voice to you, blow carefully, I have no home, hallooo!" She stopped near a large rock jutting out over the slope on the south side of the trail. She felt disembodied and thrust out her arms to steady herself. The wind wrapped around her and she became its hollow center, spiralling higher till their whirling broke with a whistling sound against the pines. She felt held in the wind's eye, in the teeth of the wind, and in its circle she was free.

After the wind's passage the temperature rose and in the morning the sun was brilliant. Neither Lidia nor Richard could stay indoors where the sunlight quivered in squares on the floor and reached out like a fisherman's net. The snow had melted and frozen again and it caved in and split into chunks as they walked up the woods road. Their tracks were mis-shapen, defining only the weight of the body. Lidia's were smaller, barely indented into the thick crust and Richard's splintered like jagged glass. She followed behind him, watching for branches he would let fly backwards, a thing she had learned about him. The brilliant sun created a double world of purple shadow falling forward of each thing, a cooler world, she noticed, as the road passed through a dark hemlock grove.

"It's only here that it's like this," she said suddenly, "these forms, this color. They're not in the other world." He didn't answer nor had she expected it. "Maybe it's all shadows there."

He turned halfway and gestured for her to come closer. She saw the sun lighting up his gray hair. "Are you thinking about Morley Skiles?" he asked.

"Yes, I dreamed about him last night. He seems so present in December." The memory of the dream rushed out of her and she did not let him walk on. "I saw how hard it was for him to come back, to come back in his old form. I had so much to tell him but he couldn't listen. He struggled to sit still and to say one thing, and then he got up and walked away, like he wanted or needed to go back."

She fell silent, hoping Richard would not dismiss her offering. Finally he said softly, "And what did he say?"

"He said to me, 'You're an extraordinary woman. Just do what you can there', and that was all."

They stood still, waiting for something. The wind blew up and they watched it carrying their frosty breaths away. "Let's go back," Richard said. "We'll go on our own tracks, the same way."

By mid-afternoon the sun was wan, faintly gold like a moon. The dogs crept into the straw in their barrels, the cats slept indoors under the stove. Lidia moved the plants to a south window for more light. How much the seasons govern us here, she thought, when really they're only material for us to use. I'm using this cold creeping into my bones, my bones that hurt because I've betrayed them. When Richard comes downstairs I'll give him all the letters, all the poems written as honestly as I knew how. I'll give him all this that has made no difference. She reached up to her left eye where a nerve was twitching. Richard, you *could* try to see, you *could* try to see clearly. One of us has got to say I've come to the end of patience, and this is the cold gray afternoon that's turned me to stone.

She felt reckless, cold as ice. She laid her hand on the box where she'd put all her letters to him, letters of entreaty, hope, despair, all the poems she'd written at Stone Hill. She heard the shuffling of papers in the upstairs study, a groan, and then Richard's footsteps on the stair. She felt the cold wedge itself behind her eyes, the cold that was her friend and would not now allow her body to weaken. Richard went to the stove to poke up the fire. "Wretched day it turned out. I'm having a little drink. Where's Mary-Molly?"

"School got out at noon. She went to Jessie's. Richard," she began, "I'm not drinking. I want to feel like a real person."

"Oh? As opposed to what, Lidia?"

"I feel dead, Richard. Look, Mary-Molly's at Jessie's for dinner. Can we sit by the stove awhile?" His body stiffened and she saw his face begin to move like a dis-connected thing, conflicted.

"What is it now? I'm sick of talk."

"Yes, but what else is there?" she asked, and from a desire that over-whelmed the cold of her resolve, she said "I love you, Richard."

"We'll see about that."

He sat down with her by the stove. She struggled to tell him she was missing something. "A hand held out, just some kind of look that means I see you, I know you. My hope isn't for having anything, just for know-ing, seeing. I can't explain it, I guess it can't be explained. What is it *you* want?" she asked desperately.

Still in its early flush of well-being, Richard's body was relaxed. "I know exactly. I want someone to be in bed with me and hold my hand."

She felt disarmed but struggled on. "Richard, I want to be in a place where you are just you and I am just me. Do you understand that we've never done that? I mean, away from this place?" The abrupt movement of his body told her the question had moved them off the firm ground. She went on quickly. "I want to grow old with you, to share Stone Hill together, but Richard…"

"It's the goats, the damn goats, Lidia, you know we can't leave here, there's no one to milk the goats!" The air around him filled with exas-perated vibration. They were spinning and she didn't know how to pull them out.

The cold rose in her spine. She felt her eyes turning to ice. "Richard, I'm having trouble eating. I mean I don't feel like I'm worth it. I'm dreaming terrible things. I told you about all the tools taken away. I'm not clear, but if you want to think about separating from this property that holds us, there's a legal way."

He didn't answer, he wasn't hearing her. Oh my God, she thought, this drama isn't what I wanted. But she persisted. "Richard, listen, you're not wearing your wedding ring, where is it?"

"Lidia, for Chris' sake, I lost it. It was too tight. I lost it." He rubbed his cigarette out in the stove and slammed the glass door shut. "Will you please leave me alone?"

Darkness began to fall. The box of letters remained unacknowledged on the table, by the north window in the cold drafts of wind.

No one had noticed that Lidia wasn't eating. It seemed to her she hadn't eaten for weeks. She was spending the days alone, her stomach shrunken with fasting, her brain ticking like a machine spinning out endless reels of euphoria and memories. Still she walked at night, to avoid the light on the snow, she told the others. And she wrote...

> *I'm not afraid if I have to walk all night with these deep sighs, these deep sighs that are the trembling of what's being born. Walking is a prayer to help me escape from mystery, from my passion to change what I cannot change. It clutches me and won't let me go. I'm glued to the ceiling of a dark cave, like a bat head-down escaping light. I am at this heart of darkness, the rising and falling that does not resolve. Do not diminish my trying to create a sacred space for you. And for the children. My longing is too great. Yes, to be blind and see only the deep well where I really live. At last I am known to myself and I am split in two.*

In this chaos she was not afraid. She was diminished, as though a light inside her was going out. She watched for signs. On one day a book fell from the shelf and a photograph slipped out onto the floor. She took it to the window to see clearly, aware of the sudden fluttering of expectancy around her heart, like a small bird shifting its wings at night. She knew it was hope, hope that this chance discovery might be a symbol full of meaning for her. It was a dark figure hulking against the light, its arms raised, groping, menacing. She remembered why she had saved it. It reminded her of a Picasso painting, a small girl in white holding a candle or lantern. She is leading a huge donkey who stands upright on its hind legs, its mouth wide open in an agonizing bray. He is blind.

The photograph could be anyone groping in a dark place after coming out of the bright sun. No features were discernible but from the hunch of the shoulders it was clearly Richard. Her hands flew to both sides of her head as though it was bursting. "Why don't I feel compassion for you like this child? I've been leading you for years!" To see no light coming from him, this helpless groping, made her crazy and full of fear, for herself, her own feeble light, her own child's voice. She felt *herself* caged, and dark and monstrous as he had showed her how to be.

But something was surfacing, something greater than self-pity. It focused her, moved her out of the numbness of the days. In late December she met Merle, by chance, at the feed store in Garrison.

"Reuben's dyin'. It's why I don't come up there. He's afraid and he won't let me go anywhere." Merle looked into her face. "Looks like you need someone too, Lidia, so thin and peaked."

She put her hand on his arm, acknowledging him without words. "It's a hard winter, you were right about the snow. It's piled up to our windows now. How are your birds?"

"Haven't lost a one. The snow's keepin' them warm." He was not diverted by her conversation. "I'm comin' up there, Lidia. It's too much for you. I'm shovelin' for Piri and then I'll just walk up to your place. The roads are clear."

"I know, I've been walking. But don't do that Merle, don't come, it won't help now, please. I have to be alone." She struggled to keep back tears.

"So, that's what it is, you're alone?"

"I am Merle, I need to be."

"You're not alone, isn't he there?" Merle's voice was cold.

"Not really," Lidia said, "not alot of the time. Merle, I have something to give you. Will you wait?"

He thrust his hands deep into the pockets of his ragged jacket. "I'll wait, but Lidia? I don't like it, I don't like it." He lifted the feed, grain for the chickens, goats and the horses, into the trunk of her car and came to stand by the car window.

She handed him a dark fragment of metal, irregular, a piece of something broken. It was pure iron shaped into crevices with a rounded edge designed for one specific purpose, a crux which allowed other iron parts to move and perform their function. It was a man-made thing but burnished by wind and water into a piece of art. She'd found it long ago lying beside her car on the roadside of a northern town far back in the hills. She'd gone there to see the woman of psychic powers who had told stories of Lidia's past life as the daughter of a Native American chief. From where it lay on the ground, the metal fragment had exerted a force that pulled her to it, like a stone dropped from a high place. It was this fragment she held out to Merle. It lay smooth and dark in his large hand. "Keep this in your pocket now. I've had it a long time."

Merle did not smile. He said nothing in reply but held up the sculpted metal in his open palm. His eyes were full of blue space receding into darker shadows. His body, tall and bent, leaned slightly toward her. He said what he always said, "Take care now, you take care."

The snow continued falling, hiding old tracks, spoiled garbage, the dogs' frozen pee. The falling entered their heads, and only Mary-Molly stayed connected to the outer world. Richard could not claim any of her territory and was constantly in battle with her. "This confinement is boring," he told Lidia. He packed clothing, put his skiis on the car and drove off into the snow leaving them giddy and laughing in the midst of rising energies.

"It's not like Dad. Mom, d'you think he's going to see Aunt Belle?"

"No dear, he wouldn't go that far. I don't know where." But without knowing, she *did* know. She knew he was going some place to meet Crete. And about that she felt ----- nothing.

Turning up the volume of music, Mary-Molly began painting a mural on the wall of her room. It was a large winged goddess wearing a silver net and emerging from the sea with tiny mermaids by her side. In the living room Lidia dumped coils of grapevine and long strips of honeysuckle in piles on the floor. She turned up the heat from the furnace and began sorting vines, plunging them into a pail of water to soak.

She chose six ribs and laid them by three's in the form of a cross, then wove them together at the center with softer vines. She started

weaving, beginning to push apart the thick ribs, widening the space between them and inserting weavers, widening and weaving till the bottom
of the basket was complete. She bent the ribs upward with pliers and
kept on, choosing the weavers carefully to raise the sides of the form
upward. The structure suddenly assumed a life of its own, twisting in
her hands and shifting, resisting the new weavers that would make it
grow. As she struggled to subdue it, the coarse vines lacerated her fingers. The coiled tendrils Piri had said would make it beautiful clutched
each other and the rows tangled. Her frustration turned to anger. She
could not overcome its resistance, she did not want to. She would not
work with this basket that would not grow! She threw the crooked mass
into the open stove where it smoked and then flamed up quickly.

"How's it coming now, Mom?" Covered with blue paint, Mary-
Molly came back into the living room and slumped down in a chair. "I'm
hungry."

"I gave up. It wasn't fun." Lidia stuffed the remaining vines into a bag
and threw it outside in the snow.

They made sandwiches and sat by the fire. "Mom, if a thing isn't fun
you just don't always give up, right?"

Lidia looked gravely into her face. "No, sometimes you can't, sometimes in the middle of a thing, maybe half-way, you have doubt. It would
be easy to give up then because it's painful."

"What do you do then?"

"At that moment of doubt something may happen that helps you if
you allow space for it, if you stop and let your body listen."

"If you allow space for it," Mary-Molly echoed.

"It may be the tiniest thing, like hearing a bird land in a tree and fly
away again. Or a small sound your body makes, or..."

"Or maybe tears that burn your eyes. Mom, it isn't a thing, it's a
person. It's Jessie. She's not my friend any more. She's different now. She
said I'm not like her and she can't be my friend."

"And she has new friends now?"

"They're so picky and la-de-da, la-de-da." Mary-Molly stood up
shaking her hips and screwing up her face. "But Mom, it's so sad." She
sat down again and looked at the floor.

"It is sad, it makes me sad." Lidia was silent a few moments, then took a deep breath and spoke slowly. "Dear girl, here's something I want you to allow space for, to see how it feels, to hold it quietly for awhile." She took another deep breath. "Dad and I wondered if you'd like to go away to school, with Mouche, to Parker's Farm. To start there after the New Year, a little earlier than we thought, a head start. Then you'd have one more year to be there with Mouche."

"With Mouche, to Parker's Farm School! Pheww," she gave a low, long whistle. "Mom, that's an idea. I'll give it space right now."

Snow kept falling and the eaves of the house rounded with sparkling drifts. Paths to the barn and sheds narrowed inside deep walls of snow. It seemed like an offering to the season's celebration. Lidia yielded once more to its rising and to whatever it required. Mouche and Claire were coming.

Claire arrived first and then Mouche, their bodies and bundles making the space busy again. Indoors and out everything gathered together and spilled out and gathered in again, and would not lay still. Stone Hill was a center spread everywhere, in the house and barn, over the animals, in the sky and snow-covered fields. Even the road was drawn down and up again when Richard came from the shed pulling an old Flexible Flyer, newly painted and almost six feet long. They all piled on it and veered crazily downhill to where the road turned sharply, and they landed in a snow-bank.

"How's that for an early Christmas present?"

"Great, Dad, great, if Mary-Molly can learn how to steer." Mouche turned and pushed her down into the deep snow.

"Mouche, you just wait. Do I have something to tell you! It's about Parker's Farm School."

Claire let the goats and the two horses out of the barn and then began making piles of perfectly round snowballs. Up and down the road raced the dogs, the goats, the horses, the children and their parents, perhaps countless invisible Others engaged in the pursuit of war. More snow fell and then the sun gleamed out. Icicles melted and then grew. On the pond they skated around the small plowed place Richard had made with the snow-blower. Some of them made tracks with snowshoes and skiis in the deep woods. For all of them, the place had become the Center of the World.

Claire had said she wanted a bonfire for the New Year, and across the road a pile of logs and old lumber grew steadily. They called the neighbors to invite them too. When the sun disappeared on the last evening of the year, Mouche thrust a burning torch into the center of the pyre. Flame shot out and spread along the dry timbers like a burning wheel. The big logs shifted and fell together sending up a flight of sparks. No one spoke, but there was an audible murmur when the sparks reached high into the dark sky and hung there to join the stars.

"It's true we can't exist without connection to the sky." Lidia was standing alone. Through the flames she saw Lorion Olevsky with his arm around Piri's shoulders, and at that moment they were both looking up. Claire stood near them, Claire who lived so close to the energy of fire. Mary-Molly and Mouche stood together, and Richard, a little apart, his body moving gently from side to side. Others arrived and joined the circle. Some stood with Richard and some watched from outside the firelight till Mouche drew them in.

Claire came half-way around the circle to whisper in Lidia's ear. "Mom, I found another magic being, one that lives in fire. We have to read about it. It's made of fire so it can endure the flame. It's a salamander, a kind of big lizard. Don't you see one in there?"

For a time they looked into the leaping flames. Then Lidia turned to Claire. "Yes, I see the salamander now. She's gold, she's beautiful."

January was not a beginning. The sun made prisms on every branch and purple shadows reached out of the woods, but it was disconsolate beauty with bitter winds and cold. The children went to ski with Mouche's friends at school. Richard's eyes were healed but still he did not nurture himself. What had he learned, Lidia asked herself, from his loss of sight? Why can't he *see*? She watched the shadows reach across the meadow till they darkened the doorstep. When the moon is full I will leave, she promised herself.

Two days before their twenty-fifth wedding anniversary she wrote him...

> *I give you my letters so they will not burden me anymore. Perhaps some day you will answer them. Today, in the silent winter, a Brahms piano concerto enfolds me into the wholeness of which I am a part. It makes me clear I cannot be caught in the continuing creation of Stone Hill as an extension of myself. The place is yours. There's nothing more I can do here. I am leaving tomorrow.*

Pale and shaken when he came to her, Richard was holding out a package. "This is for our anniversary. It reminds me of you."

"Richard, I can't open it. I feel sick and there's nothing to say. I can't listen to you."

"I have a question. Will you hear it? I want to know which of these four things is the reason for your leaving. One, the house is difficult to live in; two, the isolation of this place; three, because of me; four, because you need to be alone now."

Her voice was tight. "Richard? It's all four."

They were silent. She knew he could not understand her. "I guess you have to do this, Lidia. You're doing what you want to do. But I don't know where you're going. Can you tell me when you'll be back?"

She struggled to answer. "I have to go. I'm leaving you. I'm leaving this place." As he reached toward her she ran up the stairs.

In her room Lidia opened the box Richard had given her and lifted out a gown of shimmering silk, brilliant green with old Chinese characters embroidered in small medallions below the tiny straps. She held up the thin, shining pillar of green and burst into tears. She saw herself and Richard alone on a quiet river paddling the red canoe, she saw them dancing, Richard tall and serious and handsome, herself laughing, running, running, in the green silk gown.

The house was empty. She did not know where Richard had gone. Like a thief she wandered through the rooms, picking up objects, a cooking pot, pottery and books, small pieces the children had made. Stealing her own things, yes, it was easier, she was protecting herself.

In the morning Lidia moved her car up to the stone walk leading to the house and carried out her things. Richard came outside and stood on the porch, looking at her. "You're really going? Why, Lidia?"

She moved backward in confusion. "So you can be free." Richard kept looking at her. Hardly knowing what she did, Lidia backed away, got in the car and let it roll slowly down the road.

The road climbed for three miles and then turned north along the reservoir toward the highway to the city. She'd traveled several miles on the highway when suddenly she seemed unable to make the car go forward. She could turn back, she *would* turn back. Her eyes were so full of tears she could not see the road. She began pulling the car to the side and then felt a powerful presence at her back that made her turn around. No one was in the car. Turning forward she felt the presence again, powerful, urging her on. Lidia put her foot down on the accelerator and kept driving toward the city.

Part Three

The Sound of Blue Mountain

"One, seven, three, five –
The truth you search for cannot be grasped.
As night advances, a bright moon
illuminates the whole ocean;
The dragon's jewels are found in every wave.
Looking for the moon, it is here,
in this wave, in the next."

Xuedou, 11th c. Zen master and poet
--from The Blue Cliff Records

1

Richard and Merle

THERE SHE GOES, DOWN THE HILL. DAMMIT, who knows where. Will somebody tell me if this is real? I don't have a grip on it, don't have a grip on anything.

Damn bitter morning! I can't believe this. It's the day we were married, twenty-five years ago by God. The day arrives and it's shattered. She's gone. She's gone because she's sick of this place, this place *she* found. It's not magic any more, not a refuge. She's lost, she wants to be lost. Some kind of wandering in her mind. She set this up, an anniversary present of Stone Hill. It makes me weep!

Jesus, it's cold, cold, *cold!!!* Well, I'll wait it out. I'll just wait. She'll be back, right Potter? Even a dog knows she'll be back. The world isn't what she thinks it is, Potter. She doesn't know about the city. She'll be afraid and she'll come back. Damn this wind, this howling mountain. Glare on the snow. Hurts my eyes. Let's get back inside, Potter, get the fires going. It'll be warm when she gets back.

Makes me sick to my stomach, the cold in this kitchen. Nothing colder than an empty wood stove, colder in here than outside. Damn you, Lidia, don't you do this to me! It turns back years of my life, brings the past right back again… back to the big house…

…The big house where I grew up…the kitchen, and Silvie. Silvie, you're still my real mama, aren't you? Always letting me sit up in your lap. I beg you over and over to come upstairs and say goodnight. And you say, "Chile, those big eyes gonna swallow yo' up, yo' knows I'm givin' these folks dinner. I tole yo', yo' Mama say No takin' Graylin' pony up stairs to yo' room. Now g'wan up there youself. I'm tellin' her yo' in bed."

I climb the stairs. My mother's voice rises up and the glasses are tinkling and there's laughter down in the dining room. It's dark up here, dark in my bed. I wait for her footsteps down the hall but she doesn't come. I feel the sickness now, in my stomach. But I never cry. Only my mother can be angry, not the rest of us. Clomp, clomp, her shoes on the stairs. We didn't know how to be angry. We didn't know anger could rescue us.

It's a woman's voice, always a woman who keeps me down. "Oh, you're such a disappointment to me bringing that Dougherty boy here. And Patrick Scorzetti! What kind of friends are these? They don't belong in this neighborhood. Do you hear?" A woman's voice. Always a woman.

Well, by God Lidia, what you're doing changes everything now. It changes everything I feel about that past. It changes who I was. I *wasn't* weak, I survived. Survived betrayal by women who didn't care *what* I felt, didn't try to know *who* I was. And now it's you. You don't respect my ideas, you're devious, and most of all Lidia, you deny me time, my own time, *my...own... time.* You define me into oblivion! You doubt, criticize, question, you close me down! Of *course* we have issues! It's hard for me to show my heart. But it's a good heart, dammit, it's a strong, good heart. It's a heart that doesn't belong to me, it's a wounded heart.

Yeah, creep under that stove ol' dog and listen to me. How will I like it now, Potter? How will I like being an ordinary person, a man left behind by his wife? Because he searched for more. He wanted more than simple-minded enjoyments, more than just the moment. A man in midlife, doing his life by halves, his place, his work, and now, Potter?...his love. You know, Potter, love never arrives, it keeps coming and going just like this place. It opens you up, then it scatters again. It's always on the way to not being here. Love opens you up and then it scatters, it comes toward you but it doesn't reach you. So you close down. Is love that important, Potter? Is it really important? Is it important to me?"

I don't know what it is I can't get hold of. Things happen, I react. No one ever tells me anything till its already happened. I'm not a moving force, things happen to me. I'm an onlooker. I can't live with that, it makes me feel bloody rotten. Do you know what I have to say to you, Lidia? What I have to say and what I can't say, is that I need to feel I'm more important to you than Claire, than Mouche, than Mary-Molly or Piri, or Crete, or anyone else, and this I need to know, and this I cannot say to you. When you come back Lidia, I'll say it. My God, it makes me weep.

But you're not afraid, are you Lidi. I never saw you afraid, did I? It wasn't fear I saw this morning, it was bigger. And it wasn't for me. It was for this place, for Stone Hill, for leaving it behind. I know you, Lidi, I know you well enough to know that. And how does that make me feel? …Like a goat, I'm a goat, a goat!

So, what is this place after all? It looks simple, some acres of woods, a field, a house sitting here on its little road at the foot of Blue Mountain. A place to see the sky. But it's devious. It doesn't make you safe. It penetrates. It needs this, it needs that. You draw it in, chew it, spit it out again. It's a dead-end isn't it, nothing more than reflections and shadow. The place is all in your mind. D'you know that, Lidi? d'you know that? It's in your mind. But still, it's my folly. After all these years I can't imagine the place left alone, can't imagine leaving it. Makes me weep, my God.

Am I a grown man? Silvie, Silvie, it's like it was when you told me you'd be leaving, flyin' with the angels. And how you loved Lidi you said then, how she never raised her voice with the children. You loved how she laughed when you'd carry a big stick for snakes in the garden. You loved her voice you said.

Well, I'll just wait for her, Silvie. I'll wait, isn't that right?"

***

I say to myself, Merle? you know this winter's a fierce crittur. Not like winters we've had in these parts. Used t'be the snow would warm it some. Now it's a freeze, melt n'freeze, everythin' covered with ice. Jagged splinters of ice blindin' me in the sun. Dark as a cave in this house, snow and ice plowed up right over the window. Same at Enos' and Cordonnier's. No light from the backside either, this old house built right into the hill rising.

It's no sense for me t'go out now except to feed my birds. I know Lidia's gone. I feel it. And Reuben. I don't feel I have a place. Somethin's moved outta me. There's nothin' to hold to what's left. I been moved back I guess. Moved back, but I'm not lonely more'n I ever was. I'm not lonely. My heart's changed is what it is. The Fowlers all have weakness of heart. I cain't stop it pressin' on me now. If it's broke it's bigger than it ever was. Like Aunt Lacey says, it's the thing ya love that'll kill ya.

What's there to do for a man? Ol' Doc Riley tellin' me to stop drinkin' coffee after I already give up the cigarettes! I always had hard use o' my body. This coffee's special, made on the woodstove. Plenty of sugar in it too. I'm not afraid o' that. What I am afraid of is anger. It'll be anger closin' them tubes to my heart. It'll be anger that cuts my breath. They riled me up so at Reuben's funeral it put me right back in the hospital. Doc Riley tellin' me again, you're still on the waitin' list for a new heart Merle. Mebbe so I told 'im, mebbe so.

Reuben's gone now. His face keeps comin' to my mind, a bad dream. Angry, cussed to the end. The same words over and over. Helpless that's what 'e was, made 'im full of rage and full of noise like an animal. Whinin' at me to kill 'im, get 'im out of suffocatin'. His yellow eyes wild like a weasel, little slits of eyes. It was good shuttin' his eyes down at the end. All of a sudden he went out there into it quiet and peaceful. I felt him goin' out, goin' out in that space. Makes me weak to think of it, all he did. He's gone now. Reuben's gone. It's quiet. Who'm I gonna fill that stove for any more?

Mebbe I don' need people. If I'm alone it's safer for my heart. But no human crittur can live without people, I know that. Mebbe I cain't either. I don' know why it's so painful, jes' the loneliness I guess. How my body feels walkin' hours alone on the road, wandrin' the woods, doin' all my work alone. I'm alone but I'm not lonely then. Connected to somethin' real. I don't guess connection's always painful. I guess what matters is how you hold to it.

Mebbe I should call Piri. Now wouldn't that be a comfort ? She knows jes' like I do that Lidia's gone from her place. We both knew she *would* go. What I understand about all that is my affair and I'll live with it. I have my ideas. Too much of a struggle for her with that man Richad so tied up. How he needs to keep confusion around 'im. How he doesn't feel finished with 'imself, one part fightin' the other. Funny how joy's parcelled out so diff'rent. He thinks it's up to us not to disturb 'im. In his heart he don' know if he kin trust me. Rooted like a tree and you cain't budge 'im. He jes' doesn't fly up. Only the drink's a comfort. Well, it's all nothin' that bears sayin' now, not to Piri. Soon enough she'll hear about Reuben. She hears everythin' that goes by. There's just no damn reason I kin think of to call anybody now.

Nothin' for me to do till spring. Jes' sit here and think. It's that time of day, the sun sinkin' down. Like holdin' my breath. I kin' hear my mother's voice, sweet as i'twas. Sonny, she said, you take time now and be with that little Mary Molly child. She needs you. Take her fishin' on the East Fork where you go. That's good as all the work you could do. Take care of 'er.

Well sometimes I'm not easy with people. I don' take a chance. Somethin' spreads around me, a stiffness. Don' know what it is they're after. Piri, now she's a teacher, she needs me and she needs Lidia. She needs us to listen and see all she knows . Piri's desprit sometimes. Her life hasn't brought her the one thing to make it whole. Says she doesn't know what that is. But I feel safe with Piri. She doesn't trust that Montfort woman either. What does that woman want from Lidia? Somethin' not natural I guess.

Thinkin' now on the Sutherland place, how it's changed, how it changed me, how it hangs on me. I knew the place twenty years before Lidia came, in rain and wind, vines takin' it down. Before her it was Sutherland. He made all them tin roofs in town, raised six little 'uns there, the girl feeble they kept t'home, their boys like wild things fishin' and huntin'. A big man, Charlie Sutherland. Lost courage there, said it was that maple goin' down but we don' know why he left the place. Moved them all further out in the woods, Duanesville I think, that mean house at the crossroads. When he left it, that place kept somethin' of its own. Like eyes watchin' out of the cellarhole, like voices. It was waitin' for someone to see how the light fell onto it out o' the sky. Light fallin' down off that mountain. So still sometimes. Yes, I could've, I could've helped her those first years. Long before she asked.

And five years i'twas, five years before she asked me t'go up and build the dock on that pond. Crazy thing to have a pond coverin' the water line from the old spring. One of his big ideas. But no cause for trouble, I was wrong there. No trouble till ol' Clark up above cut the big oaks on his place. Now the cellar of that house is a sinkhole, water runnin' downhill in spring. Damned if I'm goin' to ditch it till she comes back. I don' want any part of it up there.

"Git, git outta there now...git! Git out from under that stove you ol' cat."
    Far as I know that place is hers. He works there some but she's the spirit of it, she's the center. Everythin' there comes out of her. It ain't just a simple place to hold things. With her the place is what's happenin', what's to be done. It wouldn't be how it is without all she makes happen there. She puts her own self into it. Without her there wouldn't be nothin' there. Knowin' by her body, how her body feels. She told me the place is like the world. She said it's movin' like the world.
    Jes' say I'm climbin' the road to her house feelin' softer comin' in to the clearing. That house is like a hut with a lantern shinin' in the dark. Mebbe there's chickens in the road, children and horses. Mebbe goats in the meadow. That house connects everythin' to it, paths in the woods, the pond, the roads and who's on 'em. Connects Blue Mountain and its sky, all that together there in the space where she is.

But somethin's not right in it up there. All the things they make happen ain't right. All the people who come and never come back to help when it's needed. Why does she do that? for him? All the times I go there, to help with the big parties, the bonfires, that Easter hunt over the whole meadow, cars parked everywhere. It ain't right for ordinary people. I knew harm would come out of it. Somethin's closed down there. Like that waterspout I seen on the river, goin' round and round. Sucks everythin' down. Nothin' can get out o' that hole. Mebbe it's his head, his way of not lettin' anyone in.

And her, makin' a whole world on that place. Everythin' she does there, all her ways, is all a gift for him. That man cain't see it. To see it's a gift, a person has to be up to it, not mean and down in spirit. My mother told us, she said when Reuben's peaceful that's a real gift to her. Well, he cain't see it. Don't let her have anythin' there without ruinin' it, the goats, the garden.

He cain't enjoy a thing and he cain't see how that bothers the others, the little one Mary jes' like her mother. And the oldest, Claire, such a one to make anythin' with her hands. She's troubled by how he stirs up her mother, how he has t'be right. Always in his head. He cain't see if you do this, that's goin' to happen. He'll throw away any kind of thing in his way, a devil in 'im sayin' anythin's possible and he kin do it. Ask 'im how far to Pittston. Oh, that's twenty minutes east, he'll say. Now any fool knows Pittston is due north thirty miles from here. He never checks himself out. Mostly I guess, he jes' cain't make up his mind and that's what makes 'im angry....I'm tired thinkin' on it, how a person is so tangled up they cain't see to love someone like her. And now she's gone and I don' know where. It's a bad thing. I cain't think on it now, jes' close my eyes.

It's worse now dammit! I see the bright head of her shinin' red with the sun, the hair hangin' on her neck. I'm lookin' up to her in the apple tree. I see her kneelin' in the barn for Vita's kids bein' born, how it's bringin' tears to her eyes. I see her runnin' down into the meadow in twilight callin' the children. My head is sick goin' on with it, thinkin' about her in ways I never done before.

It's true she don' need people so much either, the way I see her shrinkin' back at those big parties they make. She'd as soon go with me right now to find a catfish pool as talk some of that nonsense. I know it!

And I know how that Montford woman sucks the life out of her too and she cain't protect herself. She needs somebody to show her you kin do that. That man Richad don' know her like I do. He jus' cain't see she's runnin' herself ragged. She's full of a wildness she is, and I don' know how it's goin' with her, wherever she is. Now this piece in my pocket, this metal piece, I know she give it to keep me safe. I jes' hope... where are you, Lidia?

***

Slow, slow time...another March, another month of these goddamn fires. Three a day in the kitchen, two in the living room, two hundred fires. Bloody suffering in this cold. I'm not a warrior, what you always said, right, Lidi? Half the night up writing, choking on these old ideas. No one here to see who I am, no one to say...Richard? you're surviving the winter old man, you're a survivor. My father never told me that. I don't know what he thought of me. I never pleased him. A big man, big success in his world. Well, I don't know what anybody thinks of me. I'm just a speck, a speck struggling with this mountain over my head, the sound of it humming all day, crashing around at night. The wind always doing something new, little streams of air moving through from the cold. There's high power in Blue Mountain...in my head, maybe it's in my eye...going with the flow. Blue Mountain...slow time. Not a bad thing.

But nobody calls me. Only Mouche, God bless 'im. Kids don't know what they put you through! The worst of it is, I can't see your face any more, Lidi. It's just shadow. But your voice is in every room. Why didn't you take all your dreams and nightmares dammit, why didn't you take your body? I love your body, I feel really hungry for you. You don't be-long to me, that's what I see now. I lost something but it wasn't mine. It never was mine. Maybe it was meant to be lost.

What the hell's attacking me? I feel good, some days everything's pos-sible. Then I feel empty. Life and death at the same time. Two weeks into school and there's nothing new to say to them, the same old ideas, old ho hum ideas. Some part of me saying this isn't what I deeply need to do. Is that the part of me that's with you, Lidia? The part I can't get back? A feeling there's nothing to hold me, something's ripped out of myself. Are you coming back, Lidia?

God, I don't understand women! Guess I don't want to understand them. I never thought you liked being a rural wife but you liked the notion. All your perplexities, poking into peoples' lives when you don't even know them. Trying to change what no human being can change. Asking me how I feel about this, how I feel about that, always getting at something. Well, what does that mean for you, Richard, you say. I can't tolerate any more of that. I need quiet, need t'be safe. I see better from a distance. Need to listen from a distance. You had a lack of faith in me. Yes, I felt that. But I don't think about that any more.

…Longest day of my life, my recent life. Hard times, hard and lonely times. Tonight you're bugging the hell out of me. What's your body remembering? I can't tolerate these painful feelings. Use them, you'd say, they're a signal. Don't you know I suffer more than other people? Gotta get beyond self-pity into the real you say. Well, we're not of the same mind. We love each other, we can't live together, can't live at Stone Hill. I feel it, I feel it now…failure is possible, permanent failure's possible. Maybe I'll die and that wouldn't be so bad. My life turning to dust, and me with it. Tyranny of events. It's all there, you'd say, it all has to be unfolded. My God.

Nothing new in anyone's life. Have to accept the ordinary. I'm simpler than you are, Lidi, making fires, keeping up this place. Who knows? Can't answer your letters. Two, three years of letters, can't answer them. There never was an answer. Can't discuss difficulties, exhausting to live them over and over again. Even the shrink couldn't help me. But something was always unfolding around you, Lidi. Now it's all draining away. Maybe that's good, maybe it's helping to get me out of here.

"Potter, be quiet! Lie down now." My God, who's driving up here? It's almost dark. Crete Montfort! Well, she's uninvited, un-in-vited. Doesn't she know that? She preys on my mind. Some people eat you alive.

"Richard, it's me, Crete. I barely got up here through the mud. Your road's almost impassable. How are you? Why don't you let me in? Oh, it's so cold in here!"

"How *am* I, how *am* I! I'll tell you. I'm better off when I'm raging. And I'm raging now. I feel rotten. Why did you come up here? Do you know where Lidia is?"

"No, I've heard nothing."

"Dammit, then why'd you come?"

"To see if you're safe."

"Safe! I'm not safe! I've never been safe. Why now? I need someone to see what I'm doing, don't you know that? To hear my ideas, see who I am!"

"Richard, I want to stay with you. I worry about you. You don't take care of yourself. You don't know how vulnerable it leaves you."

"Vulnerable! Maybe I need to feel vulnerable. Sit over there Crete. I think there's very little about it you understand. For one thing, you don't know what it's like to be alone here in winter."

"Richard, it's a radical choice any time, to stay at Stone Hill. You don't know that do you? There's not space here to work on real problems. Look at yourself, ragged, wasted, you're so immersed in this."

"Yes, very little you understand, Crete. I'm trying to face things head on. I need silence."

"You're so full of wishes, Richard. You're drowning in magic beliefs. Do you think psychic laws don't apply to you?"

"No, they don't. I rely on my mind. It's simple. My mind observes and that's who I am. It avoids conflict. Stop therapizing me, Crete."

"You thrive on confusion. Maybe you need confusion. You have your own lens to see through. That's interesting for a photographer!"

"I'll ignore that remark. What do you expect to learn by coming up here at this hour?"

"Why you stay here, if you see yourself clearly."

"Well Crete, how about this? This place is an adversary and right now I need an adversary."

"Instead of love, Richard? You need more love than other people, isn't that true? I think you have a great need for love."

"Ha ha, love. I'm confused about love, what it means to me. Love, freedom, loyalty, you see? I don't know what those things mean. No, you don't see. You don't see that this place is about Lidia and me. She brought it to me like an offering. It was just thickets then, weeds and stones, bare stones."

"And now she's gone. Is it bare stones again, Richard?"

"Don't mock me, Crete."

"I don't, I miss her too. I never found redheads beautiful as a rule. But Lidi glows like a candle flame. You're caught in that flame, Richard, you're not a free man."

"What difference does it make to you?"

"But my heart..."

"Damn your heart, Crete. I made one mistake with you. And that was messy, it didn't go unnoticed. We both agreed it was a mistake. Have you forgotten that? What I need to tell you is that I thought it would help me to love her better. I've figured that out now. A bad business, a mistake, and there won't be another....You're tough as nails, Crete. You don't really care about Lidia. She's a convenience for you. You haven't helped her. Do you think I'm blind, not to see your need to muck around in her life?"

"Richard, don't you think we give to each other? Don't you think any of us care?"

"That's a large question, very old. I'm sorry, Crete. Will you go now? I think we're both clear. I'm safer here alone."

"You needn't rise, Richard. I'll find my way back to civilization."

"Crete? I'll stand. If it was your intention, you've made me feel better. Give my good wishes to Ferdy. He's a fortunate man."

"Goodbye, Richard."

Phew, there she goes, Potter. Phew! Damn flashy woman. Devious. Disaster. Handled it pretty well. In spite of myself, still a gentleman. But what I don't know, is the answer to that question. Do these women care for each other? *Do they care?* What kind of caring is that? I don't know the answer, Potter. It's painful. But I do feel better. It's true, without an adversary, I'm nothing. Phew! Let's go to bed. "Good night, Potter."

***

Another day, another March already. A year's passed but it's the same old struggle in my mind. It's always been the booze, since the beginning, right, Lidi? We've been through all that, lots of times. And I told you, and you remember, the cocktail hour was the only time I saw my father. You and I agreed, doctors have a drink every day, with decorum you said. All those debutantes and sporting events, that's what we did. Booze at school, serious hangovers on Saturday. You were there, Lidi, you were there. Remember carrying Claire home from a party, in one of those little portable things? You said we have to be more careful now because of Claire. Then the Orient, back and forth across the ocean on big boats, embassy parties, government people always drinking and then shooting themselves. Bizarre how that was.

Well, I want to know *what* put me here. What was it that prepared me for this? What made me think this place would be more than a beautiful dead end? It's survival, survival. What I really need is to drift a little, get away from what they made out of me in the past.

…Yes, so many, so many contradictions. I can't allow them to surface. The real question is am I fit for this solitude?

Ah, saved by the bell. "Aha, Mouche, it's great to hear you! How are you? And Mary-Molly? You're keeping an eye on her? How's it at school? Well, as good as I can be for an old hermit in the middle of March. The ides of March, mud season, spring run-off filling up the cellar again, almost a foot deep this time, more than last year. Some things don't change.

"No, I haven't heard from Mom. I'm managing. Adjusting? Hell no, I wasn't meant to live alone. Yes, Potter, he's fine, a little company but he doesn't build fires, shovel me out. It's been tough, I'm hungry as a bear, fierce. It's a little wild living under Blue Mountain…the roar of it always behind you.…Nope, not given it up, but since you asked I'll tell you. I'm cutting it way down now, can't afford it for one thing. All alone here I have to be clear in my head. Right, nobody to push me around now. What's new is I'm not denying it, I'm not denying that booze is a problem. I'm glad you could talk to me about it. It's difficult but I'm not denying it any more.

"My plans? Yes, staying here, keep the home fires burning. I decided to do serious work on the place, maybe start this summer. Push out the north wall to get more light and space in the living room. Surprised? Of course I'm attached to the place! Where'd you get that idea? I can't fool myself too long. Right, clear thinking, right. Yeah.

"No, Merle doesn't come up here. Haven't seen him around since last year, December. I guess he's suffering down in the village. No, no, not unkind. I like Merle. I think he doesn't feel at home with me, that's all. He's very fond of your Mom. Sure I miss his help, he knows what he's about. Maybe he'll come when the cold breaks.

"How's it going there, Mouche? Good, that's good. I know, I know you don't. I know you're not a scholar. That's all right, I wasn't either, just did whatever it took to get through. My advice is, do your best, you don't know where it'll take you. Woodworking? you made a chair? Well, of course you're good at it! Damned good at it!

"What? Mary-Molly? You think Parker Farm's too intense for her? What kind of trouble? Took the farm truck! What, full of sheep, where'd they go? No, the school didn't call me. Mouche, she's a highly social being, not too good with authority. She'll find a balance. Don't worry, you're helping her just by being there.

"Sure, it's lonely. Your mother, well, it takes time, maybe a little deprivation is helpful. That's right, plenty of time for that. Yes, I expect her. Certainly I expect her. You're right, time passes. I'm working hard. Not all that hullaballoo she always stirs up....Yes, the teaching's good but it's hard to fire kids up these days. No trouble in photography, I've got serious students in there. I'm working on a new course. I'm pretty pleased with it. As a woodworker you'll be interested. Well, OK, it's called a Way of Building, the Spiritual Dimension. No, to the contrary, very grounded. Deals with patterns, in rooms and buildings and towns, how they grow when the uses behind them are alive. We'll talk about it.

"Spring vacation? for three days? I'll be here. That's a good idea, do some sugaring together. It's a two-man job. That's soon isn't it? Great idea. Mom? No, I don't think so. But she'll be back soon. Maybe after this damned cold is over. No doubt she will. She's wandering. It's an old practice, being on the road, leaving old stuff and accepting what comes. That's how I see it. She has the courage. But you come on down. It'll be great having you here....Mouche? no, just a frog in my throat. It'll be good to see you. Goodbye."

Why my eyes are filling up like this, I don't know. Dear old Mouche. He keeps the old ways, a steady man. Wants to get the sap run, wants to do it together. A blessing. Worried about his Mom. We don't know, we don't know what's ahead....Well, I'll get some coffee now. Gotta do Heidegger, ol' Martin Heidegger. I think there's something in there I need.

This guy is a gift to me, he's brilliant! He's a poet, what's more he's a friend. Invents his own language, and grammar. Not easy but the ideas are there, wide ideas. Do your best I told Mouche. Claire could help me, she'd love this. She'd recognize Heidegger, by God she would. Well, where am I in here?

'Let things appear and dwelling occurs.' Is that splendid, or not? 'A thing is not *in* space but is at work in space...it radiates about a center that cuts across time, giving visions to come, visions of the past...the things utter themselves in us.'

That's perfect, perfect! Ahh! I'm rising far up with this. It's food. I love you Heidegger.

Now he writes on dwelling.

'Dwelling is not primarily inhabiting but taking care of and nurturing that space within which something comes into its own and flourishes. Dwelling is primarily saving, in the older sense of setting something free to become itself, what it essentially is...to set something free into its own presencing...Dwelling is that which cares for things so that they essentially presence and come into their own...'

Ah, beautiful! If I read this right, presence is a verb, to presence. What is this, Potter? I think you know something about it. You do it all the time. Look straight out into the Open and bring it all back into your doggy heart. Something arrives if you let it, right? If you don't try to set it all up. There's a big feeling here. I don't know, Potter, but I'm going to hang on to it, get it clear. It's an opening. It's helping me see some things. Like maybe I haven't cured all my problems, but this winter something solid's starting to form at the bottom of all this suffering. It's helping me to bear with who I am. It's an opening. And I'm going to make it through.

***

The time passin' is slow, cold for March. I'll jes' put some more wood on this stove I guess. Alone now this whole month. No one callin' me. It's these birds keepin' me alive, keepin' me movin', keepin' my heart so's I listen to it. These birds gettin' me back into myself. People say they're ordinary. Well, not to me they aren't! That little one Mary-Molly, she loves the pheasant, the ring-neck with half a wing. She loves all of 'em, the guineas and Plymouth Rocks and bantams. Specially that crow makes her laugh. She talks with 'em too, always helped me feed the guinea chicks new born. I'll jes' keep buildin' cages. Birds are a wild creature I kin take care of. Keep me busy, their little lives like playthings. I'll keep on jes' like I always did from the beginnin'.

What a racket now! Well I b'lieve it's Lacey, my Aunt Lacey. "C'mon in here, Lacey. It's cold as a witch's arse."

"Sonny? Guess you ain't improved yourself none. At least you ain't lost your voice. I thought mebbe you'd need somethin' by now. It's soup and milk and coffee, them crackers you like. There's news, the property's settled free and clear in your name. That'll give ya some spark now. Don't eat too many o' them white crackers, Merle. Like I always say, it's the thing ya love that'll kill ya."

When Lacey leaves I dial Piri's number, and it's Lorian. "Piri's been sick. She's better now. She's asking for you, Merle."

It's sudden but I know things will turn. I know that's true when the need comes to me to search the falcon. It's the same these last years, somethin' calls me to watch that falcon in her place, to go every day till she's used to me. The time's close for her to come back. She's free now before she starts huntin', flyin' so fierce ten miles along the Weir. It's early but I'm strong for huntin' her, for the search. I'll go in the mornin'.

Jes' this soon after dawn the river's got clouds and mist high on her banks. Mebbe a warm breath comin' down off Blue Mountain. Kind of like a sigh, makin' the ice break up now n' float downstream in the high water. Water movin' faster on the top than underneath. It'll spread out over the banks there, move slower. Tryin' to balance itself out is my guess. It'll take some while.

Three miles to the first bridge now. Then I'll turn north along the crick n' go along there till the ledge where she used to perch on that dead branch. Thinkin' about her this wet mornin' I know she won't hunt till the mist burns away. She'll be playful with it, circling and swooping down. Risin' up she'll hover there and plunge down on her walls of air. She'll be listenin', watchin' to hunt when the light's bright. I can see what she sees, the same shadows and light. A space of wildness for us, a space of wildness I need.

No sight of her now, not a speck in the distance. Not anywhere in sight. Mebbe north to where the orchard opens onto the river I'll watch for signs. Mebbe I'll wait three hours. I know she'll come.

…Three hours now and I know I oughtta go back. Goin' along the river to the highway. Two miles more from the river crossin' to Piri's place. Lorion's there now. He's oilin' pulleys that open the tower roof, fixin' parts of stone made loose by the ice.

Inside that tower there's a racket of wings and birds that pesters me so, to hear it when I'm missing my falcon. I know all them piddlin' little black-headed weaver birds, doves, and them pesky parrot birds Lorion brings home from all parts.

"It was worse for them than for us this winter," Lorion says. "Seven birds lost though it wasn't below freezing inside. How are you, Merle? We heard about Reuben. I'm sorry, it's hard on you." Lorion always gives me his hand.

It's true I always stand a little stiff in front of Lorion. He looks out of his eyes with that sureness sayin' he could meet whatever happens. But he always gathers me in. I forget we might have distance.

"Well, dyin's only once," I say. "You can get through a thing once. Reuben was pesky right up to the end."

"That's good." Lorion laughs his big laugh. "Let's hope it goes that way for us all. Piri's concerned. She's had problems with her legs in the dampness and she caught a cold that's hanging on. Go on in, she wants to see you."

"Merle?" I hear Piri's sharp voice from inside the house.

"See? She's waiting. If you can help me later, I'd be grateful." Lorion turns back to work again.

Inside the house Piri looks closely at me. "Merle Fowler, a sight I've been waiting for. You look the same as ever."

I take both hands Piri holds out to me. "I'm good, thinkin' about hunting again."

"Hunting? Hunting!...ah, I know, the peregrine. You hunt her every year. Is she back?"

"Not yet."

"Will she come back?"

"Piri, she'll come back. She's young but not too young. This month she'll come, if she has the mate or not, she'll come. Why're you sick? Lay back with that cough. Your hair looks purty against them pillows you made. You don' look sick."

"I'm not, it's just a cold my body seemed to need. Too much change for it this early spring. I'm glad to see you. I'm sorry about Reuben."

I didn't answer and she went on. "I'm going to need more help from you. With the planting and collecting it'll be busy this spring. I've promised a lot of dyestuff to people. If you'll give me extra time it'll save my legs."

"Be good to have work. That's a big thing."

"You're right Merle. It's work, place, and love. That's all of it, but we don't know in what order." She sounds firm now and we both stay quiet, me wondering how could she put it all together like that so neat and clear.

"Well, I'll not go up to her place now." I was sayin' what I thought was on both our minds. "I'll not go to Lidia's place awhile."

"Till she comes back," Piri says, and then tells me about her walk up there that warm day of thaw. "The boy Mouche was there helping his father get ready for sugaring. They were friendly. I stayed a short while, long enough to get this cold I guess. I felt dis-spirited."

"Yes, I'll not go up there, not till she comes back....Piri, I'm goin' out to help Lorion with the mortar now. I'll see you in a week. You'll be chipper then. We'll manage. Take care now, you take care."

Workin' with the loose mortar and stones I caint' help thinkin' about this tower. I always overlooked it, not wantin' them to know I was critical. I always thought that tower was a waste, buildin' space you couldn't live in onto a place. A child's toy, a place for children to play. I jes' thought to myself it's too much for those birds. I see now that buildin' it was enough reason for Lorion. For Piri it's where the birds make a celebration in the spring.

There's more to it than I allowed. I'll tell Lacey. It's like the water she sees underground. It has a life of its own and that's not clear to most people.

It's slow in April. Days pass before I kin go out again for the falcon. Patches of old snow lie in the north hollers and streams runnin' full down to the river. I took care again to wear the same hat and clothes she knows. Two times she watched me last year, from that dead oak limb two hunderd yards further on. I saw her eye shine yellow and her head fierce with the hooked bill. She met my eye one other time and the rage in her was clear. She'll remember me, that still and silent thing watchin' her in her world.

…Air's heavy over the river now, wind blowin' upstream. Sun's to the left and I best move to keep it outta my eyes. If she circles up to dive she'll keep the strong light between her and anythin' movin' on the ground. Waitin' like this I jes' rise right up to a place of peace.

Mebbe further upstream she'll come downwind if I keep lookin' back. Three miles to that southard orchard slope where the warm air will be movin' up for her. Must be ten o'clock now, the mist burnt

off. Blackbirds warblin', starlins, mournin' doves makin' their soft call.
Patridge flappin' out o' the orchard brush. Lidia'd be pleased my knowin'
all these birds. I'll set down on this rock in the middle of the river. She'll
come today. I'll jes' wait. She'll come today, and this is the place.

After an hour mebbe, there's a ruckus from all these birds. Before I kin
get on my feet there's currents of air movin' on the back of my neck and
there! - she cuts past me liftin' her body, drops of water scatterin' off her
wings. Then she's flyin' faster, upward into the wind, straight beyond me
turnin' with the river. I feel a kind of lightness now and I say to her, Ah
my lady, comin' from your bath, now you know I'm here.

The miles back are slow, watchin', knowing she'll perch to dry her
feathers in the sun. I pass the sign I missed before, a fresh kill buried a
little in the old snow. Mournin' dove with its breast a hollow bare to the
bone. Movin' slowly now toward the ledge I see her…there! On the dead
limb in full sun, red from the sun behind her, her breast feathers gold.
She's come back, she's come back alone, she's a glory to me! Her eyes
stare, I kin see the dark feather of her eye mask, blue-black feathers on
her back, her body strong to the tail. She's powerful and she's swift, she's
a perfect thing. Haven't I known her all my life? But she's new again. She
gives me space. She gives me joy. I kin go home now. I have her in my eye.

Summer comin' on in a month. I don' know what I'll do. Some people in
town come to give me work and I tell them there's too much work now
for me to do. Some of them I started with but I became dis-satisfied.
Piri needs the help. She made promises to people.

I like workin' at her place. "This season it's red, red and purple dyes
they want," she says. "Coreopsis blooms and elderberry for the reds. The
yellows are easy, most folks gather their own."

We sit on her porch in the sun and I say to her, "It's contradictry,
strippin' all the leaves and roots of those plants. But you believe in it,
I guess." Piri doesn't answer very quick. We're listenin' to the birdsong,
seein' some early butterflies. When she speaks it's a little sharp for me.

"Being consistent isn't always a virtue Merle. There's a middle way in everything. It isn't always straight. The plant world produces abundance for childrens' joy. Am I right?"

I don' know if she's right. But we both laugh, because of her sharpness, because we know she's not clear in her mind to me. Because it's June and warm again.

We're together in the woods these days. Piri shows me what she knows about plants. I know coltsfoot by the shape and St. Johnswort now. I dig roots of wild indigo for her that come up every year, their flowers like a yellow pea vine. She wants bushels of that weak-stemmed vine that crawls, bedstraw she says. The wet places for elderberry and dry places for the old nut trees. I know them all now an' I'm pleased. We hang blooms to dry. "Merle," Piri waves her hand over the reds and golds, "soon we're coming into July. It's bold, it turns everything inside out. It fulfills all the promises."

It was then I told her somethin' I'd found out by myself.

"In the beginnin' Piri, all the bloom starts with green that's tender, and then a color like peach tree blossoms comes in. It's jes' like skin, color so soft you don' know if it's real. From what I see that's the way they all start, the green and then the peach-blossom color. It's in all the leaves and then it's in the bloom."

She stands still. "Merle? Do you have anything more to say?"

I push my cap back and smile. "Alot I see now I owe to you Piri. Things changin' their space and growin', the leaves of the plants all movin' themselves around to where they get light."

"I guess we both have hopefulness," she says.

Suddenly I feel there's so much between Piri and me now. July is long and my falcon's come back and Reuben's gone and Lorion's alright. And then there's our work together. It's all a background for the thing we don't speak about, and that's Lidia's return.

2
Piri

LIVING ON THE SIDE OF A MOUNTAIN, I don't have the usual sense of time passing. The light rises and falls and rises again. I see that light is the mover of all things. It moves time and the seasons that follow it. I see the strength of it pushing everything into growth. Its absence allows everything to rest....That's all there is, the rise and fall of light. It's a flowing, almost a sound I can hear. It becomes part of my body.

Every year, when the thin spring light was beginning to strengthen, I looked for Lidia's return. Every spring I said to Lorion, she'll come when the earth is just tilting towards the fulness of summer, toward the sign of Leo when she was born. I feel the loss of her but I can't do a thing to get her back. I don't have courage to walk up to her place. I feel the loss of that connection too. Six years have passed now, seven springs, and it's moving again toward the light of summer.

How do you think we knew, Merle and I, that it would be the seventh spring? He came to work yesterday and said −so quietly- that he'd seen Lidia at the old mill a day ago when he bought grain for the birds. He said she was there with a woman, "that tall one with hair wrapped around her head."

Perhaps it's strange how Merle and I hide our joy. Knowing Lidia's back fills us with happiness. But by now I've learned a way to laugh without laughing, to cry without crying. It keeps me safe. As for Merle Fowler, I think he's lived the life of suffering that is unmoved by changes of fortune.

As we stand by the tower today listening to the birdsong cascade and spiral in the early light I see Merle's attention heighten. "Piri, someone's coming up the road. It's Lidia... I'm sure." In a few moments the figure comes into view. She sees us and begins to run.

"Piri!" She runs toward us with her arms out. At last. I enclose her like a small ship at harbor.

"Let me see you, I've waited so long for this. Let me look at you."

For a long while I hold my hands on each side of her face. Letting her go, I see Merle's blue eyes filling with tears that begin to fall as Lidia puts her arms around him. We're all silent under the sound of warbling birds. And, as we stand listening, the air suddenly fills with small silvery pale-brown wings of flying insects coming from the edge of the woods out into the sun. They fly up everywhere so quickly and in such numbers that it seems like another country, some tropical space. Light quivers on their wings. The air seems to be trembling.

"A good hatch of moths," Merle says. "They're for you, for your coming back."

"What are they, they're so beautiful," Lidia wants to know.

"Moths," Merle says simply.

"Yes," she smiles at him.

"Plume moths. I know them. The larva feed on the wild grape leaves. See the fringe, it's like plumes on their hind-wings. They never hatch this early. It's great for the birds. Merle is right, Lidia, it's a good sign for you."

I wonder if she sees Merle's eyes so full of joy and I wonder what she feels for us both. She doesn't speak about herself except to say her help is needed here. She's found a place in town and will stay while it's necessary. No, she hasn't thought about where else to go.

Merle is silent, not moving his eyes away from her face. I can see her holding carefully the yearning that always changes him in her presence. She contains it with gentleness. We speak very little for awhile and then Merle turns to go.

"I'll come again soon," Lidia says, as Merle starts toward the road. His long body turns once and once again, to look back at her. She watches until he disappears. I see she's pale, but that much less of the old jagged energy hangs about her body. A web of fine lines spreads at the corners of her eyes. Her dark auburn hair is lightened with shades I can't describe. I feel the change in her. The meaning of her absence --almost seven years-- overcomes me so suddenly that it's hard to speak.

"It's been so long, Lidia."

"Yes," she smiles sadly. Then her eyes brighten in the old way. "I loved the city Piri, its brick sidewalks and gardens. I learned how people live, how a wider view is possible…how it's necessary. A poet I heard said when you're troubled, go to the poor. And he's right. It was right for me to work with poor people, many of them sick and not going to get better. Many of them accept death and old age. It gives them a certain kind of freedom. I think I'm shaken down a little, do you see?"

Yes, I do see. Around her is a small golden ray instead of the old metallic red. But I say nothing.

"The tower's still the same. It's the same, isn't it Piri?" She has the plain look of a child.

"No, nothing's ever the same. Everything's always changing. The moths, see? They've disappeared."

"Piri, I can't stay. I have work now. My car's down on the main road. As soon as I can…"

"I'll wait," I interrupt, "but Lidia… come soon."

Two weeks pass without her coming, so I feel relieved when Merle says he has news. We sit, earlier than usual, drinking coffee at the kitchen table.

"I saw Lidia. She's thin as a candle. The place she's livin' is poor lookin', roof fallin' down over the porch, squirrels takin' it, runnin' right up the walls on an old wire onto the roof. There's furniture and burned out pots all over the grass, renters' stuff I guess. She wasn't there. I think she works somewhere beyond Garrison. I went back again after supper and asked her to come out to your place. She did say she'd come…and I'll keep an eye out for her."

"I'm waiting too."

At last Lidia comes to tell me what I already know, that her reason for returning is to see Richard. I'd been pondering that. I want her to see from my eyes how the place is now, what's changed there. She comes early and a mist is still falling. The morning doesn't have a match for as long as I can remember. All week the rain and clouds held back the full bursting of leaves. Today the branches are delicate against gray skies. The brilliance of greens shines like a looking glass. With birdsong and answering stillness, the New England spring always pulls at my heart… and pulls farther, back to my own village sweet with lilac blooms..

Guided by his sense of Lidia's presence, Merle appears suddenly and stands with us before starting to move loads of compost into the garden. "Soon everythin's goin' to bloom, everythin' that should bloom," he says seriously, and then with a smile, "and we're part of it." He looks steadily into Lidia's eyes before I steer her away through the tower and into the house.

She's restless so I know there's little time. Yes, she's going up there. She can't be here longer without seeing Stone Hill.

"About Richard, I don't know if he's had any one to talk to. Your friend Lucretia was going up there. Not since he came back from the expedition though."

Lidia looks evenly at me. "Last fall? You mean you haven't seen him since then?"

"Maybe once, but I'm afraid of disturbing him. Several times I passed him in town and he looked restless. He didn't notice me and I didn't speak. I could see he was pared down to survival."

"And the place?" she asks simply.

"It's not like it was when you left. It's very still now. He's made changes. I think the place has a hold on him even stronger than it has on you. Maybe a peace he doesn't find anywhere else." Her body stirs and seems on the edge of flight. It isn't time to speak my thoughts so I keep to the facts I know. "The land's the same but he's changed the house, pushed through the roof for a dormer and added glass to the north side. You'll find it different." I can't watch her face.

"Oh, I don't think I'll mind. Listen, I had this dream, what's it saying, Piri? I dreamed I had some old oriental rugs, silver pieces and gold jewelry things. I took them to a museum but they didn't want them. I put the things in a boat and went out onto the water. The boat overturned and everything went under. A few of them I rescued but when I looked back, I saw the rug shining down on the bottom of the sea. All the other things were sparkling too, scattered there but not lost. Beautiful under the clear green water."

"Lovely. Yes, you'll manage everything, all the changes. Go now, be with him. I think it's what you desire. But here's one thing more. It answers your dream. Lorion read to me an ancient Indian writing that tells how all things in the universe are part of a net. Where each thread of the net joins is a diamond mirror that gathers light. All the images reflect each other and each one contains all the others. We can't see one alone without seeing all the rest."

As she listens, I see Lidia's eye move to something high above the horizon. A wide-winged hawk is tracing loops of energy over the westward mountain range.

"I see, I do see. The Diamond Net, it means nothing is ever lost. It means that hawk will always exist for me. It always has." She's quiet a moment. "Piri, I have to go now."

In the garden, Merle straightens up and comes toward her. She holds both his hands in hers for a moment and then turns to go down the road. How could I know this is the last time I'd see them together.

I don't dream any more about the Sutherland place. It's settled into me like warp threads buried in my weaving, threads that hold and direct the course of the cloth. I see the place in a different way now from how I first saw it. It's more of a promise than a reality you can hold to. It's a promise that keeps fragmenting and disappearing and dissolving into the world. Just like all the things I love.

A place made sacred becomes the center of the world, Lorion says. It reaches to the stars and planets and to the waters underground. A sacred place repeats all the stories of the past and makes time disappear. But it's difficult to reach because the center of the world moves everywhere. The center's really just where I am, and that's all I need now.

3
Lidia

I'M GOING BACK, BACK TO STONE HILL. It seems like yesterday. Seven years, it's been seven years. But it looks like yesterday, an October morning with early asters blooming, leaves falling across these flats, the landscape washed clean by summer rain. The same stillness flows down off Blue Mountain.

Turning onto this road makes me want to stop and feel the damp earth on my feet. The big pines begin here and the stream, running back into the woods, still reflects the sky. The road rises now where the wolf pine grows and levels out toward the house. Maybe Piri's right about desire. If you yield to it, it will transform you. She says to turn the desire back into my own heart. But what I found is that the heart can't live with longing, it isn't good for the heart....Well, Lidia, here you go, up the hill right to the front door.

"Spectacular entrance. But you're late." The screen door slams and Richard comes out.

"You said it was soup. That keeps doesn't it?"

"For years."

"But...wasn't it only yesterday, Richard?" I feel a little reckless.

"Not on my calendar."

"The house looks so silvery gray in the sunlight! And you look so... so revealed!"

"And you have a feather haircut! Are you coming in?"

"I don't know how long I can stay. I don't want to be sad, Richard."

"No, we're just having soup, Lidia. I think that's all we can manage. Sit down."

"There's cobbler for dessert, black raspberries I picked. Good summer for raspberries."

"Was it...oh." His hands lie on the table, large and still, like small animals, his long fingers thickened and rough, the skin on the longest fingers split and creased with dirt. I didn't know coming back here would be so delicate. I didn't know I would feel like a flower unfolding. The table's set perfectly and there is fresh vegetable soup in a rich broth. We eat in silence that's alive with unfolding, all the meanings Richard holds and keeps here. I feel respect, I feel fear. He looks shaggy, his shorts hooked up with suspenders, his great shock of hair, his eyes deep gray, the lines in his face almost noble. I feel fear again.

"D'you know, Merle came up here two days ago. He knows you're back."

"Yes, I've seen him."

"We're clearing brush around the meadow. You won't believe how it's grown in, alot more than you remember. What is it, Lidia?"

"Nothing." My throat suddenly constricts and tries to swallow. It's all the old problems again. I don't want to remember. Richard goes on.

"And he's starting to dig a trench across the back hill east of the house. To stop the run-off. He hasn't come all these years you've been gone but he says it's not too late. We can stop it now. He's doing it for you."

"Yes, he told me that. But it's crazy don't you think?" The old problems again, the things we were so good at. "You know Merle, once he has an idea there's no way to stop him."

"You seem lighter, Lidia."

"Oh...heavier I think. From living with silence. It's growing in me. So, I'm heavier I guess. But a bit light-headed right now. Is that confusing?"

Richard nods as though I'm clear, and my words keep coming out in a rush. "Do you know what I collected the whole time in the city? Bread recipes, can you believe that? Why're you smiling Richard?"

"Yes, I can believe that, I can. And you know, I've been living with silence too. It rolls off the mountain, the heaviest sound you can imagine. Now come, I want to show you one thing."

"It's not a big thing, is it? I can come back again." I feel a desperate need to escape as he leads me out to the terrace.

"No, not a big thing, though," he says slowly, "there are big things. C'mon. I think you'd like to stand here, under the sky."

I can see the woodshed beyond him as he looks down into my face. "Oh! the trumpet vine, it's beginning to bloom! For the first time in years..."

"I knew you'd say that, you always say that. Oh Lidia." His arms reach around me and I lean in to his rough shape as if it was one of the old maple trees. A peace rolls out from me on dark waves. But my arms won't raise up around him. My body stands still keeping everything inside, like a vessel trembling full to the brim with water.

"There are some things I need to tell you."

"Yes. And maybe some things can't be put into words."

"I'm going to try. Could you live with me again, even awkwardly? I'm changed, Lidia. Will you think about it? Will you?"

"Yes, Richard, I'm changed too."

A strange mercy falls on me suddenly and it gives me peace. What I see now is that I've never forsaken this place. I haven't forsaken Richard. He didn't withdraw from suffering. He stayed in it and I stayed with him in my heart. But now I'm clear about what I know. I know that I gave myself over to the dream of making a garden at Stone Hill. Its beauty held so many possible events I might reveal and unless I gave it all my energy, I imagined it wouldn't become real. I gave myself to things I thought would pull me toward completion. Perhaps they did, but there were many consequences....I know these things only in silence. I know them when I feel this sadness at the bottom of my heart, when I feel the radiance gone out of my face.

"Yes, Richard, I'm changed too."

A car pulls up. It's Mary-Molly. I run to meet her and see, in her face, all the radiance I thought was lost. "Mom! I was hoping you'd be here today. Did you know that Merle's here? He's been digging. And this is Harry. He loves this place. We came to help Dad harvest all his stuff. Mom," she whispers through the open car window, "Harry and I are really close. It's serious, it really is, Mom."

"I'm so glad for you. I'm glad you met him. Let's go in. I want to see what Dad's doing now."

"You go, I'm staying outside with Harry. We'll pick apples. Go see everything. Dad's going to make juice and he's so happy."

On my way back to the kitchen I can see Richard through the window. A cloud of steam rises up to envelope him. I notice how the house is full of earth smells, pungent and ripe in the hall from pots of marigolds, moist smells of parsley and mint and sage hanging from the high beam in the living room, the sweet odor of seckle pears and apples in bushels in a new, open pantry. With his back turned, Richard is pouring the hot juice he's extracted from the wild grapes into a row of glass jars. I sit on a high stool and wait for him to finish.

"I see, Richard, you're much more of a gatherer and harvester than I was."

He turns and begins to laugh, in a way so startling that I stand up to watch him. And then I remember his different laughs. One I always rejoiced in filled my body with joy, a laugh I haven't heard too many times. It comes from deep down, rich and layered with music. When I heard it I'd say to one of the children, listen to Dad, and they would listen too. It held the deep resonant quality of an organ welling up from rolling waters and filling all the space around us. And I remember a laugh that wasn't really him at all. Like a brittle mask of tightness. Perhaps it came out of all the unnatural adjustments he made to conform to others' expectations.

He turns half way toward me now and laughs with his whole body in grace and youthfulness. His eyes light up to almost blue. His face thins and lengthens, and his body bends over as though in a dance. I stand like a tree, solid, as he seems to dance before me all movement and sunlit. I feel clarity in him, as though he's thrown off a tight garment. I stand there wondering if he knows the meaning of his laughter. It's only a moment in which he seems transfixed. I think of Piri and the crack opening between the worlds.

"There's something in your face, what is it, Richard?"

"I don't know but I do have some things to say. I have a dream to tell you. Can you stay till I'm finished here?"

"Mom! Mom!" Mary-Molly's voice is loud and insistent as it reaches the house. "Mom! Come right now, something's happening to Merle!"

I start running, running, praying "No, no, please God, no." I haven't seen it but I know where Merle is digging, across the brow of the steep slope east of the house. The dirt road reaching there is rutted and rocky from streams running off Clark's clear-cut far above. I run, staggering, up the slope. It's crazy, a crazy scheme. "Merle, Merle!"

The ditch is deep, at least three feet, and wide. Fresh earth is piled up almost six feet on either side. Merle's been digging for three days. I can't see his face. His upper body is collapsed over the ground above the ditch. Mary-Molly's right behind me.

"Lift his legs, lift out his legs!" We struggle with his weight till Merle's body lies stretched out on the ground. His face is white, his breath coming slow.

"Call the ambulance, quick." I push piles of earth under him to raise his legs, and Merle opens his eyes.

"Pain alright. Scared," he mutters.

I put my mouth next to his ear. "My bird, my poor blackbird. Merle you're safe, you're alright." I lie close to give him strength till the ambulance arrives. Merle's eyes are closed now.

"He'll be alright. I'm following them. No, I'll go alone, Richard."

"Oh my God, Lidia." Richard's eyes are wild.

Following closely on the road to Garrison I can see them in the ambulance pushing down on Merle's chest. They stop, then push again. At the hospital they wheel him quickly inside, and I wait.

Two hours, three, and a nurse appears. "Did you come with Merle Fowler? He wants to see you. He insists. It's unusual, but we know Merle. He's not stabilized so don't speak please. Just two minutes."

I tell my heart to breathe and I enter the room. He knows I'm here and opens his eyes, deep pools of darkness against the thin white skin. I lean over him and hear the word..."finished."

"Yes," I whisper, 'it's finished. The ditch is beautiful, no more water running down the hill." A light blazes in his dark eyes. I haven't understood.

"Finished? No, Merle, you're safe, you'll be alright." The light still blazes. "Finished." I struggle for his meaning. "Finished...yes. Merle, I love you. Take care now. On the way take care." Merle's eyes become peaceful and I reach down to hold his hand. Then...a great light goes out...everything is changed.

It's hard to come back here on this day. I try to tell Mary-Molly that Merle is part of her that will never change, part of her mind and her body, part of her strength. "Merle had a special quality. Because he was a simple person, it allowed us to get very close to him, and we could see him as clearly as he saw us."

"Did you see him clearly, Mom?"

"What I saw was the most lovely man. He suffered, but he knew that suffering was part of life. Whatever happened, he accepted as part of living. Merle lived in space where time isn't a burden. All his rituals, hunting, his falcon, fishing, being in the woods, how he worked, they made time disappear. So, in a way, if you saw him clearly, Merle Fowler lived like the seasons, returning and returning, but always new."

"That's a very rare person, Mom, don't you think?"

"Yes, it is. It's a person of quality. And this, when he's leaving us, is a very important moment."

"I'm going to tell Harry all about Merle. We have to go back now, we have classes tomorrow." She turns on her way out the door. "Merle wouldn't want us to be sad in this important moment, would he." Her blond hair falls over her face as she struggles with tears. "I don't see how I can live without Merle. Maybe Harry can help me now....Dad, we'll be back soon. Goodbye, Mom. Goodbye..."

Richard clears his voice loudly. His eyes are full of tears. "What is it? Are you sad because they're leaving? Or..."

"No," Richard's face was moving, "well yes, ...but... it's just that I wish I'd learned as much from Merle as you did, and Mary-Molly too. Everything's changed. I have some things to say Lidia, some things I know now. You won't go yet will you?"

"No, but Richard, I just need space now." Space where I can hold the meaning of Merle's life. Already his death makes it clearer.

Merle helped to make this possible, this moment of opening to ourselves. His way of watching and listening, allowing all things to rest in their own light. He wasn't frightened to live in the purity of his own heart. My words come out brokenly. "His brightness, look, I can see Merle's brightness now!"

"Lidia?"

"Yes, I'm here." I try to give space to him. "I want to listen. But can I say it first? It's that you don't want me here every day, waking in the morning, complaining with an unhappy face. I'm very witchy."

"Yes, Lidia, you are." Richard's face keeps moving. We stand in the kitchen that now floods with light from the setting sun. The gold lights his body and I see again how it's filled with all colors of the rainbow. I stand still, drawing all my energy to one place, like a newborn baby struggling to make a small sound.

"It's short, my dream. It's a towering figure, a giant. His body's covered with scars. Scars shaped like swords. And they're silver, they shine with silver. His eyes are silver. Lidi, it's not just the dream. I'm finding the one thing that's possible for me to do. It doesn't frighten me to give up my ideas of how to be, to give up a life that always seemed like chaos. I don't need a right way to be. I'm staying here, on this land you found. On this place I'm part of now. Photography is the way I talk about the place. Just understanding the changes that happen. I need to be here, to see it happen over time. The landscape's not always pretty, it has a darker side. The gift of it is seeing the changes. It changes with what I know, what I'm learning. I accept this for myself. But you could stay too if you would. I hoped you'd see it's possible for just the two of us now. I hoped, by my staying here, you'd see it was possible and you'd come back."

I feel the old grief coming toward me again, how we lived here, the price we paid for living out childhood dreams. The old images flash by, the celebrations, the mandalas of the Moon and Moss Gardens, the Pond, the passion plays of flowers and colored vegetables preserved in jars, the parade of animals and people as witness to all our performances. The temptations will be with me till my last breath, the beauty of Stone Hill, of Richard's body. But I have to answer him. I have to turn my desire back into my own heart.

"Stone Hill is alive with dreams and desires, Richard. It always was. It always will be. For so long I let those desires become my own. But I can't yield to them now. There's no magic anywhere. We have to say what we need. I have to make some more things happen for myself. That's so hard. I'm accepting that now. And I'm not abandoning the things here. I need to free them for someone else to hold. Don't you see? I've been giving Stone Hill to you all these years. And look, look how you're keeping it. You've made it far more beautiful. More space and light for things."

"But you found it, you found this place."

"For you now, to make something that will be a safe part of your life. I'll always love you Richard, always...there's nothing to forgive, is there?" I hear him drawing in his breath.

"No, there's nothing to forgive."

"I'll go then."

On my way outside I stop on the north terrace. In the waning moon I see my shadow against the black maple tree. It's true. I'm here now. I *was* here, under Blue Mountain, in this place we called Stone Hill.

*****

As time passes it reveals more about a place you've yielded to. Stone Hill still reveals many things to me, and some are about grief. Grief is like the pond in our woods. It holds so much under a smooth black surface. Reflections come and go when a wind blows. Rings ripple out till they reach the edge and keep moving on into the center of the earth. A huge log has floated in the pond for years. Sometimes it bobs up and bangs into the wooden dock or hits the shoreline. It disappears and suddenly appears at the surface in another place. I have to stop to remember where it came from. The pond is quiet, always there, in my mind.

Besides grief, a place reveals many things about love. Richard and I had a great need for what we perceived in each other. We both came to Stone Hill with a hunger and thirst for love. I would say now, the way we lived there helped to fill that hunger. Giving the place our care made a radiant unity of so many of our days. The ordinary things became refuges –the blue fence, the trumpet vine, the falcon, the ship rock, the moonlight. Living with them required a vulnerable watchfulness, listening, giving safety, almost a state of prayer…it was a weaving of love you might say.

I think a loved place is a bridge between two worlds of light. Light falls on it and reflects the people and how they live there. Far above, higher than the falcon flies, far higher than Blue Mountain, there's a more pure and simple light. Stone Hill exists in both worlds. Perhaps it's only once in a lifetime that a person can make a sacred dwelling place for all beings of the earth and sky. That's what a place does, one you recognize and love. It receives you and takes away your heaviness. It's like food that builds toughness into your bones. A place takes you on a journey and, if you allow it, it brings you home.

I have abandoned nothing at Stone Hill. I go back to see Mary- Molly and Harry and their little ones. "Look Mom," Mary-Molly says, "see how Harry left that patch of wildflowers when he mowed the meadow? Isn't it lovely in the sunlight!…Can you come inside and help me? Even after all these years, sometimes I just despair of making the space work for all of us in this old house."

Afterword

READING THE WORKS OF MANY WRITERS HAS prepared me to write this story. But the two listed below I will never be finished reading. Martin Heidegger (1889-1976), searched the origin of the word `dwelling' and gives us his understanding of what it means to dwell with awareness of the wholeness of earth and sky and with attendance upon our fellow beings and the return of fugitive gods. I am also grateful for the work of Johann Wolfgang von Goethe (1749-1832), whose science of qualitative wholeness complements the analytic and causal explanations of modern science. In attempting to realize this conscious participation in the natural world I was helped to define the main characters of my story.

Bortoft, Henri, *The Wholeness of Nature* (Lindisfarne Press, 1996). This work is a comprehensive, accessible path to understanding Goethean science.

Heidegger, *Martin, Poetry, Language, Thought*, "Building Dwelling Thinking" trans. A. Hofstadter (Harper & Row, N.Y. Colophon edition, 1975).

von Goethe, Johann Wolfgang, *Goethe on Science, An Anthology of Goethe's Scientific Writings*, Floris Books, 1996

I give thanks to the following people for their help to me in the present and in the past: first, Elizabeth Scheffey for her intuitive drawing which has become the book's cover; to Steve Strimer for his heart and courage as a publisher; to Sarah Patton for her generous technical assistance; to Patricia Lee Lewis for vital editorial support. I give thanks for my teachers: Edith Sewall, a peerless Jungian counselor, and Pat

Schneider, both of whom said to me, "Now write!" At the age of eight I shook the hand of a "real writer" and have never forgotten her. Among others, she wrote one book called "Barefoot Days" and signed it for me with her magical name, Anna Maria Louisa Perrott Rose Wright. Most of all, I give thanks for my parents who taught me to finish what I started.

Alice Scheffey, October 2014